THE THIRD
TWIN

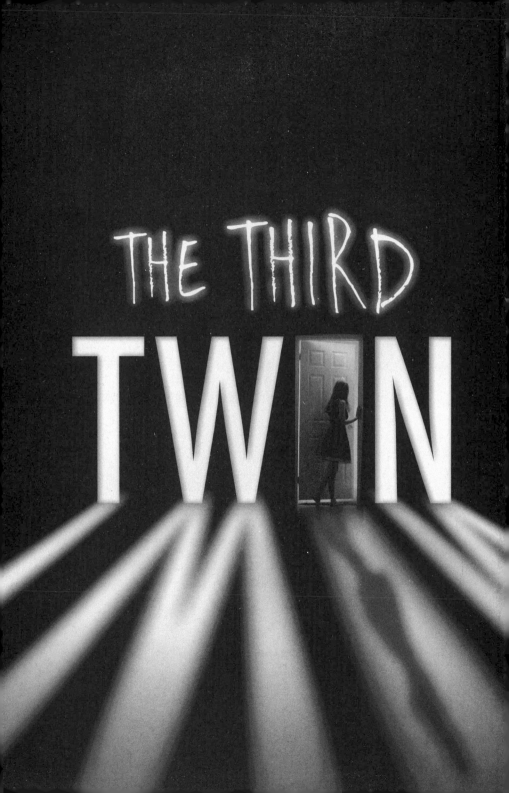

CJ OMOLOLU

DELACORTE PRESS

Text copyright © 2015 by CJ Omololu
Jacket photograph © 2015 by Allison Nading/Getty Images

All rights reserved. Published in the
United States by Delacorte Press, an imprint of Random
House Children's Books, a division of Random House LLC,
a Penguin Random House Company, New York.

Delacorte Press is a registered trademark and the
colophon is a trademark of Random House LLC.

randomhouseteens.com

Educators and librarians, for a variety of teaching tools,
visit us at RHTeachersLibrarians.com

Library of Congress Cataloging-in-Publication Data
Omololu, Cynthia Jaynes.
The third twin / CJ Omololu. — First edition.
pages cm
Summary: Ava and Lexi, high school seniors and identical twins, created an
imaginary triplet, Alicia, to date and dump boys but now they are being stalked
and impersonated by the sister they invented and their former dates are turning
up dead.
ISBN 978-0-385-74452-2 (hc : alk. paper) —
ISBN 978-0-385-39024-8 (epub) — ISBN 978-0-375-99171-4 (glb : alk. paper)
[1. Sisters—Fiction. 2. Twins—Fiction. 3. Dating (Social customs)—Fiction.
4. Serial murders—Fiction. 5. Murder—Fiction. 6. Adoption—Fiction.
7. Identity—Fiction.] I. Title.
PZ7.O54858Thi 2015
[Fic]—dc23
2013050396

The text of this book is set in 12-point Minion.
Book design by Heather Kelly

Printed in the United States of America

10 9 8 7 6 5 4 3 2 1
First Edition

FOR PATSY AND PEGGY
AND THEIR THIRD TWIN, PENNY

CHAPTER 1

We have three rules for being Alicia: always wear the diamond pendant; never sleep with any of the guys; and after five dates, they're history, no matter how hot they are. Right now, I'm especially glad for rule number three, because this particular guy seems determined to break rule number two.

"Come on, Casey. Take it easy," I say, pushing myself away from him—as far as I can in such a small space, the door handle pressing uncomfortably against my back. The car has that musky, skunky smell of old pot smoke, and there are two half-smoked joints in the cup holder, right out in the open for everyone to see. Makes me wonder who else has been in here recently.

"What?" he says with a smile, a lock of his blond hair falling into his eyes. Damn, Ava was right—he is really hot. Of course, my sister would never get Alicia involved with someone who wasn't good-looking. High cheekbones and tight abs are the prerequisites for dating Alicia, even if Casey does drive a dented 2007 Camry and work at the Cheesecake Factory. Guys with expensive cars and a real future go out with Ava.

Casey drums on the steering wheel with his fingers. "Not like this is the first time we've gone out or anything."

There's no way I can comment on that, because technically this *is* our first date. Ava swore that nothing happened between them the other times, but he's so handsy, I'm starting to doubt her story.

"And?" I say, sitting up and straightening my shirt.

"And . . ." Casey leans toward me. "You don't expect me to be a good boy forever. I mean, come on . . . look at you."

I glance down at the short black skirt that Ava put on me earlier this evening and wonder what she would do. He obviously hasn't been able to tell the difference between the two of us. Over the years we've found that, given enough cleavage and lip gloss, most guys aren't all that observant.

Casey must think that my hesitation means I'm caving in. "Come on, babe," he says, his breath hot on my neck as he swoops back in for another try. "You know you want to."

Babe? Did he really just say that? "I don't *know* anything," I say, using all my strength to keep him away from me. "Except that I don't want anything more to do with you. Get off me."

Casey grins and leans back against his seat, his profile sharp in the dim orange glow of the Cheesecake Factory parking lot. I can see my car out the passenger-side window, all alone in a pool of light under the streetlamp, now that everyone else has gone home. I suddenly want so badly to be in it, seeing nothing but his car in the rearview mirror. I grab my bag off the floor and reach for the door, but just as quickly, Casey's hand is on my arm.

"Not so fast," he says, biting his bottom lip. "We're not done here."

"I think we are," I say, twisting my arm hard, but I can't get him to let go. The strength of his grip is surprising and unsettling. A jolt of fear ripples through my body as I stare at his fingers, which turn white as they clutch my arm.

"Then once again, we'll have to agree to disagree," he says, pressing his mouth against mine. I'm clenching my teeth so hard that they grind against my upper lip, and I taste the metallic tang of blood. He pulls back just a little, and his grin gets even wider—he's loving this. "So that's the way it's going to be? Fine with me. We can do this the easy way and you can sit back and enjoy it, or we can do this the hard way. Your call." All I can smell is the spicy scent of his aftershave, and I feel like gagging. I can't believe I kind of liked the smell when I met him here after he got off work. Tall, handsome, polite—when Casey walked with me down by the pier and bought me ice cream at the stall on the boardwalk, he was everything Ava had said he'd be. Now that nice person is completely gone, and I can feel the force of his desire to control me wash over us in this cramped front seat.

My mind is racing, and I'm pissed at myself for getting into this situation. I should never have gotten into his car in the first place. All those self-defense classes Dad made us take a couple of years ago, yet here I am alone in a dark parking lot with a guy I barely know. Idiot.

"I said no!" I shout, shoving him, but he seriously outweighs me, and the harder I fight him, the more he seems to get off on it. The sharp edges of panic start rising in my chest. We were just having fun. This is not how it's supposed to go.

"God, that's hot," he says, bending down and biting my shoulder so hard, I feel his teeth pierce my skin.

"Get off me!" I scream, louder this time, the sound echoing and desperate in my ears. I can feel my heart beating fast and my breathing turn shallow as ideas flash through my brain, trying to figure a way out of this car, out of this night. I push him one last time and then drop my arms. There's no way I can fight him off. I'm going to have to try something else.

"Aw, come on. You're not giving up that easy, are you?" he asks, his voice lower and his breath quicker than it's been all night.

"Look," I say, knowing that if I give in to the panic, it will only feed the moment. "Just let me out of here. I'll get in my car and go home and we'll forget about it."

"I'll give you something you won't forget," he says roughly. "Don't you worry about that, Alicia."

That name rips right through me. Alicia. I can feel my heart slow for just a moment, and I inhale deeply. Tonight, I'm not Lexi; I'm Alicia. Strong, confident, and infinitely capable. I might give up, but Alicia would fight this asshole to her very last breath. I close my eyes and realize that I'm gripping my bag with my right hand. Casey's pressing himself against me and doesn't notice my fingers slipping into the opening of the soft leather. He doesn't hear the soft metallic clink as my hand closes around what I've been looking for, the weapon they taught us to use if we were ever in a situation like this. His eyes are screwed shut as I pull the keys out of my bag and, before I can lose my nerve, rake them across his face with as much force as I can manage.

"What the fuck!" he shrieks, jerking back and clamping one hand to his cheek.

I know I have only a few seconds, so in one quick motion I flip the handle, push the car door open, and tumble out into the dark, damp air, gulping it in like I've been underwater for hours. I hear commotion behind me, but I don't stop to look as I scramble to my feet, unsteady in the high heels I'm not used to wearing. It seems to take forever to reach my car, but I finally manage to open the door with the keys that are already in my hand. I slide into the front seat and slam and lock the door behind me.

"You little bitch!" he shouts from outside the car, his breath making a circle of fog on my window. I see a line of blood on his cheek, and my stomach clenches, knowing it's only fueled his anger. If he gets hold of me now, there's no way he's letting go. He pounds on the glass, and I flinch. For one agonizing second I can't find the ignition button as I run my hands desperately over the dashboard. He's still shouting, his face just inches from mine. I'm afraid he's going to put his fist through the window, when the engine roars to life and I squeal out of the parking space, my headlights zigzagging across the dark asphalt. Only when I reach the parking lot entrance do I pause for a second and notice the dark flecks of blood on my fingers. As I wipe them quickly on my skirt, I find the tiniest grain of satisfaction in the fact that I caused it, imagining the story he's going to have to tell about how he got his stupid face ripped open. Turning onto the main road, I allow myself one glance into the rearview mirror and see a lone shadowy figure leaning against the small red car under the dim lights.

It's cold in here, and I realize I left Ava's sweater in his car—the new blue one with the beading that she let me borrow. She's going to be pissed about that, but if that's the worst thing that happens tonight, I'm good. I adjust the mirror, and my face comes into focus. For a second I don't recognize it. It's not just the heavy eyeliner and sparkly purple shadow Alicia wears, or the diamond-filled letter *A* on the pendant that catches the light from the street. There's something behind the physical transformation that my sister crafted so carefully earlier this evening, a hardness underneath that makes me momentarily uneasy. Alicia isn't scared, and she isn't sorry. She's glad that for once, a guy got what he deserved.

———

Alicia started as a joke. The ultimate imaginary friend, our pretend triplet was handy to have around when we were little. All of Cecilia's warm chocolate chip cookies disappear? Alicia did it. A bunch of expensive games get downloaded onto Dad's phone? Just blame Alicia. They both went along with it back then, figuring it was just some quirky twin thing, but if Dad found out that we were still pulling the Alicia business after all this time, he'd kill us. Now that we're seniors, Alicia's the first one into the pool and the last one to leave a party. Ava resurrected her a few years ago when she gave Alicia's name to a guy for fun, and I play along sometimes just to blow off some steam. I don't date. At least, that's what everyone thinks. Dad likes to brag that I'm too busy with school, clubs, and volunteer work to worry about boys. And he's right, mostly. But every now and then it's fun to get dressed up and go out, no strings attached. At least, it was until tonight.

I unfasten the necklace and lift it off my skin, the diamonds in the thick script *A* pendant catching fire in the glow of the recessed kitchen lights. As I coil it on the countertop, I can feel the last remnants of Alicia fall away until I'm just Lexi again, sitting on a kitchen stool in baggy sweatpants listening for Ava's key in the lock.

"Hey," she says with a giggle when she finally lets herself in through the kitchen door. "How did it go? Isn't Casey cute?"

"Jesus, you can really pick 'em," I say, downing the last of the cold coffee in my mug. It's almost two a.m., way past the curfew that Dad imposed but doesn't enforce, and the whole place is quiet. His wing of the house is far enough away from the rest of us that he never hears anything even if he does happen to be home.

"What are you talking about?" Ava says, and I don't miss the slight slur in her voice.

"How much did you drink tonight?" I ask. I know she's going to get annoyed, but I can't help myself. My mind flashes to the very earliest photo we have, of right before Dad adopted us, the one of the two of us on an old-fashioned flowered couch. We're already six months old, and I'm sitting up grabbing my feet, but Ava's so tiny that she still seems like a newborn propped up against one of the pillows, the feeding tube taped to her cheek, and her arms grasping at thin air. I look like a hulking giant next to her. There isn't any evidence of us earlier than that—no newborn pictures, no plastic hospital bracelets pressed into a photo album, no cards with imprints of tiny feet dipped in paint—it's like we materialized right at the moment he found us on his restaurant steps.

Ava reaches absently for a glass and pours herself some water from the fridge. "None of your beeswax," she says, like we're four years old again. "I was good—Maya drove." I can smell the beer on her breath when she talks.

"So, what happened with Casey?" She grins a little wistfully. "Maybe not the smartest guy in the state, but definitely easy on the eyes."

Casey. Just the name alone leaves a bad taste in my mouth. I slide off my stool at the counter and walk over to the espresso machine on the wall. Might as well make some more—not like I'm going to get much sleep tonight anyway. "Does this look easy?" I ask, and pull at the neck of my sweatshirt so that she can see the deep purple bruise he left with his teeth.

"Oh my God! What happened?" she asks, suddenly looking a lot more sober. "Casey did that? I totally thought he was a nice guy. He never pulled anything like that on me."

"Lucky you," I say coldly, shrugging my shirt back on.

"Where were you?"

The dim orange glow on the asphalt flashes through my mind. "In his car in the Cheesecake Factory parking lot." My eyes start to tear up. "Everyone else was already gone."

"Did he . . ." She searches my face, her green eyes full of worry. "You know . . ."

"No," I say. I sniff and take a deep breath, trying to get myself together. "He didn't. But not because he didn't try."

Ava wraps her arms around my neck, and I relax a little. That's usually all it takes, and she knows it. I've never been able to stay mad at her for long. "I'm so sorry," she says. She pulls back and looks into my face, and I know she's seeing a version of what I see looking back at her—the same curly brown hair and green eyes, but it's nothing like looking into a mirror. Ava's the beauty and I'm the brains, and it always amazes me when people can't tell us apart. It's not just the fact that I'm an inch taller—that's only noticeable when we're standing next to each other. Because she was so sick when we were babies, Ava seems so delicate, so fragile. Two words I can't imagine ever being said about me.

Her eyes lock on mine, and she pulls the serious face she wears when she wants me to really listen. "I never would have asked you to go if I thought in a million years it would end like that. I know Casey's working again tomorrow night. We should go kick his ass." She gives a waist-high kick that's impressive, not just for the fact that she's bombed but also because she's wearing sky-high heels and an insanely tight skirt.

I allow myself a tiny grin. "Well, he might actually need some stitches on his face."

"No way." Ava looks at me in disbelief, and I'm almost offended that she thinks I can't take care of myself. "Did you hit him?"

"Better." I hold my fist up. "Keyed him like they taught us in self-defense. It actually worked."

Ava shakes her head. "You could have been killed! They also said that the first goal is to walk away."

"I know. I got lucky. But I started thinking about what Alicia would do, and decided that she wouldn't let it end without a fight. No matter what happened after."

Ava lets out a low whistle. "I'm just glad you're okay. You should have called me."

"I did," I say, staring at her. "I tried you a million times, but you never picked up."

"Oh. Right." She takes a sip of water, and her face goes instantly red.

For the first time I notice the matching diamond *A* pendant around her neck. Oh, crap. "*You* were out as Alicia too? I thought you said you had to go to a surprise birthday party."

Ava puts a hand on the pendant, knowing she's been caught. Rule number four is that only one of us can be Alicia at a time.

"I did! For Maya's sister's friend. Out near the university." The grin on her face is a dead giveaway.

I'm not letting her get away with it. "What's his name?"

"Why does it always have to be a guy?" She goes for a hurt look, but I'm not buying it. Whenever Ava does something stupid, it's always about a guy. "Okay, fine. His name is Dylan Harrington," she says excitedly. "Tall and ripped—plays basketball on the college team."

I sigh. "You knew Alicia was already out with Casey. What if someone figures it out?"

The guilty look on her face tells me all I need to know. Ava follows rules when they serve her purposes. Everything else is merely a suggestion. "I'm sorry!" she whines. "Except for Maya, nobody we know was there. I swear. I went to the party as me, but then he showed up. . . . I just couldn't let him go. It was an Alicia emergency."

"So what's wrong with him?" So far, he sounds like a guy Ava would keep for herself.

"He's from Bakersfield," she says, her nose wrinkling. "I swear I could still smell cows on him." She looks wistful. "But his arms . . . Oh, man. So it looks like Alicia's going to be extra busy for the next few weeks."

Which gives me just the opening I need. "I've been thinking," I say, watching her out of the corner of my eye. "Maybe we should quit Alicia. We're going away to college soon, and it's time for Alicia to disappear before she gets caught. Or worse."

"No! I don't want to quit Alicia." Her face registers shock and betrayal, just like I knew it would. "Come on," she says, her voice softer, with a singsong lilt she uses to get her way, even though she knows it doesn't work on me. "It's all just for fun."

"Does this look like fun to you?" I pull at the neck of my sweatshirt again so she can see the mark Casey left. For a split second I see his face hovering above me, his eyes shut tight in ecstasy or anger. Sometimes it was hard to tell the difference. "It's stupid. And dangerous. We've been lucky so far, but what if one of the guys finds out you've been lying to him the whole time?" I reach around and grab my wallet out of the bag that's hanging on the back of the chair. "Here." I slap Alicia's fake ID onto the counter and slide it toward her. Ava got it made last year because she almost got caught with her real license by one of Alicia's dates.

Ava's hand slides over the card just as Cecilia shuffles into the room in her robe and slippers.

"What are you girls doing up so late?" she asks, yawning. Her brown hair is puffy on one side, and she has sheet marks on her face.

"Sorry. Did we wake you up?" My heart races, and I know I look guilty. Cecilia must really be tired, because she doesn't call me on it.

"No," she says, heading for the cupboard. "I fell asleep reading and I need some water before I go to bed."

Ava's eyes widen at me when Cecilia's back is turned, and I shrug. To the rest of the world, Cecilia is just a housekeeper, but to us, she's as much of a mom as we've ever had, and just as guilt-inducing. Cecilia looks at Ava's outfit while her water fills at the fridge. "Ava, tell me you're not just getting home."

"No, I've been here for ages," Ava says with a straight face that makes me jealous. I've never been able to lie like she can. "We were just hanging out."

Cecilia nods and then turns to me as she takes a sip of water. "I didn't even hear you come in. Did you get your English project done?"

It was hard enough lying to her about where I was going tonight. I don't want to have to continue it now. "Mostly," I say. I take my cup to the sink and keep my back to her while I wash it out.

"Well, as long as everyone's home safe. Good night, girls." Cecilia gives us a wave and disappears down the hallway.

"You don't think she heard anything?" Ava says quietly as soon as we hear Cecilia's door shut.

I shake my head. Cecilia always calls us out if she thinks we're up to something.

Ava glances down the hall and then leans in close to me. "I still say we can't let Casey get away with it."

Picturing Casey's leering face sends the same shiver of fear and regret down my spine and I wish I'd never even heard his name. "No—drop it. It's done, and I don't ever want to see him again," I say. "But I think we should quit Alicia while we can. Before someone really gets hurt."

CHAPTER 2

"Alicia!"

I'm sitting on the patio of Café Roma when I hear that name, and my heart starts to pound. *Don't look up. Don't even glance his way. Pretend you didn't hear him and he'll think it's a mistake.* I focus on the laptop in front of me and hope the guy goes away. He shouldn't be here. This is exactly why we don't do Alicia close to home.

"Alicia?" The guy says it softly this time, with more of a question on the end, like he's not exactly sure anymore. That little catch in his voice is what makes me finally look up.

I take a deep breath. I don't know what I expected—Casey, or someone even worse, but this one looks fairly harmless. I guess they all do at first. It takes only one glance to figure out why Ava must have given him the Alicia business. With dark brown hair and light blue eyes, he's cute enough, but everything's just a little "too" for him to date Ava—hair a little too long, jeans a little too worn, edges a little too rough. He looks about our age, maybe a little bit older, but everything about him screams punk rock, not premed. Not what my sister would think of as a keeper.

I reach for my latte and give him a sad smile that goes with my slightly stained Stanford sweatshirt. "Sorry. No."

I can see the light in his eyes dim a little as he studies me, and I glance down to see what he sees—three-year-old sweats and scuffed UGGs, never mind a serious lack of makeup and my hair piled into a messy bun. He must not know Alicia very well if he thinks I'm her—Alicia doesn't leave the house unless she's camera-ready. We work hard to make Alicia look effortless. I just don't make much of an effort.

The poor guy looks so confused, I almost feel sorry for him. "I'm Lexi," I say, wondering how much of this I'm going to have to explain before I can get rid of him. How much did Ava tell him, anyway? "Not Alicia."

The confusion starts to lift from his face as he puts the pieces together. "Oh! You must be one of her . . . sisters." Now he just looks embarrassed. "I met Alicia at a show in Leucadia a couple of months ago. . . . We went out a few times. I um . . . had to do some things up north and just got back into town." He hesitates. "How is she?"

"Fine."

"Good," he says with a slightly uncomfortable smile. "That's good."

I nod, silently urging him to move along. Nothing to see here. I'm not the one you're looking for. When they realize it's just me, guys usually vanish.

Instead, he puts one hand on the empty chair across from me at the table. "Do you mind if I sit here?"

"Um." I look around, trying to come up with something other than a flat, bitchy "Yes," but there's something in his blue eyes that makes me hesitate. The café patio has filled up since I sat down. I've had my face so buried in my laptop, I didn't even notice.

The guy follows my glance. "It's just that it's packed out here." He nods toward my laptop. "I won't say a word. I promise."

I shrug and kick the chair toward him. All he wants is a place to sit. "It's fine."

He sets his drink and little plastic restaurant number on the table. "Thanks."

I turn pointedly back to my laptop, but it's impossible to concentrate with him sitting across from me, even though he's not doing anything I can pinpoint as irritating. Just distracting.

He drapes his jacket over the back of the chair and squints across the sidewalk toward the beach, where the sun is starting to break through the midmorning fog. "Gonna get hot soon."

I don't look up. "Yep." Sweat is starting to trickle down my back, but I can't take the sweatshirt off because the T-shirt I'm wearing is in even worse shape.

After settling in, he pulls an actual book out of his bag, so I slowly let my eyes wander past the laptop screen to see what he's reading. *Pride and Prejudice.* Seriously? I watch his eyes to see if he's just holding the book for effect, but it looks like he's actually reading it.

We sit in silence for a few minutes, until Cheryl brings his burger and fries to our table. She winks at me as she sets the plate down, and I smile, praying with all my might that she won't start some random conversation. Everyone around here knows we're twins, not triplets, and I'm too far into this to have to explain it now. I relax a little after she walks away without a word, and he slides the plate toward me. "Fry?"

I don't look up. "No. Thanks."

"It's only fair. You share your table with me. I share my fries with you."

The salty smell hits me, and I look over at my empty glass. That latte is the only thing I've had in the two hours I've been sitting here. "Okay," I say, reaching for the plate. "Just a couple. Thanks."

One of the fries barely grazes the floor before a watchful seagull dives from the railing and scoops it up in a blur of feathers and squawking. I laugh as the guy jumps back in his seat, obviously not familiar with the vultures masquerading as harmless seabirds that are the real overlords of this place. It makes sense that he's not from around here. Ava would never pull an Alicia this close to home. Alicia is strictly for guys we'd never bump into in real life. We hope.

"You'd better hold on to those fries. The seagulls are ruthless," I say.

"Duly noted."

My phone buzzes, and I jump, just like I've done every

time for the past few weeks—the waiting is killing me. I click on my email, but it's only junk. Nothing from Stanford. Not yet.

The guy grabs a couple of fries and gestures toward my phone. "Expecting something?"

I turn back toward my laptop and type a few words. It almost feels like I've been caught doing something embarrassing. "I thought we agreed no talking."

"*I* thought we were on a break." He smiles, revealing prominent canine teeth, a defect that I secretly love.

"I wouldn't want to keep you from your heavy reading," I say, nodding at the book.

He turns it over and looks at the front like he's just noticing it for the first time. "Yeah. I thought I should see what all the fuss is about."

"Let me know when you figure it out," I say, glancing at the book. I can't stand Jane Austen, with all the preening and dancing and girls who are interested in a guy only when they realize he has money.

He looks right into my eyes, a piercing gaze that makes my stomach flip. "Not an Austen fan," he says quietly. "Good to know."

I look down at my hands and shake my head. What am I doing? This is one of Ava's rejects, and I'm sitting here stealing fries and talking about Jane Austen when I should be studying for that statistics test on Monday. After the catastrophic end to last night's date, I need to keep my focus. Eyes on the prize, as Dad always says. I seriously don't have time for this.

He peers over the top of the screen. "What's so important that you're hunkered down here typing away on such a beautiful day?"

"'Hunkered'? I don't hunker." Who under the age of sixty uses words like that?

Without even looking up, I can tell he's smiling. "I don't know. You look pretty hunkered to me, and one little text got you all twitchy. I stand by my word choice."

"I'm just waiting for an email." He doesn't comment, so I go on. "From college. Admissions acceptances are due this week."

He nods thoughtfully. "Sounds important. Where did you apply?"

"Stanford."

There's a beat of silence as he waits for more. "That's it? Just Stanford?"

I put my hands in my lap and look at him. It's obvious he's not going anywhere anytime soon. "No, that's not it, but it might as well be. The first thing I ever wore was a Stanford onesie. My father's had the Stanford Dad bumper sticker ready for his car since I was nine. Stanford's the only place that matters." It doesn't help that I applied for early action and got deferred. Deferred. As in a definite maybe. My life feels like it's been on hold the past few months.

"But why?"

I stare at him, amazed that anyone can be so oblivious. "Um, because it's the best?"

The guy shrugs and gives me a little grin. "The best for what? The best for meeting your very own Mr. Darcy?"

I turn back to my laptop, irritation bubbling up inside

me. Why am I even bothering trying to explain myself to this nouveau-grunge *P & P*–toting hipster? Not like this conversation is ever going to matter. "Only the best university on the West Coast. For everything," I say into my keyboard.

"Prelaw?"

"No." I hate the smug look on his face. "Business."

The look of derision in his eyes isn't subtle at all. "Hmm. Serious."

"What's wrong with that?" I can hear the defensiveness in my voice, but I can't help it.

"Nothing. Lots of kids want to grow up to be CEOs."

I try to tell myself to shut up, but I rarely listen to my own advice. "I'm going to be a partner in my dad's company," I say before I can stop myself.

"What kind of company?"

I hesitate. I usually hate telling people what Dad does, but this guy looks expectant, so what the hell? Not like I'm ever going to see him again. "They make Andy Bars."

"Your dad is *that* Andy?" The guy's eyes are wide.

I smile tightly. His actual name is Alvaro, but Dad thought "Andy" was catchier, back in the days when he started making his nutrition bars in small batches in the kitchen of his restaurant. Now that he's practically famous, it's too late to change it. "Yep." I wait for the next question, which is always "Can you get me some?"

But he just seems surprised. "Interesting. Is that what you've always wanted to do?"

I don't like the way he's looking at me, like my family is

all entitled or something. "My dad's family came here from Guatemala when he was five. His father was a custodian at a high school. Dad put himself through college by bussing tables and got his MBA from Stanford. He does a lot of charity work through his corporation." Not to mention being the only parent to his adopted twin daughters after his blond trophy wife bailed on him. Okay, maybe she wasn't blond—I don't know because Dad got rid of all of the pictures of her—and not exactly a trophy wife, because they didn't have a lot of money back then, but that's what I imagine when I think about the woman he was married to once upon a time.

Dad saved the newspaper article from almost seventeen years ago. It's on the front page of our baby book. I love the headline: FOUNDLING TWINS LEFT ON RESTAURANT STEPS. When I was little, I thought a foundling was something out of Harry Potter, some mythical creature with tiny shimmering wings and secret magical powers, not that it was just a nice word for an abandoned baby. Dad decided that the fact that we'd been left at his restaurant was a sign that he'd been chosen just for us. They spent months working on our adoption, only to have his wife decide before we were two years old that maybe the whole parenting thing wasn't for her. But he stuck around.

"So you feel like you have to do the same thing in order to measure up?"

Yes. "No. It's just what I've always wanted to do. If he was a doctor, I'd probably want to do that. He's one of the best people I know."

"I see," he says quietly, and I can't tell if he's mocking me or not.

I glance at him. That turned into a lot more of a moment than I'd meant it to be. "So, what did you want to be?"

He stares at the sky. "At first, I wanted to be Superman, but then I realized that leaping tall buildings and bending steel is not exactly a skill set you can learn. So then I wanted to be a rock star."

"And you're studying Jane Austen because it will help you at rock star school?"

"Something like that." The guy smiles, revealing those big, square teeth. "Right now the school of life is a better choice than Stanford for me." He leans back in his chair. "Okay, future CEO, what about Harvard? Yale? Dartmouth?"

I glance out at the bicycles on the path in front of the sand, their riders in shorts and flip-flops despite the fact that winter is barely behind us. "I don't believe in snow."

He lets out a sharp laugh. "You don't *believe* in snow? How can you not believe in it? It exists. I've seen it myself."

"I believe in it for other people, just not for me. I hate it. And all the other Ivy League schools have snow, so it's Stanford or nothing."

"Obviously." He leans back in his chair so that the front legs lift off the ground. "Now that you've explained it to me, I totally see your point."

He goes back to eating, and I try to focus on the statistics problem in front of me, although my mind is whirling and I'm having a hard time concentrating. I have no idea why I just told him all that.

"So, Lexi? Alicia told me that your other sister is Ava. Ava, Alicia, and *Lexi*?"

I pointedly take my hands off my keyboard and put them in my lap. "Alexa," I say. "Lexi is short for it. Ava, Alicia, and *Alexa*."

He laughs a little and nods. "I see what they did there. Why do people always name twins and triplets things that rhyme?"

I don't even remember how we came up with the name for the third twin, but once we started calling her Alicia, it just seemed to fit. "Technically they don't rhyme. But honestly, I don't know. I didn't exactly have a say in it."

He waves to a bunch of guys as they take over an empty table in the corner.

"Let me guess," I say, looking at the group. It's full of way too much hair, visible tattoos, and those ear gauges that make a person look like an escapee from *National Geographic*. "Your band?"

He grins. "Is it that obvious?"

I look from the table of guys back to him. He fits in perfectly. I'd bet money he's the lead singer. "Yep. It is."

"So much for conformity in individuality." He thumps his chair onto the deck as he leans forward, and I feel the heat from his body as he closes the space between us. I wonder what Ava wore the night she met him at the show, if she put her hair up in a ponytail like she does sometimes when it's hot, if she wore the shorts Dad hates because her ass plays peekaboo when she walks. I wonder what she said to him over the loud music at the club, if she leaned in close in the steamy air, her lips brushing his ear as she shouted her answers. If she smiled in that annoying way she has when she gave him the fake name to go along with the fake personality.

He tilts his head, and for a split second I wish I was wearing Alicia's pendant. Instead of sitting here going on about Stanford and the joys of business school, Alicia would probably put her hand on his arm, brush the soft skin of his wrist with her finger. She'd look straight into his eyes with a gaze that would leave no doubt about how she felt, a look that would leave him grasping for words. Alicia can get a guy to do anything she wants.

"Maybe I'll see you around sometime," he says, pushing himself away from the table and shooting me a smile.

"Right," I mumble, my eyes on the wooden tabletop, embarrassed, as if he could read my mind.

He pauses as he turns to go. "Must be fun having other people who look just like you," he says, studying me. "I bet you could have a great time with it, you know? Sitting in each other's classes, taking each other's tests—fooling people into thinking you're the other sister."

I watch him as he wanders over to the crowded table across the deck, pulls out an empty chair, and flips it around before sitting down with his friends.

"You poor dumb bastard," I say into my keyboard, trying to get his face out of my head. "You really have no clue."

"What are you muttering about?" Zane Romero asks, pulling the chair out and flopping into it. Despite the fact that it's still freezing at the end of March, he must have gone out surfing, because the ends of his curly blond hair are still wet and his hands are red. Zane cups his hot chocolate in both hands and takes a big swig, his brown eyes on me.

"Nothing," I say, staring at my keyboard. Whenever I see Zane now, I miss him. Not this six-foot surfer version of Zane, but the little kid with the unruly hair and killer train set complete with hills and tunnels and little tiny people placed carefully in the painted landscape. Before his mom and dad got divorced, we lived next door to each other and spent hours playing with the train set that took over his entire garage. Until his parents decided it was weird for a ten-year-old boy to hang around with a ten-year-old girl all the time and they started finding other things for him to do. Soon after, Zane discovered surfing and I discovered studying— eventually, when we saw each other in school, we didn't have much to talk about anymore. This year he ended up in my Spanish class, and it's been nice having him back, even a little bit.

"Who's the guy?" he asks, nodding in the direction of the crowded table.

"I don't know," I say, not looking over there. I feel stupid for letting myself get all worked up over some band boy. I glance up at Zane and know he's not going to be satisfied until he hears the whole story—besides Maya, he's the only one who's in on it. "One of Alicia's rejects."

He raises his eyebrows without saying anything. But he doesn't have to, because I've heard it all before. I shrug my sweatshirt higher onto my shoulder to make sure Casey's bite mark doesn't show. No way can I explain that right now. "I know, I know. I just told Ava that we should quit."

25

He takes a slow sip of his drink and watches me squirm. "You know you're better than that."

I look him straight in the eyes. After all this time, what does he know? I can hear the guys at the other table talking and laughing. "Maybe I'm not," I say quietly.

I can tell by the look on his face that he's not going to take the bait. As much as he would disagree, Zane doesn't know everything. Just because we were neighbors once upon a time doesn't mean he can pass judgment now. It's not like we're still running through the sprinklers in our underwear. Times have changed.

Zane glances at the guy. "So, what's wrong with him?"

I shrug. "Knowing Ava, his car is probably more than three years old. That's enough to make him un-dateable, as far as she's concerned. He thought I was Alicia."

Zane laughs out loud. "How could he possibly think that?"

He doesn't actually look at my sweats and grungy boots, but I get what he means. "Thanks a lot."

"Don't be like that." He leans the chair over on two legs and gives me a wet, sloppy kiss on the cheek. I get a whiff of the sea and sunscreen. No matter what the weather, Zane always smells like summer. "You're much hotter than Alicia."

"Not working," I say, wiping my face with exaggerated movements.

He laughs. "Remember the time you cut your hair really short? And blamed it on Alicia?"

"First grade," I say, nodding. The moment was immortalized in our school photos that year. I did it when Ava got invited to Vanessa O'Neill's birthday party without me—an attempt to finally make myself different from her. Except it felt so weird, like I was the one being punished. Once my hair grew back, I never did it again. "I looked like a boy for months."

"Didn't Alicia pour some live goldfish into the pool once?"

"The hot tub." I scrunch my eyes shut with the memory of the colorful fish bobbing to the surface like carrots in a giant bowl of chicken soup. "She thought they were cold. Cecilia was so mad." In my mind it's almost like there was actually a third twin with us. Even when we were kids, Alicia was fun and daring and not afraid to get into trouble now and ask for forgiveness later. "Even though she was imaginary, Alicia seemed so real then."

There's big rolling laughter from the table in the corner, so we both look over. I catch the guy's eye as he quickly looks away from me with a sly smile. He's exactly the kind of guy Alicia would go for.

Zane looks from the table back to me, and for a split second, I'm sure he can tell what I'm thinking. "Good thing you're not doing Alicia anymore," he says softly, so no one else can hear. "That girl was nothing but trouble."

CHAPTER 3

"I'm out of here!" Dad shouts, his voice echoing through the two-story entranceway. "The car service will be here any minute."

Ava rushes him as he walks into the kitchen. "Bye, Daddy!" She gives him a hug and then pulls back to take a better look. "That's what you're wearing?"

He looks down at his jeans, which are cuffed and just a bit too tight. "What's wrong with these? I just got them."

Ava looks over at me because "I just got them" is code for "a new girlfriend took me shopping." We know that Dad dates—with his full head of dark hair just starting to get gray around the edges, his height, and his money, he's a catch—but he never brings any of the girls home. "You're not even wearing socks!" she says with a wrinkled nose.

Dad looks down and waves a loafer at the two of us. "I've been told I have sexy ankles."

"Gross," I say.

"Anyway," Dad says. "I'm going to check out the new school building in Soweto, not walk the runways in Paris. Nobody cares what I look like as long as I bring the money."

"Fine. But when you get home, we're seriously going shopping," Ava says. She reaches over and grabs the flat cap off his head. "And this has to go."

"Like I said, as long as I bring the money," Dad says, running his fingers through his disheveled hair. He walks over and gives me a quick hug around the shoulders, the kind you'd give a teenage son if you had one. "Have a good week without me." He winks. "Heard anything?"

I pretend to glare at him, but I know he's as anxious to get the Stanford email as I am. "You know I'll call you first."

"That's my girl," Dad says, giving my shoulder one last squeeze. "Keep your eyes on the prize. Even if you can't reach me right away on this trip, keep trying. I want to be the first to hear the good news."

"I will," I say.

"And how about you, my baby girl?" Dad asks Ava. "What are you going to do while I'm gone?"

Ava shrugs. "I don't know. Hit the beach if it gets warmer. After this summer, I won't have any time to lie out anymore." Which is ridiculous, because she applied only to state schools that are less than twenty miles inland. She purses her lips into a pout, and Dad laughs, gathering her into a big bear hug.

"Somehow I think you'll find the time, no matter where you end up," Dad says.

He turns to Cecilia as she walks out of the pantry, her

arms full of ingredients for dinner. "Now, you have the credit card?" he asks.

"I do," she says, as if she hasn't been through this routine a hundred times. Dad is constantly flying off to far corners of the world, checking on this orphanage in Guatemala or funding that school for underprivileged children in Africa. Apparently adopting two needy babies wasn't enough for him—he has to save the world.

"And I left some cash in the envelope on the hall table." Dad's phone buzzes, and he checks the display. "Car's here. Cell service is awful in that part of South Africa, so I may not be very reachable, but I'll check in as often as I can. Be good," he says, and with a wave, he heads toward the front door.

Cecilia grabs a cutting board and starts chopping onions vigorously as Ava checks her phone, Dad's departure barely causing a ripple in our routine.

"What are you making?" I ask Cecilia.

She doesn't look up from her chopping, even though I know that she could do it blindfolded and still make tiny, perfect pieces. "Chicken parmesan."

"With homemade sauce?"

Cecilia glances at me but doesn't bother with an answer. The only time jarred pasta sauce sees the inside of one of our pans is on her night off. Before she was with us, she was a cook in Dad's restaurant, and she more than knows her way around a kitchen.

"Can I help?" I ask.

She answers by putting the knife down and moving to

the sink to wash some tomatoes. She knows I'll do it right, because I do it her way. Over the years, she's taught me everything she knows in bits and pieces, and I like to cook.

Ava's fingers fly over her phone. "A bunch of us are going to the movies later," she says, her eyes on the screen. "Want to come?"

I glance up from the onion, my eyes already stinging. "It's a school night."

Ava pretends to slump forward onto the granite countertop, her hands up in surrender. "Seriously. It's Sunday," she says, her voice muffled. "You have got to get out more."

"Seriously," I repeat. "I've still got, like, two hours of homework to deal with." I lean sideways, away from Cecilia. "I wasted a ton of time on Friday night, thanks to you."

Ava pulls herself back into a sitting position and shakes her head. "Hey, if it weren't for me, you'd have no social life at all. Don't blame me if you end up living alone with twenty cats someday. You know what happens when you die in a room full of cats? They eat you."

Despite pretending not to listen, Cecilia laughs out loud. "Good Lord, Ava," she says, shutting off the water in the sink. "Leave your sister alone. You should be grateful that she wants to make something of herself. Gets you off the hook."

Those are fighting words to Ava. "Are you saying that I'm not smart enough to be some stupid business person? That Lexi's the only one who can get into Stanford? I could do that too if I wanted to."

Ava's played right into Cecilia's hands, just like every

other time. "Stop being such a poonch," I say, using the word we made up when we were kids.

Cecilia glares at me. She hates the word "poonch" but can't do anything about it because it doesn't actually mean anything. "I'm not saying that at all," she says as she bends over to look for another cutting board in the cabinet. "You're plenty smart enough. You just don't make it a priority. Maybe if you actually stayed in from time to time instead of running all over town from one party to the next, you'd be able to get into Stanford too."

Listening to the two of them have their standard argument only reminds me of the one part I'm not looking forward to—going to college alone. Ava might be smart enough to get into Stanford, but she wasn't dumb enough to apply, not with her grades the way they are. At this point, we're going to be hundreds of miles apart. Even in this big house, we shared a room until seventh grade, when Ava decided she needed her own space. When Dad finally broke down and bought a new bedroom set for the room down the hall from mine, I snuck in with a blanket and my pillow and slept on her floor for weeks, just to hear her steady breathing at night. As crazy as she makes me, I can't imagine not seeing her every day—it would be like a piece of me was missing.

Ava's arguing back now, but I tune them out, concentrating on making little perfect onion squares like Cecilia does. I glance up at the screen of the small TV that Cecilia had Dad install below the cabinets, where it squawks away most of the day. I'm always trying to get her to use the tablet we bought her so she can use the movie apps, but she says the TV is good enough for her. It's just the news on now, but as I'm starting to look away, a familiar image flashes onto the screen.

"Lexi!" Ava insists. "Will you please tell her—"

"Shush!" I say, waving my hand at her, even though the reporter's talking so fast, I can barely catch a word.

There it is again—the red car from the parking lot Friday night, although now it's daylight and surrounded by yellow crime tape. The reporter stands several yards away from the car, but I can still see a dark puddle on the ground by the open driver-side door.

"Shhh! What is that? What are they saying?" The whole scene looks surreal. Did someone call the cops after all? Did they find out what happened?

Cecilia looks up from the sink and frowns at the screen. "I saw that story already. A boy was found dead early this morning in the parking lot of the Cheesecake Factory." She waves the knife in my direction. "I bet it was the gangs. Drugs and gangs."

"We don't have gangs," Ava says, oblivious to the truth that's starting to dawn on me.

"Dead? How? Did they say what happened to him?" I scan the screen, but all I see is the reporter talking, and my heart is beating so fast that I've totally given up trying to figure out what she's saying.

Cecilia focuses back on her tomatoes. "With a knife." She makes a slicing motion across her throat with her finger. "That's how they do it with the drug cartels." She looks at us both with a shrug. "I saw it on *Nightline.*"

I glance over at Ava, and her mouth is hanging open as

the conversation catches up with her. "Wait— The Cheesecake Factory? Is that . . ."

"I think so." Any doubt is erased as a grainy photo of the guy from Friday night is flashed on the screen. His hair is longer and he looks a little younger, but that's definitely him.

"Oh God. It's Casey," she whispers. She grabs me by the arm and pulls me into the laundry room.

I suddenly feel hot all over, and my skin prickles like it does just before I'm going to be sick. I slide down the wall on top of a pile of clothes. "Do you think he's dead?"

Ava's concentrating on her phone, and she settles in beside me. "They wouldn't have it on the news if he wasn't. And I know he works closing on Saturday nights," she says. She scrolls down on the screen for a few seconds, her eyes darting back and forth as she reads. "Holy shit."

"What?" I say, leaning over to get a look.

"There's a bunch of news reports, but there's not much in any of them." She looks up at me, her face expressionless. "The short version is that someone stabbed him and he bled to death sometime overnight."

I can feel my mouth go dry. Someone I was with just the day before is dead. "Oh my God." I grab the phone from her, but she's right, there are just a bunch of short articles, and they all say the same basic thing: that he was found at dawn and police estimate that he'd been dead about five hours. They're withholding his name pending notification of next of kin, but one of the reports has a photo of his car. The very same car I bolted out of on Friday night. There's no doubt it's Casey. A jolt runs through my body as I reread the story.

"He was killed in the very same spot where we were parked."
I stand up and start pacing in the tiny room, needing some
kind of physical motion to go with my racing thoughts.
"What if whoever did this was in the parking lot that night
too?" I take a deep breath and try to calm down. "What if
they were watching? I might have ended up the same way.
Jesus, Ava, we have to call the cops!"

She looks at me, and I can't believe how calm she is.
"What for?"

"I don't know," I say, feeling lost, like I should do something, but I have no idea what. "I guess I was some kind of
witness or something. Maybe I saw something and didn't realize it." I pause, picturing a figure emerging from the shadows and attacking Casey.

"*You* didn't see anything Friday night," Ava says. "You
weren't out with him. Alicia was. The last thing we need is to
have to explain Alicia to the cops."

"Why would they care?"

She looks at me like I'm an idiot. "Hello? Fake ID?"

I glance back at a news photo of the black pool of blood
next to the car. More blood than I thought a body could
hold. Just the thought of it makes my stomach turn. "What
is wrong with you? Casey is dead!" Ava frowns, as I'm practically shouting at her, so I lower my voice. Yelling at Ava only
makes her shut down completely. "Look, someone killed
him . . . *murdered* him . . . the night after I was with him. In
the very same spot. The cops aren't going to care about some
stupid fake ID."

"You don't know that." Ava stands up. "Besides, this

has nothing to do with us. Maybe Cecilia's right and it had something to do with drugs, and no way do we want to get involved with that. Calling the cops will only drag us into something that is none of our business."

I picture Casey's shadowy figure leaning against his car under the streetlamp. "Oh my God! What if they got my license plate number? What if whoever did that to Casey thinks I know something? They might be able to track us down here!"

"Stop it!" Ava says, grabbing me by the shoulders. "For the last time, this has nothing to do with us." She shrugs. "I know Casey smoked a lot of pot—was probably dealing it too. Maybe he had it coming."

I can't believe she said that so calmly. "He was a total asshole," I agree. "But did you see the photo?" As the image pushes its way back into my mind, I wonder if he knew what was happening. If he was killed instantly or if he lay on the ground, helpless, as the life seeped out of him. "Nobody deserves that."

Ava reaches for the door handle, and there's a distant look on her face I haven't seen before. It's almost like this has happened to someone on TV, not someone she knew. "Maybe," she says slowly, considering it. "Maybe not. After all, they say that karma's a bitch."

CHAPTER 4

"So everyone's talking about that guy Casey being killed yesterday," Maya says, barely loud enough to be heard in the crowded hallway. She looks almost pleased to be able to share that news.

"You didn't say anything, did you?" Ava asks, slamming her locker shut. "I don't want people to know that Alicia went out with him."

"Of course not!" Maya glances at me. She's friends with both of us but takes her orders from Ava.

"Did anybody here know him?" I ask. "He graduated from Claremont. That's pretty far away."

She shakes her head. "I don't think so. Not personally. But a guy in my bio class knew his cousin or something."

Even though I let Ava talk me into not going to the cops, just thinking about that night makes me uneasy. It's like a bad movie; scenes from the car and then the news keep flashing through my mind. Casey's eyes as they narrowed in on me. The feel of the keys as I clutched them in my hand. The wide pool of blood by the driver-side door.

"Don't even think about it," Ava says to me, her voice edged with warning.

I'm pulled out of my thoughts and blink like I've been caught in headlights. "What?" As if I don't know. As if she can't tell what's going on in my head.

"You've got a guilty look on your face," she says, leaning toward me. "Nothing you can tell the cops is going to help them find whoever did this. It has nothing to do with us."

"Can we talk about something else? Please?" I beg.

"It's just so totally creepy!" Maya says, completely ignoring me. She puts one arm around my shoulder. "I mean, imagine something like that happening to someone we knew."

"He wasn't all that innocent," Ava says, looking around to make sure nobody overhears her.

Maya gapes at her. "You mean he got what he deserved?"

"That's exactly what I mean," Ava says, turning her back on Maya, signaling that the conversation is over. They both wait while I reorganize my backpack. "Are you coming to lunch?"

"In a min—" I'm interrupted by a whooping noise from down the crowded hallway. Over the sea of heads, I can see Joel Macy's spiky brown hair popping up and down. "I got in!" he shouts, banging on lockers as he makes his way toward us. "I got in!" Some people scowl, and others fist-bump him as he passes them—it's difficult not to get caught up in his enthusiasm.

"Did you hear yet?" he asks, sweeping me around in a circle and then setting me back down again. I glance over at Ava, and like I thought, she's staring at the two of us with a scowl on her face. Joel doesn't notice, only waves his phone at me. "I just got the email from Stanford—I got in!"

"So I guessed." I grin. Not like there was any doubt. Joel's been the one and only choice for valedictorian at our school since kindergarten. "That's awesome."

"Thanks," he says, and bumps my arm. "What about you?" Joel's grin is threatening to take over his entire face. It's nice to see him happy for a change.

"I haven't gotten anything yet." Joel was a lock; we all knew that. Nobody in their right mind takes five AP classes senior year. Me, on the other hand ... not so much. Too many nights I stayed up past midnight studying, trying a lot harder than everyone else seemed to need to in order to keep my grades up. I've done everything I can. Now it's up to the admissions committee. We're both aware that they only take 7 percent of their applicants. Now that Joel's in, there's one less space for me.

"You will! Like they're going to reject you? Oh my God, this is going to be so awesome. Stanford is going to rock next year." With that, he gives me a giant smile and continues down the hallway.

"What an idiot," Maya says, even though we all know she's just saying that for my benefit.

"Promise me that when your email comes, you won't embarrass yourself like that," Ava says, glancing down the hallway to where we can still hear Joel celebrating.

"That was not my fault," I tell her.

"I didn't say it was," she says. "I'm sure you two will be happy together next year."

"Shut up." I shove her in the arm. "I might not even get in."

Maya gives me a look. "Come on."

"Seriously," I say, trying to wrap my mind around that possibility, but they both shake their heads in disbelief.

"Hey," Zane says, peering over my shoulder. "Did you hear about the guy at the Cheesecake Factory?"

"Enough!" Ava says, and puts her hands over her ears. "I don't want to talk about that anymore."

"Sorry," Zane says, looking hurt.

"Don't worry about it," I say, shooting a look at Ava. "She's decided that she wants nothing but good news from now on."

Zane glances at Ava, then nods down the hall. "Speaking of good news, Joel Macy got his admission email."

"We saw," I say. If Zane knows what's good for him, he'll drop the subject quickly.

"Have you heard anything yet?"

"Nope," I say, feeling in my pocket for my phone. I can feel the butterflies forming—the truth of what I just told Ava is starting to sink in. What if I don't get in? What would Dad say?

"They're probably sending them out alphabetically. I bet by the end of the day." He puts one arm around my shoulder, but the weight of it just feels heavy.

"Don't jinx it," I say, removing his arm. "I don't know how much more waiting I can take."

"Won't be long now. I can feel it." Easy for Zane to say. College isn't exactly on his list of things to do. He turns, and I see a big scrape on the bottom of his chin.

"What happened there?"

Zane puts one hand up and rubs the spot absentmindedly. "I caught a sweet wave this morning but got Maytagged on the bottom."

I always think surf talk is hilarious, but I force myself not to laugh. "Sorry. Are you going out to the quad?" I ask. "I was going to eat with Maya and Ava."

"Oh yeah?" Zane says, looking over my shoulder.

I turn to see them already at the end of the hallway. Maya looks back like she wants to say something but gets swept along in Ava's wake.

"I know I'm not your sister's favorite person," Zane says.

I watch Maya and Ava walk out of the building. She doesn't not like him. It's just that he's not exactly her type. "It's nothing personal," I say.

"Yeah," he says with a grin. "That's exactly how I'm taking it."

We walk through the double glass doors and out into the sunlight, and settle onto the concrete wall on the edge of the quad. I grab my sandwich out of my backpack, and Zane pulls out a book. *Homebrewing For Dummies.* Not *Pride and Prejudice.*

I flick the edge of one page. "Home brewing?"

Zane glances at the cover. "Sure. Like a micro microbrewery. In our kitchen. Don't worry—it'll be classy. Dad's even working on some private labels for the bottles."

Figure Zane's dad for making home brew in their sink. He's the kind of parent who lets you drive the car on the back roads when you're only fourteen, and looks the other way when you take a swig of his beer at the Fourth of July picnic.

"You can't even legally drink."

He looks at me thoughtfully. "So? I can still make it. Think of it as chemistry. And I like chemistry."

I barely take another bite of my sandwich before my phone buzzes. I jump a little, enough for him to notice. "You gonna get that?" Zane asks, glancing at me.

I suddenly feel sick. "Of course," I say, reaching for it, but it's like my fingers have a mind of their own, and my phone sails onto the grass.

Zane jumps down and picks it up, but as he hands it to me, I change my mind. "You check it," I say, pushing it back at him.

"Come on," he says, waggling it in front of me. "Just get it over with. Then you can start to make plans—finally order that twin extra long My Pretty Pony comforter for the dorm room."

"You only say that because you want one." I reach for my phone, but then back off like it's red-hot. "I can't." I look up at him and clasp my hands together. "Please. Just look at this one email, and I'll be your best friend."

"Who else would have you?" Zane looks at the phone, considering it. "You're sure?"

"Positive. I've never been so sure of anything in my entire life."

"Okay." Zane taps the screen a few times.

42

"Is it from them?" In just a few short moments, it feels like I've forgotten how to breathe.

He grins. "Would you look at that? There's an email here from the Stanford University Office of Undergraduate Admissions."

"Oh my God," I say, digging my fingernails into my palms. My heart feels like it's going to beat right out of my chest. "Open it!"

Zane taps the screen again, and I squeeze my eyes shut, unable to bear the suspense any longer. My entire life hinges on the next few seconds. Everything I've worked for, all the honors and AP classes, all the class vice presidencies I've held, all the volunteer hours, they all come down to this one email. "What does it say? Just read it already!" I feel like I'm going to explode.

I hear Zane take a deep breath. "Dear Alexa," he begins, but his tone is so flat that I open my eyes to watch him. I barely register the words "very sorry" and "unable to offer you admission" before my anger flares up. "That's so not cool!" I yell at him. "This isn't the time to be screwing around!"

I expect him to smile, to push me on the shoulder and tell me he's joking, to break the thick wall of tension that's formed around us, but all I can see is the regret in his eyes.

"You *are* kidding, right?" I can hear the pleading in my voice that mirrors how much I want that to be true.

He swallows hard, and I see his Adam's apple bob up and down. "I wish I was," he says softly. Zane grabs my hand and puts the phone gently on my palm. I scan the letter, but my brain refuses to understand anything beyond the first

43

sentence. *I am very sorry to let you know that we are unable to offer you admission to Stanford University.*

"But . . . how?" These are all the words I can form at this moment. I feel numb and empty, like someone has come and scooped out all of my insides. We did everything right—I took the AP classes, PSATs, SATs; joined the Key club; and ran my ass off on the cross-country team even though I hated every second of it, because I wanted a sport on my application. I may not be in the running for valedictorian, but my grades are always above a 4.0. Dad promised I'd get in. It's all we've talked about since forever. I search Zane's face to see if there are any answers there. "What happened?"

"God, I'm so sorry," he says, squeezing my hand. Zane isn't the type to give me meaningless hope, tell me that I can always apply somewhere else, that maybe this is for the best, that it just wasn't meant to be. He understands how bad this really is.

I hear a roaring in my ears, and it feels like the future is rushing at me a million miles an hour, but instead of ivy-covered walls and long nights at the Stanford library, it's just a giant black hole. I don't even care about my phone as it tumbles to the ground. I just lower myself down onto the wall until I can feel the warm concrete on my cheek as I lie there. This is as far as I can possibly move right now. The thought of getting up and walking across the quad is impossible.

"Come on. We have to go," Zane says, trying to pull me up. "The bell rang."

"I'm staying here," I say, pulling my knees up to my chest.

He looks around as everyone slowly walks away from the grassy area and into the two-story brick buildings. All of them still have their futures wide open. They'll get emails from colleges in the next couple of weeks and celebrate by running down the hallway banging on lockers and shouting with excitement. I have nothing.

"We're going to be late," Zane says, and I hear the panic rising in his voice. He has no idea what to do next. "You hate being late."

I manage a small shake of my head. "Doesn't matter," I say. "None of it matters anymore."

CHAPTER 5

A silky sequined shirt flies through the air and hits me in the face. I peel it off and toss it with the others next to me on Ava's bed. I don't even know why I'm in here right now, except that being alone gives me too much time to think about what happened. How I've failed. How everyone is going on with their lives. Everyone except me. Every time I look at my phone, it's like that email is pulsing inside it, mocking me, but I can't bring myself to delete it. Maybe I need the reminder, to read it over and over again, the words like a bad tooth that you just can't keep your tongue from exploring, despite the sharp, stabbing pain.

"What do you think of that one?" Ava's voice is muffled from inside her closet.

Maya picks it up and holds it up to the light. "I like it. What with?"

More clothes fly out into the room. "I'm trying to find that black skirt I wore to the party downtown," she says before emerging with a crumpled black object in her hand. "Got it."

Maya looks skeptical. "The two of them together is going to look like you're trying too hard. It's just a party. You're not going to the opera or anything."

Considering her options, Ava stops and looks at the debris that lies all over her room. "Maybe. How about with those black jeans and fuchsia heels?"

"Better," Maya agrees.

Ava slips into the new clothes and, ignoring the mirror Dad installed behind her door, models her reflection in the full-length window that faces the back fence, because she says the window gives her a better "feel" for her outfits. Once she has examined it from every angle, she turns to me. "What do you think?"

It feels like I've been watching all of this on TV, like I'm not really in the room. I'm a little surprised that one of the characters is addressing me directly. "Whatever."

"Come on," she insists, turning to admire the bright pink top. "It's for that party on Friday."

I blink slowly, feeling Ava come into sharper focus. "It's only Wednesday."

"Exactly," she says. "So, what do you think?"

I try to put my level of not caring into words, but I can't seem to form that as a linear thought. "It's fine."

"You're not still grinding on that Stanford thing, are you?"

I feel a flash of frustration pushing up through the nothingness. "Yes, I'm still *grinding* on it. My entire life is over. I'm sorry if that's a problem for you."

Maya leans over and gives me a quick hug. "It's not over," she says. "You can always apply again."

"No. I can't." I knew they wouldn't understand. "Once you get rejected by Stanford, that's it. No second chances."

"There's always Cal or UCSB or one of those other schools," Ava adds. "I'm sure you'll get into one of those."

I feel the tears push up through the backs of my eyes. "Not the same." All I can think about is the conversation I'm going to have to have with Dad. How disappointed he's going to be after all the work we've put in. How I'm a total failure. The one thing we always talked about was me following in his footsteps at Stanford and then getting my MBA. And now that's all gone to hell.

"You're being overly dramatic." Ava kicks off her jeans and shimmies into the short black skirt. "There are plenty of other schools that would take you in a second." She turns and admires her ass in the reflection of the floor-to-ceiling window. We're basically the same height and weight, but somehow clothes look different on Ava, if that makes any sense. The same black skirt that hugs her curves makes me look Amish.

I lie down on her bed and grab her pillow. "A UC school," I repeat. So not the same. Dad's going to freak out.

Cecilia opens the door a crack. "Dinner, ladies."

"I don't want anything," I say, burying my face in the pillow. Everything is starting to feel totally overwhelming— Casey's death and now the Stanford email.

I feel the bed shift as Cecilia sits down. "Are you sick?" She brushes the hair off my forehead and feels for a fever.

"No," I say without turning my head. I'm afraid that if I look at her, I'll tell her everything, and I don't want to talk about this right now.

"A boy?" she asks.

"No." I push myself into a sitting position and glance at her. Cecilia's wearing a concerned look on her face that rightfully belongs to Dad, and I wonder if he handed that expression over to her like a set of house keys the day she came. "It's nothing. I'm just not hungry."

"It's chicken curry," she says in a singsong voice. "The kind you like with the carrots and mushy potatoes."

I feel my stomach rumble at the thought and wonder if she hears it too.

"You can eat with us," she says to Maya.

"Thanks," Maya says, already texting her mom. Nobody passes up an invitation to eat anything that Cecilia makes.

Cecilia turns to go, but stops and takes something out of her apron pocket. "I forgot—this came in the mail today." She glances at the front of the envelope and frowns. "It's addressed to Alicia Rios." Cecilia looks from Ava to me. "You wouldn't know anything about this, would you? You girls promised."

I glance at Ava, but I know she won't tell. Maya I'm a little less sure of, but Ava gives her a look that would make anybody keep their mouth shut.

"Alicia?" I say, hoping that I sound at least a little bit innocent. "No."

"You know that we haven't done Alicia for years." Ava reaches out and takes the envelope from Cecilia's hand. "What the . . ." she says, ripping it open and pulling out the paper inside. "It's a speeding ticket from a couple of weeks ago. But it was in a Honda." She flips the paper over.

I get a weird feeling in the pit of my stomach. It's got to be a joke—someone who knows about Alicia. "Where was it?"

"On Rancho Santa Fe Road," she says. "Going fifty in a forty." She looks up at me. "It's not even that fast."

Cecilia's looking at her, waiting for an explanation.

"This isn't either one of us," Ava says, waving the ticket at her. "Someone's screwing around. I don't even know anyone who drives a Honda."

"Let me see it," I say, taking the paper from her. It looks real enough. "We just have to tell them that it wasn't us. This Alicia Rios must have given the wrong information, and the ticket came to our house by accident."

"Identity theft is everywhere these days," Maya says.

Cecilia shakes her head. I can tell she's suspicious. "You'd better give that to your father to deal with when he gets home. You know he's not going to be happy if Alicia's back."

"She's not," Ava says, sounding so indignant that even I almost believe her. She catches Cecilia's stare. "I'll give it to him, I swear."

"Ten minutes until dinner," Cecilia says, glancing around the room at the piles of discarded clothes. "And do something with this mess."

"Okay, Ceyaya," Ava agrees, and leans over to give her a

kiss on the cheek. Ava started calling her that when we were little and she couldn't pronounce "Cecilia." I think Cecilia secretly likes it. "What do you think of this skirt?" She twirls, showing flashes of her red lace underwear.

Instead of answering, Cecilia just crosses herself and backs out of the doorway with a sigh.

As soon as the door closes, I turn on Ava. "How do you explain that? Somebody knows about Alicia. What if this has something to do with Casey?"

"God, relax," Ava says. Her face shows no emotion at all. "It's not like the name Alicia Rios isn't all that common. I bet if you Googled it, there would be thousands of Alicia Rioses running around. Maya's right— you hear about cases of identity theft all the time. We should have picked something more exotic, like Amber or Amaryllis."

"We were kids," I say. "Not like we were thinking something like this was going to happen."

"Nothing's happening," Ava insists. "Don't be so dramatic. Maybe the cops looked up that name and put the address from the fake ID in the system instead of this girl's real address."

"That's ridiculous," I say. "It's a fake ID. How would they even have our address?"

"I don't know," Ava says. "They've got everything on their little cop computers."

I shake my head. Sometimes Ava confuses even me. "So, what are we going to do about it? You know the minute Dad suspects something, he's going to start sniffing around."

Ava puts her hands on her hips. "We aren't going to do anything about it. It was a mistake. We're going to forget about it. He'll never find out."

"I thought your dad was home," Maya says from her perch on Ava's bed. "Didn't he just come back from the Galápagos or something?"

"Yes," Ava says, while I say "No" at the same time.

"No, he's not home," I repeat. "And the last trip was to India."

"It was the Galápagos." Ava stands up straight and looks at me, tossing the ticket onto a pile of papers on her desk. "He took that cruise on the small boat to fund some ecology studies."

"Hang on," I say. I walk into my room and pick up a snow globe from the bookcase. Dad's been bringing me snow globes as a souvenir since I stole one from him when I was five. Now the bookcase is practically full. "See—the Taj Mahal. India," I say, shaking it as I come back into the room. "This was from the last trip."

Ava tips it upside down, and fake snow pours over the building inside the plastic dome. In a place where there's never any real snow. "Oh. Maybe you're right," she says, examining it.

Maya's eyes light up. "Hey! Maybe that's it—you guys are from India! Maybe your birth mother was Indian royalty who was living here but got pregnant by a commoner, which is why she couldn't keep you. Oh my God, that's so romantic, like your dad made you his very own princesses or something."

"One of us is a princess anyway," I say under my breath.

Ava looks in the mirror. "Maybe." She shrugs and turns sideways.

"You could always get one of those online DNA tests done. They're not that expensive. It won't tell you who your parents are, but it will tell you where you're from," Maya says.

"No." Ava's tone is sharp and final.

"But wouldn't it . . ."

Ava turns on her. "I said no."

Maya looks at me, but I just shake my head. I've had this argument with Ava before, and there's no point. Dad adopted us when we were babies, and that's all she wants to know. Any talk about birth parents, and she freaks out. I might do it, try to find out when I turn eighteen. I don't know if I could keep it a secret from her, though.

Maya leans back against the wall and wiggles her feet, admiring the boots that Ava is letting her borrow. "So where is Mr. Rios off to this time?"

"South Africa," we answer together.

Maya frowns. She hates any display of twindom, like we're doing it on purpose. I pull my phone out and focus on the screen.

Ava and Maya are still arguing over clothes, when she comes over to see what I'm doing. "Really?" Ava asks, tipping the screen back. "You're on Casey's page again? Why do you keep obsessing over him? All that has nothing to do with you."

I scroll through all of the new messages left by friends and old classmates. A lot of people have been posting pictures of him from high school and even from elementary school, and it's hard for me to picture the leering guy who didn't understand the word "no" as the adorable blond kid on the swings. I feel bad about this version of Casey. "It does have something to do with me," I say. "Twenty-four hours after I saw him, he was dead."

Ava reaches over and grabs my phone. "Stop. Casey was an ass, and now he's gone. Good riddance."

I stare at her. Ava tends to skate across the surface—her highs never seem that high and her lows never seem that low, but this is pretty callous, even for her. "I can't believe you said that."

"I said it because it's true. Everyone else is moaning about what a great guy he was, but we know better." She turns to face me, and I see a flicker of pain cross her face. I'm instantly sorry I confronted her. If this is how she wants to deal with it, I should let her. She points to the fading bruise on my shoulder. "He wasn't what he seemed to be, and he deserved what he got from the universe."

"Fine," I say quietly.

Ava looks like she's gearing up to say something else, when her phone vibrates on the desk. "Huh," she says, tapping the screen. She frowns at me with a puzzled look on her face. "Did you talk to Eli the other day?"

I shake my head. "No. I don't know an Eli."

Ava looks up from the phone. "Tall? Gorgeous? In a band?"

And then it all makes sense. The guy at the café. "Looks like he works at a gas station?"

Her eyes narrow. "That's mean."

I'm always surprised to find where Ava draws the line. "Fine," I say. "Looks like he should be on a gas station calendar? With his shirt off?"

She smiles a little wistfully. "Exactly. Where?"

"I was studying on the back patio of Café Roma, and he showed up. Thought I was Alicia."

Maya is watching the two of us, eyes darting back and forth like at a tennis match.

"He's been gone for so long, I almost forgot how cute he is." She grins and twirls a piece of hair around her finger, remembering. "And you know how I am about guitar players. Especially guitar players after a show, when the tips of their hair are a little bit damp from all the sweating, and they've been baring their soul onstage, with every girl in the place wanting a piece of them."

"So why don't you just go out with him?"

"I told you, I'm exploring other opportunities right now." She piles her hair up on her head and makes a face in the mirror. "Opportunities named Dylan Harrington. Plus, Eli drives a pickup that must be at least fifteen years old."

I try not to picture Eli in my head. How cute his canine teeth were when he smiled. How easy he was to talk to. I can't do this again. I shouldn't. "Let me introduce you to a new word. It's called 'no.' As in no more Alicia. Not after what happened."

Ava turns back to the closet. "Eli's nothing like that, I can tell."

"You sure couldn't tell last time," I say.

55

"Maybe it's good to try it again," Maya adds. "You know, get back on the horse and all that."

I turn to her. "The last guy Alicia dated ended up dead. If the date had been twenty-four hours later, I might have been with him."

"Stop being so dramatic," Ava says.

"I don't want you going out with Eli," I say. "Not as Alicia."

"Don't worry so much. It's fine." She tosses her phone to me, and it lands in my lap, the text from Eli still on the screen. "Besides, I'm not going out with him. You are."

"No. I'm not." I toss the phone back to her.

She taps the screen a few times, then looks up at me. "I already told him that Alicia would love to see him again."

"Then you'll just have to tell him the truth."

"Look, you've had a rough week. You could use a nice night out. Just do it one last time, and if you still want to quit, then fine, I'm with you. Think of it as your big farewell," Ava says, sensing my resolve crumbling. "Just stay in public places. Nothing's going to happen, I promise. What have you got to lose?"

That question hits me in the gut, just like she knew it would. Because she's right. There's not much left to lose.

CHAPTER 6

I'm calm as I sit watching the restaurant from the front seat of my car. Alicia doesn't worry about this stuff. She knows that all guys want her and all girls want to be her, and acts accordingly. I take out a small mirror from the clutch that Ava loaned me and check to see that the heavy eyeliner and lip gloss she helped me apply are still in place. As I move, the big, diamond-encrusted pendant around my neck catches the fading light. I actually hate this pendant—thousands of dollars' worth of diamonds set into a big gold *A* is a stupid gift for teenage girls, and as proof, I lost mine a few months ago, and Dad had to get it replaced—but it's Alicia's trademark, so I'm wearing it.

My phone vibrates on the seat next to me, and I jump a little, but it's only Ava and Maya texting to see how it's going. I answer that it isn't yet and shut off the ringer completely. I'm thinking that I don't even remember what Eli looks like, when I see him walking toward the restaurant wearing a leather jacket and jeans. I take in his slightly floppy hair and easy smile and have to admit I was wrong—I'd recognize him anywhere.

I get out of the car and carefully smooth down the skirt that is way too short for Lexi but for Alicia is just perfect. I'm not a skirt person, but Alicia is. Plus it goes with the ridiculous high heels that Ava picked out. One thing's for sure—nobody would ever mistake me for Lexi at the moment. I can't help but notice that if the zombie apocalypse should happen sometime during this evening, Alicia would be one of the first people caught and converted into a walker, because no way can I run in all this stuff.

I walk slowly and carefully toward Eli, aware that his eyes are on my body as I approach. I'm not in any hurry because guys always wait for Alicia.

"Hey," I say as I get closer, inwardly congratulating myself on the casual spin I manage to put on that one word. Like I just happen to be walking by this particular restaurant and am pleasantly surprised to find him here too. As he approaches, I wonder if he's going to give me a kiss hello. Ava said they went out twice, but I have no idea how far things got. What's the protocol for a third date?

"You look great," he says, leaning in smoothly to give me a kiss on the cheek. Friendly with just a hint of something more. Interesting approach. "I'm glad you came." His leather jacket creaks slightly as he moves, and there's a musky, spicy smell that lingers for the smallest second as he pulls away from me.

I give him just a hint of a smile and look up at him through my lashes like I know Alicia would. She's shameless when it comes to stuff like that. "I'm glad you asked." I inwardly gag just a little, but his returning smile tells me I got it right. Being Alicia is basically doing and saying the opposite of everything I normally would. Easy.

Eli tilts his head and gives a little laugh—not mean exactly, but now I'm confused.

"What?" I run my hand over my hair, wondering if something's out of place.

His smile is unreadable. "Nothing." Eli glances up at the restaurant's sign. "So I know I told you to meet me here, but I was thinking we might be able to do something a little more fun."

"Like what?

"It's a surprise. Feel like going for a ride?"

The thought freezes me, and my mind flashes back to the last time I was alone in a car with a guy. I look back at Eli's easy smile. "Okay. But I'll drive."

Eli looks like he's going to say something, but changes his mind. "Great. It's not too far."

He walks to the passenger side of my car and squints at the hood. "I thought your car was silver?"

Crap. I didn't even think that he'd seen Ava's car. Dad gave us each the same car when we turned sixteen, but mine is white. I try my best to look casual. "Nope. It's always been white."

"Oh," he says, nodding. "Must have been the streetlamps outside the club that made it look silver."

"Yeah. Must have been." I hope that sounds more convincing than I feel.

He gives me some directions as he slides into the passenger seat. It's uncomfortably silent for the first few minutes. "So I think I totally embarrassed myself in front of your sister last week."

I think back to his expression when the seagull stole his fry, and suppress a smile. "Oh yeah? How?"

"Well, for one thing, I thought she was you."

I shrug, keeping my eyes on the road. "That's not embarrassing. People think I'm Lexi or Ava all the time."

I can feel him staring at me. "You really do look a lot alike," he says. "I've had friends who were identical, and I could always tell them apart, but I see why you get mistaken for each other."

"Hand me my phone," I say, when we get to a red light. I scroll through the photos until I come to the right one and hand the phone to him. "There's a picture of all three of us we took last year." It's really a picture of the two of us at our cousin's wedding, with an extra Ava added in with Photoshop. I glance over to see if Maya did a good enough job to fool him.

"Wow," he says, studying the picture. "This is you on the left, isn't it?"

We've got on matching hideous purple satin dresses. I wonder if he just got lucky.

"Right! How can you tell?"

"I can tell," he says mysteriously, and hands it back to me.

I laugh and twirl a strand of hair around my finger, something I've seen Ava do a million times when she's talking to a guy. It feels so fake, but his eyes follow my movements. "At least we don't dress alike. Lexi doesn't exactly make an effort," I say. "We're always on her to trade in that nasty sweatshirt for something nicer, but she really doesn't care." The light changes and I keep driving toward the freeway.

"You think so?" Eli asks with a frown. "I liked talking to her, but she's really . . ." He trails off like he doesn't know how to finish that sentence without being rude.

"Nerdy?" I volunteer. "Plain? Boring?"

"I was going to say 'serious.' Or 'intense.' You're pretty hard on her."

I sit back. "Lexi brings it on herself."

"She's definitely focused on going to Stanford," he says.

I flinch, remembering my favorite Stanford sweatshirt that is now at the bottom of our trash can. I couldn't even bear to put it into the donation bag. "She didn't get in," I say, biting my lip to keep my emotions steady, glad I can look at the road, because I don't want to look at him. It's the first time I've actually said that out loud.

"Really?" He looks surprised. "Well, maybe it just wasn't meant to be."

For some reason I don't want to kill him for saying that. Coming from Eli, it sounds almost reasonable. Not meant to be—like a good parking spot at the beach or the last sesame bagel at Roma on a busy Saturday morning. Or a future.

"Maybe you're right." I'm feeling like this conversation is circling uncomfortably close to my real life. "So, how's the band going?" Ava told me what his band is called, but I'm totally blanking on their name at the moment.

"Good. We're putting out a demo sometime next month. Adam's got a studio going in his garage, so we've been recording there as much as we can."

"Is that what you want to do? Play music?" I can hear the challenge in my voice and realize I sound just like Dad. Next I'm going to be telling him that he needs to have a backup plan and an English degree so that he can at least teach when his music career goes down the toilet.

He raises his eyebrows and looks amused. "Is that a problem?"

"No. It's just that only a tiny percentage of musicians ever make it." I shrug, wondering why I even started in on this. Not like Alicia would care if he ended up some broke musician living out of his dented Econovan.

"Well, someone has to be successful," Eli says with a confident grin. "Why not me? Why bother doing anything you're not passionate about?"

I have no idea if he's any good or not, but at this moment, I'm not sure it matters. I try to push all of the Lexi responses out of my head and figure out how Alicia would think and feel. Lexi knows that he'll probably end up playing in dive bars for seven drunk people who won't even notice he's there, long after he should have been discovered, but Alicia . . . Alicia might just believe in him. She'd be able to picture Eli at the front of a stage that overlooks thousands, even hundreds of thousands, of people, all screaming in unison for the first notes from his guitar.

"Listen," he says. "I'm sorry about Rebecca that night at the club."

I'm caught totally off guard—Ava didn't say anything about a Rebecca. "It's fine," I say noncommittally.

"She can be a real bitch sometimes, but that's no excuse," he continues. "She's had a hard time since we broke up, and sometimes it comes out in unexpected ways. Rebecca's crazy, but I kind of feel bad for her. It's like the band became her family."

"Don't worry about it," I say, hoping that's the right response. You think Ava would mention a fight with a crazed ex-girlfriend.

"Thanks," Eli says, looking relieved. "I was hoping you'd understand."

We get off the freeway somewhere near the zoo, in a neighborhood I've never been to before. "Where are we going?"

"Just up here," he says, pointing out the front window. "Take a left at the light."

"The drive-in?" I didn't even know there were still any drive-ins left.

"Sort of," he says, still grinning maniacally. "Just be patient; it's worth it."

"I'm not really the patient type," I say as we turn into the giant parking lot.

"Really?" Eli says in mock surprise. There are a ton of other cars parked around the edges, and a bunch of brightly painted trucks are arranged in a sloppy semicircle toward the front, where the screen rises several stories into the air.

"Taco trucks?" I turn and look at him.

"Not exactly," he says, opening the door. "Although some of the best are the original taco trucks."

We get out of the car, and my stomach starts rumbling right away at the amazing smells coming from the far side of the lot. People are scattered all over the asphalt, some just sitting together right on the ground. Some are perched precariously on thin concrete parking bumpers, and one group has set up a table and folding chairs in one of the parking spots, complete with a tablecloth and tiny vase filled with roses.

"It's Food Truck Friday," Eli explains as we walk toward the trucks. Each one has a fairly long line in front of it, and I squint, trying to read the menu boards posted on the sides.

He rubs his hands like an excited little kid. "Where should we start? Sliders? Soup? Vietnamese?"

"You do this a lot?" I say, enjoying his enthusiasm. The choices are kind of overwhelming.

"Enough," he says. "You can follow them online and find out where they're going to be. You said you liked good food, so I thought you might like this." He inhales, a happy smile on his face. "I've thought about being a chef sometimes. How cool would it be to have your own truck, be your own boss?"

I look around at the mostly young crowd, all focusing on the food that's being handed through the tiny windows on the sides of the trucks. Everyone looks like they're really into what they're eating, even if they're sitting on the ground to do it. I look around again. I really want some truffle fries, but Alicia would let the guy lead. "You pick."

Eli steers me toward a bright yellow truck. "I think we

need to start with some pulled pork sliders and then go next door for parmesan truffle fries."

"Sounds perfect." I watch the people in the trucks work. Their movements are compact and efficient, like people who are good at their jobs and like what they do. Everyone looks pretty young, and I wonder which one of them owns this truck.

We get our food on paper plates and walk toward an empty spot of asphalt.

"Next time I'll remember to bring the table," Eli says, nodding toward the fancy people a few parking spots away.

"I like this," I say, settling carefully down on the ground, the asphalt still warm on the backs of my knees. It's been hot for April, and while this skirt is okay for the weather, it's not exactly an eating-on-the-ground outfit.

"And I like that you like this," Eli says. He holds my gaze a second too long before looking back down at his plate.

I take a bite of the slider, the obviously homemade sauce dripping down my chin. There is a burst of salty and sweet as I crunch into the coleslaw that's perched on top, and it's one of the most perfect bites I've ever taken. "Oh God," I say, chewing slowly and then swallowing. "That's awesome."

"Try one of these," he says, handing me the basket of fries. "Real truffle oil on those suckers."

"Insane," I agree, taking a few from the basket. Eli knows his food. "So would you really open your own food truck?"

Eli looks around at the different options. "Maybe," he says with a shrug. "More fun than sitting in a boring office all day."

"Is that instead of or in addition to becoming Superman?" I inhale sharply the minute the words leave my mouth. Stupid! Alicia didn't have that conversation with him at the café that day—Lexi did.

Eli doesn't miss it. "Superman?"

I brush some hair away from my face to kill time. "Yeah. You told Lexi that you wanted to be Superman when you were little." I slide a sideways glance at him. "Sisters do talk, you know. I thought it was cute."

"I'll have to remember that," he says, but he doesn't look mad. "I think that life isn't so much linear as it is a bunch of different rooms. At one point in your life you're a student, then you can be a rock star, and when that gets old, become a chef and open up your own food truck. Or work the Superman angle. Don't get me wrong—I love music, but I think getting stuck in one thing for years and years has got to be kind of boring."

I realize as he says it that my life has only ever had one room—Stanford. "Don't your parents care?" I realize how bad that sounds. "I mean that you don't want to go to college or anything?"

He frowns, and I can tell by the shadow that crosses his face that I'm in unwelcome territory. "No. They're not around." His voice is flat and emotionless.

I feel terrible. "I'm so sorry."

Eli looks over at me, and I can tell he's deciding how much to say. "They're not dead or anything. At least I don't think so. We just . . . we just don't communicate. I lived with Danny from the band since junior year, and when we graduated last year, we got an apartment in Carlsbad." He sits up straighter. "It's nice. I can do what I want."

I wonder what that would be like—to not have any parental expectations at all. I can't even imagine it. I lean into him slightly. "Maybe I'll get to see it someday."

There's a mischievous light in his eyes. "Maybe."

As soon as he says it, I feel guilty. I got so caught up in the Alicia moment, I forgot I'm not supposed to be sitting here enjoying myself. After tonight, Alicia is going to disappear. We eat and watch the people as they gather in line, then finish up their food and drive away to wherever they're going next on an early spring night.

Eli points to the bright orange food truck. "The slider guy sometimes parks outside this club in Oceanside," he says. "Nothing better than a good pulled pork sandwich after midnight."

I briefly wonder who else he's had sliders with after shows, and feel a flash of jealousy that I know I'm not allowed to own.

Eli folds his empty plate. "What next? How about some pho? And then maybe dessert."

"Sounds good." I start to push myself off the ground, but Eli stops me.

"Wait here. I'll go get it."

I watch him in line at the Vietnamese truck, how he easily starts a conversation with the couple in front of him, tilting his head back and laughing at something the guy says. Everything seems to be easy with him, free of the subtle vibrations of stress that always seem to be the undercurrents of my life.

I wonder if I'll ever really learn to not worry about life after high school, about getting the best grades, running Dad's company someday. For all the good worrying does me now.

"Okay. I brought you a surprise," Eli says, sitting back down beside me. "And you have to eat it first, because once they cool off, they're just gross." He holds out a small round pastry that looks like a donut.

"What is it?"

"Deep-fried Oreo with white chocolate sauce. It's like redneck tiramisu. Amazing."

"Wow," I agree, eating dessert first, and then I dive into the fragrant soup. I don't register the chilies floating on top until my mouth explodes in flames. "Oh, crap." I cough and reach for a napkin to stop the tears that have already started to flow.

"Sorry!" Eli says, handing me the french fries. "Have a couple of these—it should help."

I take a few, and it does help, the heat in my mouth dulling to a pulsing ache. I can feel sweat on my upper lip, and my cheeks are wet from the tears that have been running down my face. As I bring my napkin away from my eyes, I see that it's streaked black with mascara. I must look like a wreck, another thing Alicia would never do, chilies or no chilies.

"You okay?" he asks when I finally pull myself together.

I nod quickly, not trusting my voice.

"I had them put extra chilies in," he says apologetically. "Last time we went out, you said you like your food as hot as you can get it."

"I do," I say quickly, my voice rough and ragged. "It just

68

went down the wrong way." Of course Ava would say that Alicia loves hot food. She carries a tiny bottle of Sriracha around in her bag. I can't stand it. "I'm fine."

Eli looks concerned, then lifts his hand and wipes my cheek with his thumb. "You had a little . . . um . . ." He suddenly looks embarrassed by the gesture.

I run my hands over my face. "I must look like a wreck."

He meets my eyes. "No, you don't. You look beautiful." The moment hangs heavily between us, and I wonder if he's going to kiss me, when he suddenly stands up and gathers our empty plates. "Want anything else?"

I look up at the trucks again, slightly disappointed that the moment passed. "No." I look away, knowing that I have to stop this before it goes any further. Turns out I really like Eli. I have to tell him the truth. "Listen . . . there's something we need to talk about."

"Okay." He glances away from me. "But hey, the line's gone down. How about another helping of Oreos for the road?"

I swallow hard. Maybe this isn't the right time anyway. I can only imagine the silence as we drive home if he gets pissed. "Sure. That would be great."

While I'm waiting for him to get back, I feel someone watching me, the way you do when the sense is physical, like a hand just brushing the skin on the back of your neck. I look around and see a familiar figure with dark hair and a light pink shirt vanish behind a parked car. What the hell is she doing here?

"I'll be right back," I say as I pass Eli by the Oreo truck.

The sun is low enough that it's getting hard to see in the shadows. When I get to the car there's no one behind it, but I glimpse a pink shirt vanishing behind one of the trucks. I'm a little pissed that she feels like she has to spy on me. Like I can't even get this right. "Ava!" I shout, walking around the long line to the back of a truck, but there's no one here. I walk back around to the front, looking quickly from side to side, but I don't see her anywhere.

I pull the phone from my tiny purse and punch a few buttons. "Where are you right now?" I demand as she answers. I brace myself, half waiting for her to jump out and scare the crap out of me any minute.

"At home," she says casually. "We're getting ready to go out." I hear Maya say something in the background. "Maya says hi."

"You sure you're not screwing around?" I say, looking around the parking lot.

"What are you talking about? I don't even know where you are."

"You swear you're not somewhere around here? You're not lying to me?"

"No! God. Hang on a second." I hear some muffled rumblings on her end, and then my phone vibrates as Ava gets back on the line. "Check your phone. I just sent you a photo."

I pull the phone away from my ear and click over to see a photo of her and Maya flipping me off from what is clearly her bedroom. "Got it. Thanks," I tell her.

"So, what's going on? Why the phone call in the middle of your hot date?"

"Nothing," I say, looking around, but whoever it was has disappeared. "I just could have sworn I saw you a couple of minutes ago."

"Not me," Ava says. "How's lover boy? Did he end up taking you to a fancy restaurant?"

"He's good," I say, looking at the growing crowd in the parking lot. I realize that for the first time in days, my stomach isn't in a knot. Eli walks over with a paper plate and sits on a parking barrier. "At this moment we're sitting on the ground in a drive-in parking lot downtown eating deep-fried Oreos from a paper plate."

"Classy," Ava says. "And a good argument for not dating band boys."

"Hmm," I say noncommittally, sitting down next to Eli. "I have to go."

I shove the phone back into my bag as he hands me a hot, fried Oreo. "Everything okay?"

"Fine," I say.

Eli grins at me, a tiny bit of batter on his upper lip. I have a sudden urge to reach out and touch him. He must see me staring, because he wipes his mouth with a napkin. "You said you had something we needed to talk about?"

I lick some powdered sugar off my finger, then look up into his blue eyes. Once the words about Alicia are out of my mouth, I won't be able to take them back—maybe Ava's a little bit right. I shrug and shake my head. "It was nothing."

CHAPTER 7

I glance down at my phone and hit IGNORE, despite the pang of guilt that follows. It's Dad again, calling from the land of lions and tigers and sketchy cell service. I can't talk to him about Stanford right now. I can barely think about it without a wave of hopelessness washing over me. I have no idea how I'm going to tell him I failed. He pulled himself up from nothing to be a very big something, donating millions of dollars to endless good causes and changing thousands of lives in the process. I've had it easy, and I can't even do a simple thing like get accepted to Stanford. How can I tell him that I'm not good enough for his alma mater? Not good enough to run his company? Not good enough to be his daughter?

I stare at the open page on my phone like I have been for the past hour, Casey's picture on the funeral announcement staring right back at me. Glancing at the clock, I see that I still have time to make it. Maybe I should—some part of me seems to need closure. Go. Go. Go.

"Who was that?" Cecilia asks from the other side of the couch. She nods at my hand. "On the phone?"

I turn the phone so she can't see what I've been looking at. "Nobody."

"If you say so." She grabs a piece of popcorn from the bowl on the coffee table and points to the TV. "It's just that you've been so distracted lately. You're not even paying attention now."

I glance up at the telenovela on the screen. She's right. I have no idea what's going on, and usually I love *Fuego y Hielo*. Dad tried to teach us Spanish when we were little and Cecilia's fluent, but these days I can barely follow along on TV. "Why is Fernando at the beach? I thought he was in the city with Maria?"

Cecilia sighs and hands me the remote. She refuses to use it, saying that all the buttons are too confusing. "Want to go back?"

"No. Thanks," I say, standing up. "I just need to get out of the house for a little while."

"Is everything okay?" she asks. "You've been acting funny lately."

"Fine," I manage, just before my voice starts to break. "Thanks." I lean down to give her a kiss on the cheek, then quickly turn away so she can't see my face.

I'm dressed in jeans and an old fleece jacket, so I quickly change into the black dress I wore when Abuelo died a couple of years ago, and sneak out of the house through the garage. I don't bother with the Alicia makeup or heels. I just want to be another anonymous teenager at a tragic funeral.

By the time I pull into the parking lot, I can tell that the church is totally packed. I manage to find a space in the very back, and as I lock the car, I notice two cops in a police car sitting a few rows away. I wonder what they're doing here—expecting trouble at a funeral? Probably just paying their respects. Casey's death seems to have hit everyone hard.

I take my place in the line of people still waiting to get in, behind a soccer team in full uniform. I knew Casey for only one night, but it's hard to reconcile the sneering guy I met with the compassionate, handsome boy in the picture that's propped up on an easel in the lobby. An older couple is stationed by the main double doors, the woman with her face red from crying and the man with his back ramrod straight as he greets the newcomers. Must be his parents. I turn and am heading for a side door to avoid them, when a woman with long, graying hair grabs my hands.

"Alicia!" she says with a sad smile. "I'm so glad you came." She glances toward the older couple. "Such a sad, sad day for all of us."

I'm so surprised, I can't think of anything to say at first. Ava said she'd gone out with Casey only a couple of times. She didn't say anything about meeting his family. "Right," I finally manage, hoping that the sadness on my face mirrors hers. "It's just awful."

"Did you come with anyone, dear?" she asks.

"No," I say quickly. "I'm here by myself."

"Then you have to come up and sit with us," she says, and before I can reply, she takes my arm in hers and leads me through the main doors and up the aisle to a pew in the front that still has some space in it. "Settle in here," she says, guiding me to a spot next to a woman in her twenties. "I'm going to go help in the lobby, but I'll be right back."

"Thanks," I say, feeling trapped. If I get up now, everyone's going to notice. I look around the church at all the people crammed into pews and lining every wall, in some places two people deep. There are people my age and people who look like friends of his parents. As I turn back toward the front, I'm startled to realize that the coffin is set on a pedestal only a few yards from where I'm sitting. Shiny dark wood draped with flowers, it has another picture of Casey on a smaller easel perched on top. Thank God the coffin is closed—but if he got his throat cut, it probably had to be.

"Just tragic, isn't it?" the woman next to me asks, dabbing her nose with a tissue.

"It is," I agree, nodding slowly. I wonder if Alicia knows her too.

"He was just the best," she says, shaking her head sadly. "And I can't believe he's gone."

She slides toward me a couple of inches. "You know," she says quietly, looking around to see if anyone else is listening, "they're saying it wasn't random."

Now I look up at her. Her eyes are dry, but her face is still red and a little blotchy. "What do you mean?" I look around too. "Like he was targeted?"

She nods slowly, sitting back against the pew. "Nothing

was taken. His wallet was in his pocket when they found him. But I can't imagine why anyone would target him." She sniffs. "Casey was an angel. An absolute angel. I can't imagine who would want him dead."

I can't exactly contradict her out loud, so I just smile weakly and hope I look like I agree.

"At least he didn't suffer," she says, blotting at her eyes.

I think of the pool of blood by the driver-side door. It must have taken a while for him to die. "How do you know that?" I move closer so nobody can hear. "I thought he was . . . you know." I can't bring myself to say the words out loud, so I make a small slashing gesture at my throat.

"That's just what the police told the media," she says knowingly. She puts one hand on the back of my neck in the little divot where my skull meets my vertebrae, her touch so light, it makes the hairs on my head stand up. "Whoever killed him knew what they were doing. They plunged a knife into this soft spot right here. Cut his spinal cord clean in half. He died almost instantly."

My mind forms a picture from her graphic description, which is worse than what I imagined just a few seconds ago.

"The cops have been spending a ton of time at the house," she says. Her eyes dart to a couple of men in dark gray suits that are standing on the left-hand side of the church. "And I think those guys are plainclothes officers. I've been watching *CSI* from the beginning—Vegas, not Miami—and the killer almost always shows up at the funeral."

I remember the cop car in the parking lot. "Why would

anyone want to kill Casey?" I ask. I can actually think of a couple of reasons, but I wisely keep them to myself.

"That's the million-dollar question, isn't it?" she responds.

My mind is reeling when the organ music kicks into high gear, and we all rise to our feet as the family starts walking slowly down the aisle to their seats.

———

The hearse is still in front of the church as I pull out onto the street. I barely remember anything about the funeral—one teary relative after another trying to make a sad joke or tell a funny story—because all I could think about was Casey's last moments. I'd been with him only the day before. The thought makes me sick.

When I get to the main intersection, I quickly flip on my signal and turn right instead of left and head toward the freeway. I just need to see it.

I can tell which parking space was his before I even turn into the Cheesecake Factory parking lot. The bright yellow police tape is gone, but there's a small shrine of plastic-wrapped flowers, soggy teddy bears, and burned-out candles leaning against the light pole where Casey's car was parked. This shrine is like a wave of memories and emotions cascading into the empty parking space—memories and emotions that have absolutely nothing to do with who he actually was. Casey might have been someone's son and someone's brother, but he was also a wannabe rapist and a creep.

I let the car idle, and I look around, the images of that night flooding my brain—the misty orange glow from the streetlights; the anger on his face as he pounded on my window; the shadowy silhouette of him leaning on his car as I drove away. I look around the parking lot at the few cars that fill the spaces that were empty that night. Could someone have been hiding in the bushes over to the left? There's still a faint rust-colored stain on the cracked asphalt, and I wonder what would have happened if the murder had been the night before. Would there be two shrines instead of just the one?

At the front of the lot, there's a brown four-door backed into one of the parking spaces, and I see two figures in the front seats that make me uneasy, so I put the car in gear again. I can't see their faces, but I can feel them watching me as I drive past their car and turn right onto the main street. I glance back as I pull away, but neither of them seems to move.

Suddenly I need to feel the mist on my face and hear the roar of the ocean in my ears. I hit the gas, and in half an hour, I'm pulling onto Eighteenth Street and into a parking space on the side of the street right before the sand starts. In summer, you have to drive miles for any kind of parking spot, but on a damp, foggy day at the beginning of April, I've got the place practically to myself. The cold, wet air creeps down the back of my neck as I walk toward the water, my feet digging into the narrow strip of sand between the two-story houses that stare blankly at the ocean. Just past the concrete retaining wall, the beach opens up in front of me, and it feels like

I'm all alone out here. I slip off my shoes, the sand cold at first but then warmer beneath the top layer as I walk toward the ocean. I sit down at the edge of the dry sand, where it slopes down slightly to the constant pulsing of the water crashing in wavelets on the shore before slipping and bubbling back into itself. I can feel the cold and damp seep through my dress, but I don't care as I stretch my legs out toward the waves. Out past the break there are half a dozen surfers in the lineup, all alike in their slick black wet suits. They sit on top of their boards as the waves bob underneath them, lifting them up and then setting them gently back down on the flat surface of the water. I wonder who's out there on such a cold day, but I can't see anyone well enough to tell. Locals, I'm sure of it. Nobody else comes to surf off Eighteenth Street. All the tourists go farther north to Breakers or Moonlight, and that's just fine with us.

I pull my knees up to my chest and rest my chin there. The houses that line the beach are lit up inside against the dark day, and that makes it seem even colder and more deserted out here. The faint smell of smoke rides on the damp air, and it reminds me of Christmas, only a few months ago, when everything still seemed possible. Now I'm just empty, like all my emotions are floating on the surface, waiting to be swept out to sea by the next big wave, leaving me blank and undone.

"Are you coming out too?"

I whirl around to see Zane with one arm over his shoulder zipping up his wet suit in the back.

He doesn't seem to notice that I'm not exactly dressed for the beach. I stand up next to him. "No. Just watching. Isn't it cold out there?"

Zane squints at the surfers in the distance. "You get a little brain freeze the first few minutes. Then you forget all about it." He picks up his board. "You should come out sometime."

Slater Connelly walks over with his board under his arm. "Way to go, bro! I heard the awesome news!" Slater is the definition of a surfer dude. If the turtle in *Finding Nemo* were human, he would be Slater.

Zane seems suddenly pleased and self-conscious at the same time. "Thanks," he says quietly, looking down so that the curls in front hide his eyes.

"You're getting on the ASP tour for sure!" Slater says, the look on his face showing his genuine happiness. "And winning that fifteen K."

"I hope so," Zane says. He glances around to see if anyone else is close enough to overhear.

"What news?" I ask.

"Aw, my bad," Slater says, grinning at me, his white teeth flashing in contrast to his deep tan. "I was totally interrupting here. Adios, bra!" He gives Zane a complicated handshake and then runs toward the breaking white waves, puffs of sand following his footsteps.

Zane turns back to me. "So, what are you—"

"What news?" I insist again.

He shrugs. "I got invited to an Association of Surfing Professionals junior tour event in Tahiti."

"Oh my God, that's awesome!" I say, punching him in the arm. "When?"

"In two weeks," he says, a grin creeping onto his face. I can see how happy he is about it even though he doesn't want to show it. "Dad's pissed about me missing school, but I can't let this opportunity get by me."

"The ASP is huge," I say, using up my knowledge of surfing in one sentence. "This could be your big break."

"Maybe." He nods slowly. "As long as I don't screw it up."

"You won't." Zane's always been the most focused person I know. I can't stop smiling at him. At least someone's dreams are coming true.

Zane looks out toward the surf and then back at me. "Are you going to be here for a while?"

"No. I have to get going."

"Okay." He seems suddenly slightly awkward. "Well, I'll see you around."

"Yeah," I call as he runs toward the surf. I watch as he leaps into the water and onto his board, his arms making long strokes in the waves so he can catch up with everyone else.

I sit for a while and watch the surfboards cut through the walls of water as the waves crest back toward shore. The wind is picking up a little, and the waves have a bigger head of white foam as they crash into the sand. Zane and Slater paddle furiously out in the dark water, then pull themselves up to ride the swell for a few feet before dropping off the backside. It must be nice to have nothing to worry about except catching the next big wave.

I take out my phone and stare at the email. Every time I see the subject line, I think back to the moment before Zane read it to me, back when everything was still happening. I've tried not to look at it, but I can't stay away; I already have most of it memorized. *We were humbled by your talents and achievements and by the commitment you demonstrated in all of your academic and extracurricular endeavors.* Right. I can picture the look on Dad's face when he gets home. The furrow between his eyes will be deeper and their usual light brown will be duller whenever he looks at me. I always loved the pride that was written all over him whenever grades came home. Twice a year we drive all the way up to Stanford to go to football games, each of us covered in Stanford Cardinal red. I've never disappointed him this badly.

Before I have time to think about it, I click on FORWARD, choose Dad's name, and then hit SEND. Then I press DELETE. Now Dad can have the joy of reading the nicely worded letter with the Stanford crest that tells everyone once and for all that I'm not good enough. Because suddenly all of this seems much less important than it used to.

CHAPTER 8

"Awfully fancy for a Saturday afternoon," Ava says as I pass by her room.

"You're always after me to make an effort," I say, walking quickly into my room as I unzip the dress. *Please, God, let her stay there.* I don't want to explain this right now.

No such luck. "Where'd you go?" she asks, leaning against my doorway.

I turn my back to her and pull on my yoga pants. When I turn back around, the bag I borrowed from her is open and she's pulling out a folded program.

"The funeral?" She looks at me like I'm an idiot. "You went to Casey's funeral?"

I pull my head into my sweatshirt, wishing I could just hide in here for the next few days. "So?" I finally ask, wrapping my hair up into a bun.

"Way to go keeping Alicia out of this," she says.

"I didn't go as Alicia," I say. "I went as me." Although, when I think about it, it didn't seem to matter much. "Why are you being so weird about all of this? I wanted some closure, that's all."

"Closure? Why do you need closure? Did you go to the after-party too?"

I stare at her. "You mean the reception? No. I just came home." I don't want to tell her about stopping at the Cheesecake Factory, because I know she'll only hassle me about that too. As shaken as Casey's death has left me, she seems mostly untouched.

"Good." She seems to calm down some. "Do you feel better now?"

"Not really." I grab the bag she loaned me and walk out of my room, with Ava following.

"So, what was it like?" She almost looks eager to hear.

"The funeral?" I ask. "Big. Sad. You know—funeralish." I pick my backpack up off the couch and put my wallet and keys from the bag into it.

She wrinkles her nose. "Was it an open casket?"

"No. Seriously, maybe you should have come with me."

"That would have blown their minds, two of us together at once. Alicia *au deux.*"

I remember the gray-haired woman at the front of the funeral home. "I thought you said you'd gone out with Casey only a couple of times."

"I did," she says, distracted by her phone. "Why?"

"So when did you meet his family?"

Ava looks up at me and shrugs. "His family? I never met

anyone in his family. Every time we went out, I met him somewhere. Alone."

"Well, they sure seemed to know who Alicia was," I say.

As I hand her the empty bag, I notice the message light blinking on the phone in the living room. I don't know why Dad still has a house phone—almost nobody ever calls. I reach over and press PLAY. There's a beep, and then a woman's voice comes through the speaker. "*This is Kate down at Leon's Hair Salon calling for Alicia Rios. We got your message about rescheduling your appointment to Thursday at four, and it's no problem. We'll see you then.*"

"That's weird," Ava says, shaking her head. "They must have looked up a different Alicia Rios and got this number by mistake." She reaches over and presses DELETE.

"But there is no Alicia Rios here," I remind her.

"I don't know. People make mistakes all the time!" She sounds impatient. "Kind of funny, though."

"Not so funny," I say, my mind racing. One mysterious Alicia Rios sighting is a coincidence. Two is something else. "First the ticket and now the phone message. Someone's screwing with us."

"You're just being paranoid." She's about to say something else when the front doorbell rings. "Cecilia's out visiting her sister," Ava says. "I'll get it."

I start to worry that it's Eli. I had a good time last night, but I don't want to admit that to Ava. Not yet anyway.

A few seconds later Ava comes skidding down the hallway. "You're not going to believe who it is!" she stage-whispers.

"Is it Eli?" I ask, following her down the hall.

"Why would it be Eli?" she says, staring at the closed door. "It's the cops."

I pause as I reach for the knob. What are they doing here?

"Don't get it!" she mouths.

"You're being ridiculous. What if something happened?" I ask, thinking of Dad so far away as I pull the door open. *Please, God,* I pray quickly, *don't let it be Dad.*

"Sorry to bother you," the one in the black suit jacket says. "Are your parents at home?"

"No," I say, my voice surprisingly shaky. I clear my throat. "Is everything okay?"

"Everything's fine. We're just here to ask a few questions," says the one in the green uniform.

"The department is investigating the death of a young man last weekend, and we're following up on some leads," the other guy says. My eyes wander to the big black gun that's in the holster at his side. He glances down at a small screen as if checking his facts. "I'm Detective Naito, and this is Officer Lawrence. We need to speak to Alicia Rios."

I open my mouth to say something, but nothing comes out. Ava giggles uncomfortably and says, "Alicia? There's no Alicia Rios here."

"This says otherwise." Officer Lawrence pushes some buttons on his tablet and then turns it to us. It's a copy of the license Ava got. The one with her picture and the name Alicia Rios on it.

He taps the screen. "And this is the correct address, isn't it?"

"Well, yeah, but—" I start.

"Okay, okay," Ava interrupts. "Alicia does live here, but she's not home right now."

"What? Come on, Ava—" I can't believe she's actually going to lie to the cops. She was right—everything really is on their cop computers.

She puts a hand protectively on my arm and squeezes in the universal sign for *Shut up.* "It's okay, Lex. We don't have to cover for her, because she didn't do anything wrong." She sends me a look, and at this point she's taken it so far that I don't have much of a choice.

The cops share knowing looks. "Do you know when she'll be back?"

Ava shakes her head sadly. "I couldn't guess. Alicia spends a lot of time in LA. With her acting career taking off, she's not here all that much anymore."

Acting career? We never discussed an acting career. Ava is going way off script.

Officer Lawrence checks his screen and then back up to us. "You girls look a lot like Alicia does in this DMV photo."

I decide to let Ava handle this one too.

"We're her sisters," Ava says. She glances at me. "Triplets."

"*Identical* triplets? You don't see that very often." He looks surprised and not entirely convinced.

"One in five hundred thousand," Ava replies without missing a beat. I can't believe she actually did some homework.

Officer Lawrence nods like he's impressed. "So you're one of only fourteen hundred sets. Congratulations."

I study him carefully. He's obviously not an idiot. I hope Ava knows what she's doing.

Officer Lawrence smiles. "Well, if you don't mind, can we see some ID?"

"No problem, Officer," she says. "I think our bags are in the family room. We'll go get them."

Detective Naito takes a step forward, and I can feel the mood shift. What was a friendly exchange has just become a little more serious. "Why don't we have just one of you go?"

"Okay." Ava seems unfazed. "Lex, can you bring my wallet too? It's in the Juicy bag."

I rush back down the hall, wishing we'd just told the truth. I fumble around in Ava's bag and find her gold wallet right away, grab mine, and run back to the front door. Ava is chatting with the cops, who are still standing on the porch, and if I didn't know better, I'd think she was enjoying herself. I wonder what other career choices Alicia made while I was gone.

"Here," I say, handing her the wallet. My hand is visibly shaking.

Ava doesn't look nervous at all. She opens her wallet and flashes her license at them.

"Do you mind taking it out of the wallet?" Detective Naito asks.

"Not at all," she says, and takes it out to show it to him. It says "Ava Rios."

"Thanks," he says, and she shoves it back into her wallet. "And yours?" he says to me.

As I hold my wallet, I suddenly realize that Alicia's license is sitting right in the little plastic window. I didn't take it out when I got home last night. "Right," I say, struggling to pull my real license from behind it.

"That's okay," he says, putting a hand out. "You can leave it in there."

"No," I say, tugging even harder until my license finally pulls free. "I've got it." I'm sure the detective must notice me close the wallet quickly, but he just glances at the name and my photo and then hands it back. "Thank you, ladies." Detective Naito leans forward and hands me a card. "Will you please have Alicia call me as soon as you get in touch with her? It's important."

"Can't you just tell us what you want to talk to her about?" Ava asks. "Then we can give her a message."

"I'm sorry. I can only talk to Alicia." He taps the card. "But it's important, so please let her know we came by."

"We will," Ava says, waving.

I can't get the door closed fast enough. I lean against it and stare at the little card with a tiny police shield and the name of the detective on it. "Why the hell did you start that in the first place? It would have taken two seconds to clear up the whole Alicia mistake."

She looks at me like I'm an idiot. "Because they had the license," she says. "Someone must have known that Casey was out with Alicia, and they found her in the system. I don't need to get busted for getting a fake ID."

"So you'd rather be taken in on suspicion of murder?"

"Oh, come on," she says. "Who said we had anything to do with Casey's murder? I'm sure they're just tracking his acquaintances, trying to find out where he's been, stuff like that."

I try to hand the card to Ava, but she puts her hands up. "Nuh-uh. You've got the ID. I don't want anything to do with this."

"Wait a second." I look closer at the ID. "I thought you said you got this from a guy on the Internet."

"Yeah. So?"

"But it's not real, right?"

"Of course not. I gave the guy a photo and paid him a hundred and seventy-five bucks."

I wave Alicia's license in her face. It does look real, even to me. "If this is fake, then how did the cops get it on their computer? It shouldn't be in the system anywhere."

"How the hell should I know?" she says a little defensively. "They've got everything on their computers these days."

"Something's wrong. . . ."

"Jeez, Lex. Let it go." Ava puts one hand on my shoulder. "Look, I'm sure it's no big deal. Stop worrying. It'll all blow over. I doubt they'll be back."

I put the cop's card into my pocket. "Right," I say, knowing that, like a killer showing up at a funeral, these things rarely, if ever, blow over on *CSI*.

CHAPTER 9

The drums are so loud, I can feel them through the soles of my boots, and I'm sweating so much that drops of water roll down my back. The music cascades into a wave that washes over all of us up in the front, arms pulsing, bodies writhing, and up onstage Eli is controlling it all.

My eyes are closed as I let the beat move through me, but I can feel the heat and vibrations of the crowd as they press toward the front of the stage, some people singing, others jumping and pumping fists in the air as the guys ram their instruments harder and faster, building to a crescendo that suddenly drops off a cliff to a momentary silence, before the deafening applause and whistles fill the small club. I'm so glad I caved and agreed to see Eli again. This is just what I needed tonight. An escape. From Stanford pressures. From the cops. From Ava.

The bass player plucks the intro to the next song, and many people in the crowd whistle in anticipation. Eli stands at the front of the band, looking back at the drummer, his guitar slack in front of him, one hand on the microphone, waiting for his turn to join in. His skin is glistening with effort, and I can see the glint of euphoria as he turns back to the crowd, momentarily locking eyes with me and flashing a quick smile. There's always a hum of energy around him, like something special could happen at any second, but now I can see how truly alive he is when he's up onstage, orchestrating the emotions of hundreds of people at the same time. He licks his lips and leans toward the microphone, and I realize that I'm standing completely still in the middle of the pulsing bodies, the desire I feel for him at this very moment threatening to overwhelm me.

I feel a hand on my arm and turn to hear a girl shouting into my ear. "I'm going for a drink. You want to come?" For a second I can't remember her name, but then it comes to me in a rush—Linzey, the drummer's girlfriend.

I glance back at Eli, wanting nothing more than to stand here and marvel at the change that's come over him, but I'm not so far gone that I don't recognize an opportunity when I see one. "Sure," I say, taking one last look at Eli as I turn away. She and the other band girlfriends were nice enough when I met them before the show, but there's a general wariness that hangs over all of them, and I'm guessing I'm not the first girl he's brought to a club. As she grabs my hand to lead me through the crowd toward the bar, I wonder what's suddenly changed to make her actually want to talk to me. We push through and get two tight spots against the wooden counter, and she pulls out a few crumpled bills from the pocket of her jeans and tries to straighten them out on top of the bar.

"I hate carrying a bag," she says with an apologetic shrug.

I reach into the tiny purse with the long strap that Ava loaned me and fish out my wallet. "Let me get this," I say, meeting her peace offering with one of my own.

"Thanks," she says, shoving the bills back into her pocket.

I hold the bill in my hand like I've seen other people do, not so high up that it looks like I'm waving it in the bartender's face, but high enough so that she can't miss it.

"They sound good tonight," Linzey offers tentatively, turning around to put her elbows on the bar and get a better look at the band.

I glance back, keeping one eye on the bartender. "Yeah, they do." I hesitate. I can't tell one song from another yet, but Ava said she'd seen Eli's band a few times. "This is my favorite song."

Linzey nods in time to the music. "Yeah, Eli really got this one right. I love the line about feeling like you're holding part of his soul in your hand."

I smile, because that is my favorite part too. I've tried to hold back, give myself a dose of reality whenever I can, but watching him onstage gives me a sense of longing that actually makes my chest ache. Can Alicia have a relationship? Can she have one if I don't tell Ava? The thought of never seeing Eli again makes me miss him already, but how could I possibly tell him now that I'm really Lexi? He'd never forgive me for lying to him, and besides, he'd never like the real me. I glance back at the stage. If I want to keep seeing Eli, I have to keep being Alicia.

The bartender finally catches my eye and walks over, rubbing the bar casually with a wet rag. "What can I get you ladies?"

I pull myself up to my full height. Alicia would definitely go for it. "I'll have a Corona," I say. I turn to Linzey. "You want one too?"

The bartender shakes her bright red hair and grins. "Nice try."

"I lost my ID." I give her what I hope is a sincere smile but am afraid I just look terrified.

"Look, that didn't work last night, and it's not going to work tonight."

"I wasn't here last night."

"Don't give me that crap. I have a memory for faces. You stood right here and tried to give me some story about losing your ID."

My mind races, trying to remember where Ava said she was last night. Why is she being so secretive all of a sudden? "Fine," I say with a shrug. "Can't kill me for trying."

"So a Coke for you." The bartender turns to Linzey. "I'm assuming your ID has also mysteriously disappeared?"

"I'll have a Diet Coke," she says, not even bothering.

Diet Coke. Damn. That's what Alicia would get—I totally forgot. I look at the bartender, but changing my order now would look weird.

Linzey grins at me as the bartender turns to get our drinks. "You had to give it a shot."

"Yeah."

"Weird that she thought you were here last night."

I try to play it off. "It happens sometimes. My sister looks a lot like me."

"Oh," she says vaguely. Eli must not have said anything about us being triplets. We watch the band for a few minutes before she speaks again.

"Did you hear that Melissa got them some gigs up in Seattle next week? I'm going to try to drive up with some of the other girls. Are you going?"

My heart sinks as I realize that Eli hasn't mentioned it at all. Not like I could go, with school and all, but it might be nice to be asked. I'm trying to come up with an intelligent answer, when a dark-haired girl walks up and punches Linzey in the arm. "Where the hell did you run off to? I go to pee, and you vanish."

Linzey shrugs. "I was thirsty, so sue me."

The girl glances at me and then turns completely toward Linzey so that I'm staring at the heart tattoo on the back of her left shoulder. I haven't totally figured her out yet. She seems to have some kind of relationship with Danny the bass player, but I saw him with his arm around another girl backstage, so I'm guessing it's not exclusive. She leans down and whispers something to Linzey that I can't hear, and the two of them burst into laughter. The bartender comes back with our drinks, so I slip her some money and push Linzey's drink toward her on the bar.

The dark-haired girl grabs Linzey's hand and pulls her back toward the stage, but as she goes, Linzey smiles at me

95

and raises her glass. "Thanks for the drink. Don't mind Rebecca. She's the girl Eli wrote the song about last year, and she's a little bitter about it."

Rebecca. So this is the jealous ex that Eli was talking about. As if she can hear me, she turns and glares in my direction, planting herself right in front of Eli and mouthing all the words as he sings, staking her claim. She's been around a lot longer than I have, and she's not letting go that easily. I watch Eli sing the last chorus, lifting one arm behind him as he pours all his energy into the song. Rebecca and Linzey are swallowed up by the hands waving in front of the stage.

I glance around the crowded club and feel a sense of satisfaction. Regardless of what Rebecca thinks, Alicia belongs in a place like this. She totally fits in with the makeup and the leather boots and the people who are just out to have a good time.

An hour later, the lights are on and the disgusting reality of a club after closing is revealed. One of the bartenders sweeps the grungy floor as the guys pack up their instruments onstage. Linzey and some other girls are sitting in a clump in one of the fake leather booths, waiting for the guys to be done. I don't see Rebecca anywhere, and I wonder if she's actually giving up. Eli's finished first, jumps down off the stage, and crosses toward where I'm sitting on a barstool trying to stay out of the way.

"Hey!" he says, his eyes still shining with excitement. "I'm glad you came." He puts his hand on my arm for just a split second, but that's all it takes. A small group of girls who have been hanging by the back door turn away at this possessive gesture, and I smile. Eli's taken, all right. At least for tonight. He reaches behind me for the glass that contains mostly brown-tinted melted ice. "Can I have the rest of this?"

"Of course," I say, enjoying his assumption that we share glasses now.

Melissa comes over and hands Eli a small white envelope. She's the band manager and is the only one in the group legally allowed to drink. "Here's your cut."

"Thanks," Eli says, shoving the envelope into his back pocket. He glances at the clock up on the wall above the bar. "Do you have to go home soon?" he asks me.

"No," I say. No school tomorrow because of spring break—not like Alicia would care. I almost tell him I don't have to be home at all, but I tuck that information into my back pocket like my own small white envelope, ready to pull it out if I need it later. When Cecilia's not working, she spends her days and nights at her sister's house, and her cousin Francesca comes to stay with us if Dad's gone. Unlike Cecilia, who stays up and waits for us even when she pretends she's not, Francesca is a deep sleeper, so as long as we're home by daybreak, it's fine. Information that is usually only useful for Ava. I smile up at him. "I've got time tonight."

"Excellent," he says, flashing me a smile.

Melissa's girlfriend, Amy, walks up and gives her a big kiss on the back of her neck. She's as tall and blond as Melissa is tiny and dark, but somehow they suit each other perfectly. Melissa turns and kisses her squarely on the mouth, and for a second I'm jealous—of their closeness, of the ease they have together and the permission they have to kiss each other in public. I can feel Eli standing so close to me, and I wonder if he'll ever kiss me like that.

"It's still like a million degrees out there," Amy complains. "And the AC in the van is broken."

"Let me go give out the rest of the money and I'll meet you outside," Melissa answers.

Everyone drags themselves toward the open back door, where the air is only a few degrees cooler than it is inside. It's one of those stagnant inland nights with no breeze, and for a moment I wish I could invite everyone back to my house for a midnight pool party. "So, what now?" Amy asks. "Denny's in Carlsbad? At least it'll be cooler by the beach."

"How about WaterRidge?" Linzey tosses out, one hand tucked into Adam's back pocket.

Amy whirls around. "Oooh, yes! We haven't done that for ages." Nods and murmurs go through the group, and it seems like the decision is made.

"I don't feel like WaterRidge," Rebecca says, walking up and grabbing Danny's arm possessively.

"Then don't come," Amy says, a hint of annoyance in her voice.

"Come on. What else are you going to do?" Linzey asks.

Rebecca glares at Eli and me standing so close together. I almost expect him to say something in view of such open hostility, but he doesn't, just looks at the ground sheepishly.

"Fine," she finally says. "I'll go to stupid WaterRidge with you guys."

"Put your crap in the van and let's go," Melissa agrees, and the guys shove the black instrument cases and amps into the back of the dented white panel van. I keep my eyes on Rebecca as she climbs into Danny's car.

"What's WaterRidge?" I ask.

Eli turns to me, his features made sharper by the lights of the passing cars. "You've never been to WaterRidge?"

"Nope," I say. "Never even heard of it."

"And here I thought you hadn't had a deprived child-hood," he says. "Don't worry, you'll like it." He grins. "You can run fast, can't you?"

"Um . . . ," I say, not sure how to answer that.

"Don't worry. If there's trouble, I'll take care of it."

I study Eli, who has an expectant look on his face. Everyone else in the group is already in their cars and heading out of the parking lot toward the street. Ordinarily I'd never do something like this—get into a car late at night bound for destinations unknown. Although, this is probably something Ava would do. And definitely something Alicia would do, if only to make sure that Eli isn't alone with Rebecca.

"Let's go," I say, opening the door to Eli's truck. I suddenly want to be somewhere far away from my real life. With Eli. He smiles and climbs in, and we follow Melissa and Amy out of the parking lot and onto the empty street.

CHAPTER 10

After about fifteen minutes of driving, we turn into some kind of office park—tall cement buildings with hundreds of windows surrounding tiny patches of lawn. I see a large metal sign at the entrance to one of the buildings: WATERRIDGE.

Eli glances around at the big empty parking lot and flips his lights off as all the cars park as close to the buildings as we can. Everyone is quiet as they drag themselves out of the cars, the only sounds some muffled laughter and scraping and squeaking as doors open and close. Melissa grabs a boogie board from the back of the van and hands another one to Eli.

I look around at the silent, empty buildings. "What are we doing here?"

Linzey hears me and laughs from outside Adam's truck. "Ooh. A WaterRidge virgin. Nice."

Melissa grins. "We're going swimming."

I take in the acres of asphalt and dozens of buildings. "Where?"

"There," Eli says, pointing to a giant fountain that cascades in levels in front of the tallest building. Even though it's the middle of the night, the water is flowing in chutes down the side, until it ends in a dark pool at the bottom.

"Is it legal?" I ask.

Rebecca's standing by Danny's El Dorado, talking quietly with the other guitarist's girlfriend, and laughs at my words, a short bark that echoes off the tall concrete buildings. "Right. You're not afraid, are you?"

I look up at the tall fountain, feeling a ball of fear in the pit of my stomach. I fight back my natural reaction. "No."

Eli grabs my hand and gives a reassuring squeeze. "Don't worry. Just stick with me and you'll be fine. It's all part of the fun."

Melissa pulls her shirt over her head, steps out of her jeans, and kicks them into a pile by the front tire. A quick glance around tells me that everyone else is doing the same thing. Linzey walks over to me in her bra and underwear like she's wearing a bikini at the Eighteenth Street beach. "Come on. You don't want to get your clothes wet. Just leave them by the car so you'll know where they are in a hurry."

"Here. I'll go first," Eli says, grabbing his shirt and pulling it over his head. I hope my gasp isn't audible as I take in his taut stomach and smooth skin. I had no idea what he was hiding under there. It's hard not to reach out and run my hand over his chest. "It's no big deal," he says, kicking off his jeans until he's standing there in a pair of tight boxer briefs, making exaggerated muscles with his arms. He's the tiniest bit bowlegged, but his legs are long and muscular. Too late, I realize I'm staring.

"Okay, okay," I say, taking a deep breath and quickly undoing the buttons on my top. I'm seriously glad when I realize I'm wearing one of Ava's deep purple lace bras. I feel Eli's eyes on me, and he shoots me a smile as I pull off the skirt I'm wearing and toss it down next to his jeans. I resist the urge to cross my hands in front of my chest. I just keep telling myself it's no different from a bathing suit, even if I don't really believe that.

"Let's do it," Amy says, leading the way up the concrete steps.

Eli reaches back and grabs my hand, and I feel my heart race with the possibility in that one casual gesture. I love the feeling of connecting with him, if only for this one crazy night. I feel a sense of possessiveness come over me, and I glance back to make sure Rebecca is watching. She is, her face unreadable.

We walk up several flights of stairs at the side of the building until we're at the landing of the top chute of the fountain, the water rushing out in front of us. Melissa disappears around a corner, and the lights in the pool below flick on, making colored streaks in the water.

"Turn those off!" Amy says.

Rebecca looks sad. "Aw, come on. It's so much prettier when the lights are on."

"You know security always comes faster when they're on. I want to get a couple of runs in at least."

"Fine," Rebecca says, walking back around the corner. In seconds, the water below is dark again.

"Security?" I ask Eli. My heart is racing, and I can feel my face getting hot.

"It's okay. Follow me," he says. "Melissa, let her have your board. I'll bring it right back up." He hands me her board. "It's just like a waterslide. Give me a twenty-second head start, and then you go." Eli positions himself at the mouth of the rushing water and dives in on top of the board. There are muffled whoops and cheers as he rides the wave down to the next level of the fountain and disappears around the corner.

"Go ahead," Linzey encourages. I look behind me at everyone watching expectantly, and I know Rebecca is hoping I'll chicken out. So much of me wants to hand the board to Melissa and walk back down the steps, but I can't. Because Alicia wouldn't. She would have been the first one down the chute, screaming all the way. I turn back around and take several deep breaths before pushing myself into the current. The water reeks of chlorine as it rushes by me, and I squeal as the cold waves wrap around my body. In seconds I've done the top of the fountain and stand up in the shallows to position myself for the next level. I gingerly lower myself into the waterfall and ride the next two levels, until I splash down in the darkened shallow pool at the bottom.

"You did it!" Eli laughs and reaches down to pull me out of the way.

I check to make sure that nothing's popping out up top and reach back to discreetly fix the massive wedgie I got on the way down. "That was cool!"

"Let's run these back up and give everyone else a turn." We quickly walk up the concrete steps, our feet leaving wet trails on the still-warm stone.

A couple of the guys have already gone down without boards, so we hand the boards to Linzey and Rebecca for their turns. We're so high up that the breeze is cooling everything off quickly, and I start to shiver as we stand and wait to get the boogie boards back.

"Come here," Eli says, pulling me close to him and rubbing my arms. At first I'm still shivering, but then I let myself relax into the warmth of his body, believing for just one second that nothing bad can ever happen if I can only freeze this moment. I glance over at Amy and Melissa, who are pressed up against the cement wall making out, their hands wandering over each other's bodies, having seemingly forgotten why we're up here in the first place. Eli follows my gaze and grins. "Looks like they have the right idea," he says, curling a strand of my wet hair around his finger.

I can feel the moment change as the grin slips from his face and his eyes meet mine. I lean into him just the smallest bit, giving him permission to do what I've wanted all night long. His lips are soft, gentle at first, and then more urgent as he bends down to kiss me, grabbing both my hands and wrapping my fingers up with his. I ease my hands free and put my arms around his neck, pulling him closer to me until every inch of our skin is touching.

I hear the laughter and approaching footsteps as Linzey and Rebecca come back up, and I pull away from Eli just as they round the corner.

"Break it up," Linzey says. She tosses the boards at us. "Your turn again."

Eli grins and kisses my neck one last time. It feels like so much has changed between us in just a few short seconds. I see Rebecca turn away from us and then grab Danny as he walks by, pulling him down into an embrace of her own.

"You go first this time," Eli says, walking over to the edge of the water.

"You just want to watch her ass!" Danny yells from behind us.

"Shut up!" Eli yells back, but I can see he's smiling.

"It's a free country," I say, taking a couple of running steps and jumping onto the boogie board as it gets swept away. I can hardly believe the things that come out of my mouth when I'm Alicia. Suddenly I feel a weight in my chest. I can't be her forever. At midnight or two o'clock or sometime next week, I'm going to turn back into Lexi, and everything will change.

In a few seconds, Eli lands next to me, and I push off with my arms, dragging my body through the shallow water to the other side of the pool, away from the landing site. It's so much warmer in the water that I just lie there with only my face sticking out, looking up at the stars and trying not to think about the inevitable.

Eli splashes over to me after handing the boards off to Adam to take back up. We lie in the knee-deep water, and I can feel him reaching for my hand. "You having fun?"

"It's awesome," I say, trying to keep all traces of sadness out of my voice.

He squeezes my fingers and is about to say something

else when we hear a shout from above us. "Flashlights! It's security!" We scramble to our feet and splash our way to the side, leap over the concrete wall, and land on the lawn below. I can hear muffled screams as everyone else runs down the stairs. I look up and see several flashlights flickering on the highest landing as they search back and forth.

"Head for the truck!" Eli shouts, giving me a little push in the right direction. "Grab your clothes and just jump in!" I reach the door just as I see a small white car with yellow flashing lights turn into the driveway that leads to the complex.

"They're coming!" I yell. I scramble for my clothes, dropping my skirt three times before I finally get it all and climb into the cab and slam the door behind me. Eli starts the truck and peels out of the parking spot with his headlights still off.

"See if everyone got to their cars," he says, racing to the other end of the lot.

"I see Adam's car moving," I say. "And the lights just went on in the van."

"Did Rebecca get back?" he asks. "Is she with Danny?"

I don't like the urgency in his voice. Rebecca is Danny's problem now. I see Danny's El Dorado still parked in the lot. "I don't think they made it."

Eli turns and waits at the end of the lot near the exit, peering through the windshield. "Shit. We have to go back." He starts to race back in that direction, when we see the lights in the car flick on.

"They're in! Go! Go!" I say, watching the flashing lights of the security car get closer.

Eli throws the stick into first gear and guns it out of the parking lot, followed closely by Melissa and Amy in the van. My heart is pounding as we race down the industrial road toward the freeway.

"Are the security guys following us?" Eli asks, his eyes glancing in the rearview mirror.

I look back, but see only the two cars and the white van. "I don't think so."

Eli breaks into a grin, and the car slows a little. "They don't usually chase us once we're out of the office park." He pulls over to the side of the road, and Melissa's van passes us, honking as Amy waves from the passenger seat. "Let's just throw our clothes on here."

"Does that happen a lot?" I ask as I sit back in the seat and try to calm down.

"Pretty much every time," he answers, his breath still coming fast from the excitement. "But worth it, right?"

I fish around for my shirt, realizing that I'm not self-conscious at all, even though I'm sitting in a cute guy's truck in nothing but my wet underwear and bra. Say what you want about Alicia—she knows how to have a good time.

"Totally," I answer. I look back at the parking lot in the distance and see one lone blue car off to the side, almost hidden in the shadows of the streetlamps. Someone didn't make it out. "Whose car is that?"

Eli glances back. "I don't now. I saw it too. Must be someone who works there. Nobo y in the band has a Honda."

A thread of uneasiness winds around my body at his words. I don't say anything, but I don't think it belongs to anyone who works there. The parking lot was empty when we pulled in, I'm sure of it.

———

There's a bright yellow sports car parked next to Ava's Mercedes in our driveway when I get home. It's an old car, but totally restored, down to the shiny chrome tailpipe and the Playboy Bunny ornament hanging from the rearview mirror. Charming. I expect to see Ava and whoever owns the car in the family room, but the house is quiet and Ava's door is closed when I walk down the back hallway. My hair is still wet, and I'm carrying Alicia's boots as I pass the big mirror in the hallway. Most of my eye makeup is gone, and my lips have only a hint of color on them. *Still more than Lexi would have on a good day,* I think as I stop and look more closely.

"So apparently Alicia is a little sluttier than we thought," Ava says from the doorway of her room, scaring me half to death.

"Jesus!" I whisper. "And she's not slutty. I didn't sleep with him."

Ava wanders down the hall to take a better look, peering into my face. "Hmm. Your lips look puffy and it's way past curfew."

I can't help the grin on my face, remembering how we must have looked running for the truck in our underwear. "Alicia's not slutty, but she's not Amish."

Ava takes one hand and pulls at a strand of my wet hair. "Skinny-dipping?"

"God! No!" I smile. "But close."

Ava grins too, her eyebrows raised in expectation. "And he kissed you?"

"Yeah. But I didn't break any of the rules." I hesitate, not knowing why I'm letting her get to me so much. "Why didn't you tell me about Rebecca?"

"What's to tell?" Ava says dismissively. "She's a crazy ex-girlfriend. She got in my face one night at a club. Luckily, some of her friends pulled her away, or I would have had to deal with her myself."

Somehow I doubt that—Ava wouldn't risk messing up her clothes just to take care of Rebecca. "Well, thanks for the heads-up—she's still hanging around."

"What do you care? He's just a band boy." Ava yawns and shakes her head. "Crap, girl. I'd know that look anywhere. You like him."

"He's . . . nice," I say, not wanting to give too much away.

"He is," she says. "For a pickup-driving lead guitarist." She leans toward me and whispers, "He's perfect for *Alicia*. Not Lexi."

I hate the way she says that, but I can't deny that it's true. "Right, like I'm going to tell him the truth anyway. 'Hey, Eli? You know the first few times you went out with Alicia? Well, that was really Ava. The last few times, it was really me. And Alicia doesn't really exist.' Yeah, that's a conversation I want to have." Besides, Eli likes Alicia. Guys like him don't go out with Lexi. "Speaking of cars—who owns the stonermobile out front?"

"Shhh!" Ava glances nervously at her door. I hear the toilet in her bathroom flush, and a few seconds later, a tall guy with sandy-blond hair appears behind her, wearing nothing but boxers. "Why are we up?" he asks, nuzzling the back of her neck until she giggles.

"*Lexi,*" she says, with an unnatural emphasis on my name. "This is Dylan."

"Hey." Dylan glances at me quickly and then doubles back with a leer. I'd have to be an idiot not to know what he's thinking. Twin fantasies are so old, they're cliché.

I stare at the two of them. "And you're on *me* for breaking the rules?"

Ava leans into Dylan, who puts both arms around her waist. "Some rules were meant to be broken."

"Come on, Alicia. . . . Let's go break a few more," he says, trying to pull my sister back into her room.

Ava slaps his hands away playfully. "I'll be there in a second," she says, pushing him back toward the open door.

"And who was accusing who of being slutty?" I ask the second he's gone. "Rule number two—don't sleep with any of the guys? Sound familiar?"

Ava pulls the door shut behind her. "Oh, come on," she says, glancing backward. "Did you *see* him? Like I'm going to let that go home alone."

I just shake my head. Not like I expect anything else, never mind the fact that she knew Alicia was already out with Eli. "Cecilia's coming home tomorrow, so make sure everything looks decent." I glance toward her room. "And that certain people aren't still hanging around?"

"I will, I will," she promises, opening the door and slipping quietly into her bedroom.

CHAPTER 11

Not twenty-four hours later, I'm wearing a shiny blue top, the diamond pendant, and a ton of eyeliner as we walk up to a stucco apartment complex that has a massive kegger going on in the courtyard. I check my phone for the address Eli gave me. "This is it."

"No kidding," Ava says, shouting over the music booming from the front gates.

I feel a text coming in. "Eli's coming down to meet us," I say as I read it. Despite the crowds of people in every available open space, I spot him right away on the second-floor walkway, and my heart jumps. Eli smiles and waves as our eyes meet, and he pushes through the crowd toward the stairs. "There he is," I say, pointing.

"Damn, Lex," Maya says, nudging me. "Now I see what all the fuss is about."

I whirl on her. This is why we don't let other people in

on it. "It's *Alicia*," I say, my heart racing. I look around, but it doesn't seem like anyone heard.

"Ease up," Ava says. "People might think you actually like him."

"Shut up, Ava," I say, my frustration rising to the surface. I knew this was a bad idea. I can't have one little comment wreck this whole thing. Not now. "I swear to God, if you blow this for me—"

"Don't worry," Maya interrupts. She puts a hand over her heart. "I promise I won't. I'll totally be careful."

"I'm so glad you're here! You look amazing," Eli says, and reaches for my hand. I glance around at the people near us, seeing a few nods from guys who must know him.

I know I'm grinning like a maniac, but I can't help it. "Thanks. This is Maya," I say, giving her one last piercing look.

"Hey," she says, giving him a little wave. "*Alicia's* told us all about you. And the band." The emphasis on the word "Alicia" isn't lost on me, and I glare at her. Real subtle.

Eli doesn't seem to notice. "All?" he says, with mock horror on his face.

I give his hand a squeeze. "Not all."

"And you're Ava," he says, leaning over to give her a hug. She blushes just the smallest bit and surprisingly doesn't say anything. Eli looks back at me. "No Lexi tonight?"

Ava gives a short, sharp laugh. "Right. Like Lexi would ever be caught dead at a party like this."

It's true, but I'm a little hurt, so I give her a look.

Eli grins and puts one arm around my shoulder as we

turn to walk into the complex. "I don't know, she seemed nice. A little serious maybe, but nice. I think you guys are too hard on her."

I shake my head and roll my eyes. "No, really. We're not."

The courtyard is taken up by a large pool with strips of grass and lawn furniture around the edges. It feels like almost every apartment door is open, with music spilling out into the eerie glow created by the lights of the pool reflecting on the hundreds of people who are wandering around. Nobody is in the pool yet, but I have a feeling that it's only a matter of time.

"Most everyone is upstairs," he says, grabbing my hand and leading the way through the crowd. "We're not playing for another half hour, so we've got time." Eli guides us into the apartment, and I say hi to Melissa and Linzey. I look around, but Rebecca is surprisingly absent.

"Holy mother of God," Linzey says, her eyes wide, looking from me to Ava. "I know you said you look kind of alike, but . . . there are *two* of you."

"Three," Maya says almost proudly. "They're triplets."

"No shit?" Melissa looks to me for confirmation.

I shrug. Not like being twins—or triplets—is some kind of accomplishment. "That's what they say."

"That. Is. Awesome," Linzey says with admiration.

"It's handy," Ava says cryptically, then disappears into the crowd. I doubt she'll pick up anyone, because she's still seeing Dylan as Alicia, but you can never be sure with Ava. *Please, God, let her behave tonight.*

Maya stands next to me, looking from one gorgeous guy

to the next. "Now I know where all the beautiful people have been hiding," she whispers into my ear. "They're all in this apartment." I look around and agree. She's not wrong.

"Do you know everyone here?" I ask Eli.

He looks around absently. "No. Some, but not everyone. A lot of people who live here go to the university. It's sort of an unofficial second-year dorm. And I saw some people from Claremont earlier."

Claremont. The name sticks in my head, until I remember—that was the school Casey went to. I feel a chill as I worry that someone from Claremont might recognize me. Or Ava. I'm going to have to stay sober tonight for sure. "You didn't go to Claremont, though," I say.

"No. But I went to middle school with some of those guys, so I know a lot of them," Eli says as he looks at the crowd in the kitchen. "Want me to get you two something to drink?"

"I'll have a beer," Maya says.

"Coke if they have it," I say, and then remember I'm Alicia, not Lexi. "*Diet* Coke."

"Aw," he says, with an exaggerated look of disappointment on his face. He puts his lips close to my ear as he whispers, "I was hoping to get you drunk and then we could mess around."

I squeeze his hand with just the right amount of promise for later. "You know you don't have to get me drunk for that."

"Nice," he says, his voice a little deeper than before. He clears his throat. "I'll be right back."

Maya swats me as soon as he's gone. "'You don't have to get me drunk for that'? Seriously?"

I shrug and pick my way through the room to a less crowded spot. "What can I say? Alicia's a little bit of a slut." I feel someone looking at me, and turn toward the open apartment door. Rebecca is staring straight at me, her eyes not leaving my face as she tips a bottle of beer to her mouth. I feel myself tense up, ready for whatever confrontation she's going to throw at me.

Maya turns and follows my gaze. "Rebecca?"

"How'd you guess?"

"She's the only one in here who looks like she'd like to scratch your eyes out," Maya answers.

"Yeah. Not exactly subtle."

"If she tries anything, I'll totally take her down."

I almost laugh just picturing it. "Thanks," I say, forcing myself to turn back around. No sense in giving her the satisfaction. Eli's here with me, of his own free will. Rebecca is not my problem. As I scan the unfamiliar faces around the room, I catch the eye of a tall guy with a mess of curly blond hair, muscular arms, and a deep tan.

"Crap," I whisper under my breath. I look away, but I know it's too late—Zane saw me and is headed our way.

"Holy shit," Maya says, and slinks away before he can reach us. Coward.

"Lexi?" he says, walking over and pushing the sombrero out of his eyes with his drink. He looks me up and down. "What's with the bad Ava impersonation?"

My heart sinks. I thought this party was far enough away from home that this wouldn't happen. Our real life has never gotten tangled up with Alicia's before. "Shhh," I say, looking around to make sure Linzey or any of the other girls aren't around. The truth is definitely not what I'm after at the moment. "What are you doing here?"

Zane gestures toward the kitchen and gives me a strange look. "Um . . . hanging out at a party."

I look at the crowd for anyone else who knows me. The real me. "Are you here alone?"

"No," he says. "Slater's over there talking to some girl. And we brought Bettina."

Oh God. I look around, but I don't see her anywhere.

"She's at the far end under the Sierra Nevada sign," he says, nodding in that direction. "She's been on her feet all day and is completely wrecked, but we're not ready to go home yet."

Luckily, either nobody's noticed the slightly worn-looking mannequin perched precariously on a stool at the edge of the kitchen counter, or everyone's choosing to ignore her. Today she's sporting a loud Hawaiian print shift dress and gladiator sandals. And one of those hard hats with two beers stuck to the sides.

"She's looking good," I tell him, noticing the new red wig and heavy eyeliner that may or may not actually be Sharpie. I relax a little now that we're on another subject.

"Thanks," he says with a wink, and turns away from her, lowering his voice to a loud whisper. "We got her a makeover. Some of the guys thought her look was a little dated."

Bettina has been with them since sophomore year, when one of the guys rescued her from the curb on big-trash day, and aside from a little peeling paint, she's in pretty good shape for all her adventures. She's been surfing, snowboarding, on two different Mexican road trips, and there was even a rumor of a skydiving incident last year. For being made of metal and plaster, Bettina's social life is a lot more active than mine. I try not to think about that too hard.

"Hey, Alicia!" Linzey calls from a few feet away. She holds up her empty cup. "I'm going to get another drink. Want me to get you one?"

Damn. I squeeze my eyes shut so I don't have to look at Zane. I manage a smile, hoping it doesn't look too fake. "No, thanks. Eli's getting me something."

She nods and disappears back into the crowd. I turn and see Zane watching me, not even trying to hide his disapproval. "Alicia?" he asks, folding his arms over his chest. He looks bigger all of a sudden.

I look over at the doorway, but Rebecca has disappeared. I pull Zane down so he can hear me. "Look, don't blow this for me, okay?"

He shakes his head. "I'm not going to do anything. But I thought you guys were going to quit Alicia."

"I am." I look over at Eli, who is talking to a couple of people at the far end of the living room. "I was. But Ava needed a favor. And I figure it's not hurting anyone."

Zane follows my glance. "The band guy? Seriously? Don't tell me you're turning into a professional plus-one."

I shove him in the arm. "I'm not. But he is really nice. And fun. And Alicia knows how to have fun."

117

"What's wrong with Lexi?" he says, a challenge in his voice. "Why do you have to do"—he waves his hand at my skirt and sky-high boots—"this? This isn't you."

"Exactly! This *isn't* me. This is someone who's pretty and fun and impulsive. Not boring and studious and plain." Lexi doesn't do fun. Lexi does studying and volunteer work and everything she can to make her dad proud of her. At least, she did.

His eyes widen. "That's what you think? That you have to look like this to be worth something?" He takes a step back, and the look of disgust on his face feels like a dagger in my heart. Zane seems about to say something else but instead turns to go. "I thought you knew better."

"You're not my father," I say. I grab his arm, and he turns back around but shrugs me off. Suddenly I'm angry, and tired of people telling me what I should and shouldn't be. What I can and can't be. "You can't just pronounce something like that and walk away all righteous," I say. "None of this is any of your business—I don't have to answer to you. I can dress how I want and tell people my name is Beyoncé if I feel like it." I look around at the crowd. "What are you even doing here? Did you come because you knew I'd be here? I don't need anyone checking up on me!"

There's silence between us for a few seconds, and I can see that Zane is deciding something. "That's possibly the most narcissistic thing I've ever heard you say. Like I came here only because of you? Contrary to what you might think, I don't spend my free time worrying about what you're doing. I came to hear some music and hang out with my friends."

I step away from him, more upset than I should be. This is Zane, not my boyfriend. "So go. Hang out with your friends."

Zane's cheeks turn a bright red, which is the only indication he's angry, because his voice is icy calm. "I'm going. See you around, *Alicia.*" He says the last word loudly enough so that the people near us turn around.

I turn and walk to where Eli is standing so that I can't see Zane through the crowded room. My heart is pounding, and the anger is flooding through my body. Who is he to judge what I do? So what if I want to dress up and pretend to be someone else? What's his problem, anyway?

"You know that guy?" Eli asks, nodding to where we were standing.

"Yeah. He goes to my school." I almost add "We used to be friends" but don't because that might require more of an explanation.

"Everything okay?"

"I guess," I say, taking a swig of the Diet Coke he hands me. I try not to make a face. I hate diet everything.

Melissa comes over and taps Eli on the arm.

"Time to set up," he says, nodding toward the courtyard. "You going to come watch?"

"Of course," I say, following him out the apartment door. I don't turn around, but I can almost feel Zane's eyes on me as we go. I grab Eli's hand, and he looks back at me with a smile.

I don't relax until an hour later when the music is echoing off the walls of the apartment building and Eli is wailing on his guitar, doing what he does best. Most of the crowd is crushed up against the makeshift stage, Rebecca front and center. I work my way to the back and stand next to Linzey.

"You're not coming to Seattle?" she shouts over the music.

"No," I say. "School next week." Right, school. Not the fact that Eli hasn't asked me to come. He finally told me about the trip and said all the right things, like how much he's going to miss me, but didn't mention that the other girls are going too. Just as well—not like Dad would let me go, but it might have been nice to be asked.

"Drag," she says with a smile. "I don't miss those days." She hoists her beer in a salute and takes a big swig.

I glance behind Linzey and see a pretty blonde talking to Zane by the pool. They're sitting on the edge dangling their feet in the illuminated blue water. As I watch, she laughs loudly and tosses her head back, brushing his arm with her hair and taking the opportunity to move so close to him that she's practically in his lap. So much for Zane not liking girls like Alicia. She has even more makeup on than I do. I wonder if he'll take her back to his apartment. His dad works nights a lot now, so there won't be anyone there to bother them. My mind flashes to the last time I was in his bedroom, with the Lego creations on his dresser and the hammock full of stuffed animals over his bed. It's been a long time since I was at his house. I'm guessing the Legos and stuffed animals are gone now.

Someone bumps me so hard that I take a step back on the grass, and I whirl around to see a guy with extremely short hair way too far into my personal space. "Alicia! What the fuck?" He's so close to me that his warm beer breath hits me full in the face. I try to pull back, but he's got one hand wrapped around my wrist, the huge tarantula tattoo on his forearm flexing with the effort.

"Let go of me!" I shout, trying to pull away, but that only makes him squeeze harder. I have no idea who this guy is, but his eyes are flat with anger, and my heart races as I try to twist away from him.

He pulls me closer, and the crowd nearest to us backs away, confused by the confrontation in front of them. "You think you can screw with me? Lead me on like a little pussy and then just take off when you feel like it?" He grips my arm more tightly, and I yelp in pain. I can feel the waves of his anger and see his nostrils flare with each exhalation.

Suddenly my hand is free, and I stumble into Linzey, who puts a protective arm around me.

"Don't touch her!" Zane pushes him, and the guy scrambles backward before catching himself and pulling up to his full height. He's tall, much taller than me, but even from here I can see that Zane's years of surfing have given him strength that this guy can't match.

"Is this the new one?" The guy ignores Zane completely and comes after me again. "This the guy you fucked me over for?"

He reaches for me again, but Zane blocks his arm, so he turns to Zane with a blow that smashes into his cheek before he can react. Zane pauses just for a moment before thrusting forward and meeting the guy with a fist that lands squarely on his jaw. The guy is thrown to the ground, and then staggers to his feet, his lip cracked and bleeding.

"Get out," Zane says firmly, standing between me and the guy. I can see Zane's hands clenching, and I know he's dying to hit him again.

The guy wavers, unsteady on his feet, as if deciding whether it's worth it to take Zane on again. He looks over at me one last time and aims a wad of bloody spit in my direction before turning toward the gates.

Linzey looks into my eyes, and I fight back tears, holding my arm and trying to rub out the pain. "Let me go get you some ice," she says gently, not asking for an explanation.

"Who was that?" Ava asks, rushing up to me as Zane follows the guy out.

I watch them reach the curb with some additional angry words. "You tell me," I say, my voice still shaky. "From what I can tell, he's one of Alicia's rejects."

Ava looks back at him and shakes her head. "Not one of mine. I've never seen that guy before in my life."

I stare at her. "Shaved head? A giant spider tattoo on his arm? Doesn't ring any bells?"

"No. Come on. I'd remember if Alicia had gone out with someone like that."

Eli reaches us two steps ahead of Maya. "What happened?"

"Jesus, Lexi," Maya says. "I thought that guy was going to kill you. What a freak!"

The air around us seems to go quiet as everyone absorbs what Maya just said. I hope that Eli hasn't heard her, that he doesn't realize what she just called me, but one look at his face tells me that I'm not going to be so lucky.

"Lexi?" Eli says, his voice rising above the murmurs in the crowd.

Maya puts both hands over her mouth and squeaks, "I meant Ava. Uh . . . Alicia. I meant Alicia."

"What's going on?" Eli looks from me to Ava, suspicion growing in his eyes.

"Nothing." I try to keep it light, but I can hear my voice shaking. "Maya just got confused. Happens all the time."

Eli stands in front of me. "What's your real name?"

I stand there for what feels like hours, but I can't get anything out. If I tell him the truth, it'll all be over.

Maya turns and mouths "I'm sorry" to me. But it's too late.

"You're Lexi." He shuts his eyes and shakes his head. "I knew it!"

This is not what I expected. "You knew?"

"You're the one I met at the café that day, right?" he asks, pointing to me.

I nod, afraid to say anything.

"And I met you in Leucadia at the show," Ava volunteers. "It's not her fault," she says hurriedly. "This was all my idea—"

He takes a step forward. "What? To make me look like an idiot? To get home and talk about how funny it is to fool the jackass who thinks he's dating a triplet?"

"It's not like that!" I say. I feel him slipping away from me as the crowd around us has gone quiet.

"Then what's it like, *Lexi*?" he asks, anger radiating off him.

"I . . . I'm not sure." I look to Ava for help, but she doesn't

123

seem to know what to say either. "But we didn't do it to make you look stupid, I swear."

Linzey approaches with a towel full of ice, but stops when she sees the seriousness of our confrontation. Rebecca pulls up behind her, eyes wide.

Eli looks at the two of us again. "I should have gone with my gut." He turns to me. "I knew you were different from before, but I tried to convince myself that I was being ridiculous." His blue eyes sear into mine. "You know, the sad thing is, I really liked you." He gestures to my clothes. "Even with all this, I could tell that you were the same smart, funny girl I met in the café. That's who I wanted to get to know."

I step forward. Eli knew, and he liked me. Not Alicia. "I didn't think you'd like me," I say, my voice quiet. "The real me."

He shakes his head again. "Now we'll never know." As he turns to go, Rebecca grabs his arm, but he shakes her off and keeps walking. She glares at me and then runs off after him.

Linzey stands still for a second, watching them go, and then, with one last look at me, follows them across the courtyard.

"Are you okay?" Zane asks, joining us on the grass, oblivious to what has just gone on.

"Fine," I say, my voice cracking and hot tears pushing against my eyes. I look up at his face. There's a red spot on his cheek where he got hit. "You?"

"Good," he says.

"Thanks," I say. There's an awkward silence between us. There should be sympathy and explanations, but right now there's just empty air. He walks back over to the blonde, not even glancing back at me.

My face feels hot, and my mind is racing. That's it. It's over. Everyone around us is pretending not to notice, pretending not to have witnessed my total humiliation.

"Should we go?" Maya asks, one hand lightly on my arm.

Without answering, I unzip both of my boots and let them flop over onto the grass, feeling the cool, damp blades under my bare feet. There's only one thing Alicia would do in this situation. I walk calmly toward the edge of the pool and, without hesitating, dive in, letting the cool blue water surround me, shutting out everything that's going on at the surface.

CHAPTER 12

"Finally!" Ava says in frustration, opening the car door before she's even set the parking brake. It's taken us almost
twenty minutes to find a spot remotely close to the beach,
even though it's two o'clock on a Tuesday, because almost
everyone else is on spring break too. And we're still a pretty
long walk away. She squints in the direction of the water and
looks with disgust at all the other cars parked along the road.
"I swear they need to do something about all of these people.
This part of town should be for locals only. I'm sick of having
to walk miles to get to my own beach."

"I didn't realize this was *your* beach," I say, sliding a glance
at her from under my hat. After everything that happened
last night I didn't even want to come today, and Ava's mood
isn't making this any easier.

"You know what I mean." She sweeps her hand toward
some of the cars. "All of these people probably live miles

and miles from here, and they're taking up valuable parking spaces and beach real estate. Dad didn't spend a ton of cash to live here so that we'd have to walk to the beach."

"Maybe next time we should get him to buy a house right on the water," I say, grabbing my backpack.

"Whatever," she says, but we both know that would never happen. Dad loves to stand on the balcony outside his room and take in the view of the ocean way down the hill. "Better to be up here and see the sparkling sea and white sand instead of the seagull shit and cigarette butts" is his motto. Ava squints up at the sun, strong for the first time all spring. "At least the weather's decent. I'm going out with Dylan on Thursday, and I need to get a little color."

Dylan? I can't believe she's still going to do it, even after all the trouble Alicia's caused. "I thought we were done with Alicia."

Ava shrugs. "Maybe *you* are. My Alicia is still going out with a hottie basketball player."

Even the thought of dressing up and putting the diamond pendant around my neck gives me a stomachache. "Seriously. Alicia needs to disappear. Now. We've already been caught once. You want a repeat of last night?"

"Maybe I'll quit once I cut Dylan loose," she says, walking up ahead of me so it's impossible to continue talking. "But until then, I'm going to have a little fun."

The sand is crowded with colorful towels that people have abandoned in order to bob around in the cool Pacific. Ava shades her eyes and glances toward the place where we usually hang out, waving as she sees people we know. "At least nobody's in our spot," she says grumpily. Our feet kick up arcs of sand as we trudge toward the familiar patch of real estate nestled up against the dunes that separate the water from the multimillion-dollar houses lining the beach. "Looks like Zane out there," she says, squinting at the water.

"So?"

"So. He kind of saved your ass last night."

"It was your ass too," I remind her.

"Agreed. Which is why you might want to be nice to him."

"I said thank you."

"Barely," Ava says, in a tone that makes me feel instantly guilty. And defensive.

"He shouldn't have even been there," I say, even though I know that what happened between me and Eli wasn't his fault. "And then he leaves with some trampy blonde? Anyway, you don't even like him."

"I don't *not* like him," Ava says. She looks from the water straight at me. "And since when do you care who he goes home with?"

"I don't!" I insist. And I don't. Really. Which is why it bothers me that I can't get the image of the two of them out of my head. "He can sleep with whoever he wants. It's none of my business."

We shut up about it as we reach our friends.

"I know you have something to drink for me," Ava says, flopping down next to Slater, putting her head on his shoulder, and fluttering her eyelashes at him. Even for Ava this is a little obvious. Apparently she's using the second-grade method of attracting boys.

"Share my Coke?" he says, handing her a bottle.

"Thanks," she says, taking a huge swig. "We've been walking for miles."

"Not miles," I say, dropping my backpack.

"You can put your stuff here if you want," Slater says, pointing to an empty spot under his umbrella.

"Thanks," I say, spreading my towel out on the sand. "I want to get some sun."

Apparently annoyed that I'm the one getting a little bit of attention instead of her, Ava stands up to rid herself of her tiny skirt, knowing as well as I do that every eye is on her as she performs her seemingly innocent striptease.

"I'm roasting," she says, adjusting the rear of her yellow bikini. "Anyone coming in with me?"

Slater and a couple of the other guys stand up and follow as Ava takes off toward the water. I hear her squealing in the shallows as the spray hits her ankles, and the guys start a water fight that looks like it should be the opening scene in *Girls Gone Wild! Beach Edition*.

I'm unpacking my backpack when I see Zane walking out of the surf with his board. He stops to laugh with someone in the shallow water, so I get up and brush the sand off my shorts. For once Ava's right. And I hate it when she's right.

The sand is hot between our spot and the water, so I walk as quickly as I can between the towels until I can cool my feet in the shallows. Zane's talking to a dark-haired girl in a string bikini, so I stand a little away from them, kicking at the water and watching out of the corner of my eye. Zane's back is broad and tan, with droplets of ocean still clinging to his skin, and I'm suddenly conscious of the way the girl moves toward him, one hand lingering on his arm. It looks like they're going to walk up the beach together, when she suddenly throws her arms around him and pulls him into an excessively long hug before running into the surf.

Zane turns to walk toward our towels, and I'm not sure if he doesn't see me or if he's choosing to ignore me. "Hey!" I call over the sound of the water pounding on the sand.

Zane breaks into a smile and walks over to me. He never was one to hold a grudge. "Hey yourself, Lexi," he says. He leans down toward me. "Or is it Alicia?"

I can feel my face get red, and I look away. "Stop." Neither of us says anything for a few long moments, and the air seems heavy with everything we should be saying. Finally I break the silence. "I'm sorry."

Zane kicks some sand at his feet. "I know."

"It's just that things have been kind of crazy lately, and it felt like you were checking up on me."

He shrugs and stares off into the distance. "I would have been if I thought you needed it."

I look up into his face. There's a bruise just under his eye where the guy hit him last night. "Apparently I did need it."

"Who was that guy?"

"I don't know. He obviously knew Alicia, but I've never seen him before, and Ava is claiming sudden memory loss."

There's another high-pitched squeal, and we turn to watch Ava and the guys jump through the waves. Well, I'm watching the guys. I'm pretty sure Zane's watching Ava. I punch him hard in the arm.

"What?" he asks, an innocent look on his face. He rubs his arm. "You've got bony knuckles—that hurt."

"Stop staring."

"I'm not staring. I'm thinking."

"And I know what you were thinking about."

"You don't know a damn thing," he says, giving me a crooked smile, which goes a long way toward making me forgive him. I glance up at his tall lankiness, at the way his hair is getting long at the back, although I'm not sure if he's growing it out intentionally or just forgot to cut it for the last couple of months, because he tends to lose track of ordinary things.

"Fine," I say, dropping it. I don't blame him for watching my sister. Everything about her practically screams *Look at me!* every second of every day. Her entire life revolves around achieving maximum impact, and a day at the beach with people we've known since kindergarten is no exception.

"Lex, what are you doing?" Zane finally asks. "I told you Alicia is nothing but trouble."

I don't bother denying it. "It was sort of an accident. Eli thought I was Alicia at the café that day, so I only did it as a joke at first." I dig a toe into the sand. "Doesn't matter anyway. It's over now. Eli found out about Alicia last night."

"I heard." Zane tilts his head. "He wasn't exactly understanding?"

"Not exactly." I wipe angrily at a tear that's working its way down my cheek, not knowing if I miss Eli or if I'm just angry at myself.

"I'm sorry." He looks concerned. "You really liked this guy?"

I can't help smiling. "Yeah, I did. He was fun and differ-ent." I think about WaterRidge and the food trucks. "*I* was different when I was with him."

Zane plants his board in the sand and looks at me out of the corner of his eye. "Why do you need to be different? What's wrong with Lexi?"

My eyes fill with tears. "Right now, everything. I didn't get into Stanford; the cops want to talk to Alicia, and for ob-vious reasons they can't; and I screwed up what might be my only chance at a relationship this year."

"Whoa," he says, his face full of concern. "Back up a little bit. What's up with the cops?"

I hesitate, feeling the force of my emotions and the in-formation I've kept bottled up inside. I watch Ava squeal and kick at the edge of the surf, and I envy the way all her troubles seem to roll off her.

"Sounds like you're in a little over your head." Zane flops down onto the sand and pats the space next to him. I sit down and lean against his shoulder, his skin warm from the sun, and his muscles solid against my side. "Tell me everything."

So I do.

CHAPTER 13

After a great beach day yesterday, today is foggy and miserable—perfect weather to help Cecilia.

"I think I got everything on the list," I say as I walk into the kitchen and set the grocery bags on the island. Cecilia's sitting at the table, staring into space, her face a mask of worry.

"What's up?" I ask, digging into one of the bags.

"Nothing," she says, glancing away from me.

"It's not nothing," I insist, a tiny ball of dread forming inside me. I put the bag down. "I can tell. What happened?"

She takes a deep breath, and her eyes flick up to mine for just a second before looking away again. "The police. They were here a little while ago. At the front door."

I feel my heart surge. They must have figured out the fake ID. "Did you answer it?"

She looks at me like I'm stupid. "Of course I did. I have nothing to hide. They were looking for Alicia."

Crap. "What did you say?"

"What do you think I said? That there's no Alicia here." My face must be giving something away. "Do you know anything about this?"

"Not really." I sit down beside her, sorry that she got involved in this at all. "Sort of. It's just a misunderstanding. A mistake. Did they leave a card?"

"Yes." Cecilia reaches into the pocket of her apron and pulls out a card identical to the one I already have. "One of them gave me this." She studies my face. "What have you two done? Is Ava in trouble? Is there something you need to be telling me? When your father isn't here, you and your sister are my responsibility."

"No," I say as lightly as possible. "It's really no big deal. Ava's fine. I'll take care of it." I tuck the card into my pocket and give Cecilia a kiss on the cheek. I can see that she's not totally satisfied. "Really, it's okay. I'll talk to Dad when he gets home.

"You promise?" She looks skeptical.

"Yes. I swear." I jump up and start going through the bags again, even though my brain is focused on the cops. "The cilantro looked terrible at the store, so I went to the produce place by the freeway."

Someone calls to her from the backyard, so she gives me one last, piercing glance and walks outside. I hear Cecilia's raised voice and a male voice speaking Spanish. The gardener is standing outside with the leaf blower on his back, pointing to something on the side of the house. He looks agitated, but he's speaking so fast, I can't understand a word as they walk off toward the side of the house. My Spanish was so much better when I was a kid.

I'm putting the milk in the fridge when I hear a buzzing sound and see Cecilia's phone jiggling across the counter. "Cecilia!" I shout, but she must be too far in the back to hear me. The buzzing stops, but then starts up again a few seconds later. I pick it up to put it in a safer spot, and see that she's gotten a text. Cecilia never gets texts. She hates the phone and has it only because Dad passed it down to her years ago when he finally got a new one. I glance at the patio door, even as I can't believe I'm thinking about it. Something's going on with Cecilia, and she's not going to tell me what it is. Looking back again, I slide the ancient phone open to unlock it and click on the message. *It's Rubi. She's gone again.* I've never heard her mention anyone named Rubi before. I hear Cecilia's voice outside, so I mark the text as unread and close it before putting the phone right back where it was.

"Everything okay?" I ask as she comes back into the kitchen.

"Fine," she says, but she seems distracted.

Her phone buzzes again, and she glances at me before picking it up. After reading the text, she puts the phone into her pocket, muttering something to herself.

"Anything wrong?"

She looks at me like she's forgotten I'm here, and her cheeks instantly go red. "No." She gives me an insincere smile. "My sister's having some trouble with her husband, is all."

I've known Cecilia my whole life, and for the first time, it feels like she's hiding something from me. I want to ask her who Rubi is, but I can't think of any way to bring it up without telling her that I read the text.

The gardener appears again in the doorway and says something to her that I can't catch.

"What's going on?" I walk over to him.

"It's nothing," Cecilia says, turning away from Julio. "Don't worry about it."

Julio looks worriedly at me. It's definitely something. "What's going on?" I repeat.

"Someone . . . looks . . . outside of *la casa*," he says in halting English.

I feel a shiver run down my spine. Something about the tone of his voice makes me nervous. "'Looks'? *Adonde?*"

Julio points to the side of the house near the fence.

"I'm sure he's overreacting," Cecilia says, but I'm already heading across the deck. She follows me as Julio leads us around the back of the house.

"*Aquí,*" he says, stopping outside Ava's bedroom window. He points to a pile of sunflower seed shells on the ground about three feet away from the window. At first I don't think much about it, but then I look at them more closely. These aren't random seeds that have been eaten by someone and tossed away. This is a pile of opened seeds that have been chewed and discarded in a single pile over a longer period of time. I look through the window and see Ava's entire room through the parted curtains. At night, when the lights are on and Ava's using the window as a mirror from the inside, you wouldn't be able to see anything out here. Or anyone.

I put on a fake smile and bend down to pick up a handful

of the seeds. All three of us are standing near the pile, and our shoes have messed up whatever footprints might have been made in the soft dirt. "I'm sure Cecilia's right and it's no big deal. Someone just left these here."

Julio looks worried. *"Pero debemos decirle a su padre."*

"Don't worry. I'll tell my dad," I say. I look more closely at the window but don't see any handprints on the glass. The seeds rattle in my pocket, and I glance over my shoulder as we walk back toward the patio, half expecting someone to be watching us.

Ava comes into my bathroom as I lean so close to the mirror, it feels like I'm about to poke my eye out with the pencil.

"What are you doing?" She flicks the pendant that's already around my neck. "I thought Alicia was dead."

"Hey!" I yell as she jiggles my arm and totally blows the line I was working on. She leans over and hands me a wad of toilet paper to rub it off and start again. "She is. But I have to do it one more time. I don't have any choice."

"Sounds serious." She grabs the pencil out of my hand. "You're useless at this. Let me do it."

I kick the door shut behind her, in case Cecilia is lurking anywhere nearby. "I'm going down to the police station."

She pulls back so she can see my face. "What? Why? I thought we agreed to let it go." I can see anger flashing in her eyes.

"I'd love to, but the cops aren't. They came back again,"

I say, annoyed that once again I have to clean up another one of Ava's messes. "Scared Cecilia half to death. I need to find out what's going on, because your whole blow-over theory is obviously flawed."

"Shit. Really? What did she tell them?"

"She told them that there wasn't an Alicia here. But they already know better, thanks to you." I grab some dark gray eye shadow from the drawer. "If you hadn't pulled the Alicia crap on the cops, this would all be over by now."

Ava slams the eyeliner pencil down onto the counter. "Well, I'm not going to help you do something so completely stupid."

"Whatever," I say. My hand is shaking as I wipe the shadow across my lid, and I put both hands down on the counter to steady them. I can't let Ava see how nervous I am. "But you better plan what you're going to say when they knock on the door the next time. And I guarantee that there will be a next time. Dad's going to be home in five hours, and I need to have this behind us by then." I can't let Dad know about Alicia—not on top of the whole Stanford mess. I can almost see the look in his eyes if he opens the door and sees the cops standing there. If he discovers that I'm not the person he thought I was.

"You don't think . . . you don't think the cops suspect Alicia?" Ava asks.

"I'm worried that's exactly what they think. This way, I can be on the offensive," I say quickly, convincing myself as I'm explaining it to her. "I'll go down there as Alicia and innocently find out what's going on. It'll look like we're cooperating. Alicia didn't do anything wrong, and I'm going to tell them that. We'll straighten this whole thing out, Dad will come home, and nobody will ever know."

Ava picks the pencil back up and scrapes the end with her fingernail. "I thought you were big on telling the cops the truth. That we made the whole thing up." She leans in toward me again. "Close your eyes."

I stand as still as I can while she puts on the eyeliner, glad that she's back on my side. "It's too late for that. They already saw her ID, and you gave them all that crap at the door. They said that they'll talk only to Alicia, so I'm going to let them. She hasn't done anything wrong, so I'm not worried." I wish I was as confident as I sound.

"Open," Ava commands, and stands back to take a look. "Are you sure you know what you're doing?" I notice she doesn't volunteer to go with me. Not like I expected her to.

"No," I admit. "But I don't have another choice right now, and the last thing we need is to have the cops coming around here when Dad gets home."

"No shit," Ava agrees, rubbing something out of the corner of my eye. She pauses. "Do you think he'd take our phones away?"

"The phone, the car, *and* the credit cards." I glance back at the mirror. He'd never trust me again.

Ava stands next to me as I look at our reflections. "Call me if something happens," she says.

"Nothing's going to happen." I hope I sound more sure than I feel.

"What are you going to do with your hair?"

I look in the mirror at the messy bun. "Nothing. It's the cops, not a club."

Ava reaches up to undo the elastic. "Yeah, but now that the rest of you looks good, we have to fix this too. Alicia doesn't do things half-assed."

An hour later I'm sitting in my car in front of the brick police station. I must have passed this place a million times, but I never thought I'd actually need to go into it. I reach into my bag, take my real license out of my wallet, and stick it into the glove compartment, making sure my Alicia license is the only one left in the plastic window. My palms are sweating, so I wipe them on my leggings and repeat to myself that Alicia didn't do anything wrong. I'm just here to find out what the cops want so that they'll stop coming to the house. I'm sure they'll just ask a couple of questions about how I knew Casey and I'll be sitting right back here in half an hour, laughing that I was so worried about something so small. Although, I suppose that's pretty much what the people in the movies think right before the train comes crashing through the intersection and obliterates their disabled car on the tracks.

Taking a deep breath, I get out, and then walk into the station, blinking a little in the fluorescent lights. On *CSI*, the station is always dark and foggy, but this place is lit up like Christmas, making the guy behind the front desk look a little washed-out and a tiny bit green.

"Can I help you?" His tone makes it sound like he'd rather do anything else.

"Yes," I say, taking out the card like I need to double-check, even though it's soft from use and I've already memorized the name on it. "I'm here to see Detective Naito."

The guy types something into the computer on the desk and looks up at me. "Can I tell him who's here?"

I take a deep breath and think about Dad sitting on a plane and drinking his complimentary first-class champagne, completely oblivious to all of this. I have to keep it that way—there's no going back now. "Alicia. Alicia Rios. He's expecting me. Sort of."

"Okay. Go ahead and have a seat over there." The guy points to a row of hard orange plastic chairs.

I perch on the edge of one of the chairs, feeling like I'm going to jump up and run out any second. It takes everything I have to stay in one place until the detective rounds the corner with a faintly surprised look on his face. "Alicia?"

I stand up and put my hand out, and then take it back quickly, not knowing whether you're supposed to shake hands with the cops or not. I look down and see he's got a big brown accordian folder in his hands anyway. "Yes," I say, remembering quickly that Alicia has never met him before. I look down at the worn business card in my hand for effect. "Detective Naito?"

"That's right." He nods. "Thanks for coming down. Would you come this way?" He holds out the folder to indicate the hallway toward the back of the building.

I take a deep breath and walk toward him, reminding myself that I'm just here to satisfy our curiosity and find out what they want. Alicia's not in trouble. I see his name on an office door to the left and start to turn in that direction, but he corrects me.

"Let's go in here," he says, reaching around me and opening the door to a room with a plaque that reads ROOM 1.

"Okay," I say, starting to feel a little more uneasy. Talking to him in his office is one thing. Talking to him in a generically named Room 1 is another.

"Just have a seat," he says. He pushes a small Formica-topped table out of the way and gestures to another hard orange plastic chair in the middle of the room. I glance behind him and see a mirror that takes up most of one wall. I've watched enough cop shows to wonder who's standing behind that mirror watching us. I jump a little bit when he closes the door solidly behind us.

"Everything okay?" he asks, settling into the chair next to mine. We're sitting so close, our knees are practically touching, and I wish that the table was between us like it is on TV.

"Yes. Fine. I've just never been to a police station before."

"Nothing to worry about," he says absently, looking through the file folder in his lap. "We just have some questions about the death of Casey Stewart."

"It's awful what happened to him," I say, hoping I sound sincere. "But I'm not sure there's anything I can tell you."

"We just need to get a few things straight with our investigation. A couple of questions and you'll be out of here."

"Okay." I say, trying to sit back in the chair, but it's so uncomfortable that I sit up straight again.

"Can I get you anything? A soda? Some water?"

"No. Thanks. I'm fine." I just want to answer his questions and leave.

The detective points to a tiny box on the ceiling. "You don't mind if we record this, do you?" He grins. "My handwriting is terrible. Nobody can read it, so this just saves time."

I look at the box with the little red button on top and try to smile. That's what someone with nothing to hide would do. "No. It's fine."

"Do you mind stating your name for the record?"

It's the "for the record" part that makes me hesitate. I take a deep breath, knowing that the next thing I say is probably illegal. I'm a terrible liar, but I have no choice. I can practically feel Dad getting closer as the minutes tick by. "Alicia Rios."

"Thank you, Alicia," he says, as if he's speaking to an audience. I glance at the two-way mirror and wonder if he is. He flips through some papers in the folder. "And how did you know Casey Stewart?"

I shrug, trying to look casual. "We went out a couple of times."

"I see," he says, nodding. "And when was the last time you saw him?"

"March twenty-eighth," I answer, glad that I rehearsed this part with Ava. "Friday. The night . . . the night before he died. We hung out and then talked in his car."

"In the Cheesecake Factory parking lot?" He looks like he's expecting a certain answer, only I have no idea what it is.

"Yes. I got into my car at about eleven."

"About eleven? Are you sure of the time?"

My palms start sweating, and I wipe them on my pants, even though everything I'm telling him is true. "Yes—it had to be around eleven, because I remember specifically that I got home at eleven-thirty, and it takes only a half hour to drive from the Cheesecake Factory to my house."

"And you didn't see him after that? Did you have another date with him that maybe you forgot about?"

I shake my head. Where is he going with this? "No. I saw him the night before he died, and that was the last time."

"Well, if that's true," he says, reaching into the folder, "I'd love it if you could explain this surveillance photo taken the night Mr. Stewart died." He turns a piece of paper so I can see it.

I can almost feel my heart stop as I focus on the image. I should have known that there would be surveillance cameras. They're everywhere these days. I wonder if it shows his killer—if they got the whole thing on tape. I lean over the photo, afraid to touch the grainy picture, but it's not what I'm expecting. I swallow hard, hoping my voice won't crack. "Where did you get this?"

I hope I'm overthinking it, but the detective's expression looks much less friendly than it did just a few seconds ago. "It was taken from a surveillance camera in the front of the restaurant." He points to a blurry time code at the bottom of the photo. "Taken at one o'clock in the morning on Sunday, March thirtieth, right around the time of Casey's death."

I look back at the photo. The focus isn't that great, but even I can see that it's a girl who looks a lot like me walking down the street. She seems like she's in a hurry, looking over her shoulder as if she's expecting someone to follow. But it's not me. That's the only thing I know for sure, which can mean only one thing. I suddenly notice how cold my hands are and shove them under my legs. Why wouldn't Ava tell me that she was near the restaurant that night? I look up at the detective and tell him the only part of the truth that matters now. "That isn't me."

Detective Naito spins the photo around, then holds it up to my face. "That's funny," he says slowly. "It sure looks an awful lot like you. Could you perhaps have gotten your dates mixed up?"

I feel panic creeping in as the realities start to build on one another. It was the day I met Eli at Roma. I was home that night, I'm sure of it. My mind races as I try to remember where Ava was that night. "I'm not mixed up," I say firmly. "By eleven-thirty on Friday night, I was at my house, and that's the last time I saw Casey." I can tell he doesn't believe me. "Can I see it again?" He hands it back to me, and I scan it desperately, looking for some clue that will explain this away. I can't see her face clearly, but I have a good view of a small silver sequined purse hanging from the shoulder of her red jacket. I point to the photo, relief flooding through my body. "The jacket. I don't have a red leather jacket like that. It must be someone else."

"Hmm," he says, reaches into the folder again, and takes out a small plastic bag. "Do you have an earring like this one? We found it in Casey's car."

I look at the big gold hoop. It looks like any one of the

dozens of pairs that Ava has. That Alicia wears when she goes out. I think as hard as I can, but I have no idea which pair I'm wearing right now, and my hand is halfway to my ear before I can stop it. "I'm not sure," I say. I look from the earring to the picture. "But I already told you that I was in his car the night before. We sat and talked in his car for a long time. It could have fallen off before I got out." I sit forward, trying to convince him that I had nothing to do with this. "Look, I hate the sight of blood—it makes me sick. I wouldn't even know how to cut someone's spine, much less be able to do it."

He glances at the video camera on the wall. "Why did you say it that way?" His tone is concerned, cautious.

I suck in my breath, feeling like I've made a mistake. "What way?"

"That you wouldn't know how to cut someone's spine." He watches me, waiting patiently for my answer.

I try to remember where I heard about it, but my mind's blank. "I don't know. The news. Or someone at school maybe. Everyone was talking about it on Monday."

He puts his hands on the folder, palms together. "It's just an interesting way to put it—that someone cut Casey's spine." He pauses. "Because we never put that out to the media. Most people assume that his throat was slit."

I sit back in my chair and try to stay as calm as possible. "I . . . I just heard it somewhere. These things get leaked all the time."

"It's an unusual method of killing someone," he continues. "But fairly efficient. Most often used to kill animals in

146

slaughterhouses or for dissection. It's called pithing, where the spine is severed from the base of the skull."

I lean away from him. "Well, I wouldn't know anything about that."

"What's interesting," he says, pulling another bag out of the folder, "is that we found this in the front seat of the car. Covered in blood." He turns the bag, and I see Ava's blue sweater covered with big spots of dried purplish blood. "Do you recognize this?" he says quietly.

I nod slowly. "It's mine," I admit. "I left it in his car."

The detective looks interested. "You did? It was awfully cold that night. Yet you got out of his car and crossed the parking lot without remembering your sweater?"

"I was in a hurry." The minute the words are out of my mouth, I regret it.

His eyebrows rise. "You were? Why?"

I don't want to tell him the real reason. That will just fire up another set of questions that I don't need. "Curfew," I say quickly. "I was late, and I was going to miss curfew."

"An eleven o'clock curfew." He doesn't say it as a question. "Your parents must be awfully strict."

I definitely don't want to talk about my dad. "Am I in some kind of trouble?" I hand the photo back to him. This is all starting to sound crazy. "All I know is that this isn't me, and I didn't have anything to do with Casey's death. Do I need a lawyer?"

Detective Naito spreads his hands out on the folder. "Only if you feel like you need one."

Which immediately makes me feel like I might need one. And that asking for one will make me look guiltier.

He pulls the photo out of the folder again, like he's examining it for the first time. "Look, we're just having a little friendly conversation here. And I really appreciate you coming down to straighten all this out." The detective smiles, but it doesn't make his face look any kinder. "Well, we do know of two other people who might look like this in a photo. Are you saying it might be one of your sisters?"

"No! None of us had anything to do with what happened to Casey."

He glances down at his notes. "What were you doing at the funeral?" he asks, and I know the subject change is supposed to throw me off.

I shrug. I was ready for this question. "I needed closure."

"Closure?"

"Yeah. Like I said, we went out right before he died, so I thought I'd go and pay my respects. Nothing wrong with that, is there?"

"Nope," he says. "Nothing wrong with that."

I remember the joints in Casey's ashtray and what Ava said. I need to know if we really should be worried, if someone thinks I might know too much. "Do you think . . . do you think that it might be drug related?"

He tilts his head toward me. "I can't comment on motive right now. Why do you ask?"

I didn't want to bring this up, but now I realize I have no choice. If someone thinks I saw Casey's killer, I might be the one who needs help. "Because I think someone's been stalking me. Us."

He looks interested. "What do you mean 'stalking' you?"

"There have been a few things." I tell him about the speeding ticket and the strange car at WaterRidge. He frowns at the story but doesn't say anything. I'm guessing murder is a little more serious than trespassing at an office park after hours. "And then our gardener found these just outside my sister's window." I reach into my bag and hand him the baggie full of sunflower seeds.

"I'm afraid I don't follow," he says, examining them.

"Someone has been sitting outside the window," I say. I picture a figure crouched in the shadows, silently cracking seeds as Ava gets dressed just on the other side of the glass. "Watching us."

"We'll take a look at these and see what we find," the detective says, pushing them to one side. He leans toward me. "Do you feel like you're in danger?"

I suddenly feel very exposed. "I . . . I'm not sure. I haven't exactly seen anyone. It's just that there are so many weird coincidences lately."

"Make sure you call me—or 911—if you think you're in any immediate danger." He shuts the folder with an air of finality. "I tell you what. You give us a quick DNA sample and you can be on your way."

I hesitate. "DNA sample? For what?"

"To eliminate your profile." He clasps his hands on top of the folder. "We found some trace evidence under Casey's

149

fingernails. We're thinking maybe he scratched someone during an altercation that night. If you didn't struggle with him, then your DNA won't be there. Right?"

"Right," I say. I realize that this interview *is* being watched, because a technician comes into the room as soon as I answer. "But my DNA is probably all over that car."

"Well, then the profile will just eliminate your DNA from the scene," Detective Naito says.

The lab tech puts on a pair of latex gloves as I watch, my mind racing. We have nothing to hide, but I'm not sure that handing over something so personal is such a good idea. "Maybe I should wait and ask my dad about this."

The lab tech looks at Detective Naito. "You can legally consent to a DNA test," he says. "But we can put you in holding until we get in touch with your parents, if you'd like."

"It's just my dad, and he's out of town. In South Africa— and he's hard to reach right now." The last thing I want is for the cops to bring Dad into this.

He shrugs. "Then it might take a while, but you've got nowhere to go, right?"

Everything feels like it's spiraling out of control. "I don't know. . . ."

"Look," the detective says, leaning forward in his chair. "We're going to get a sample one way or the other. You can either hang out here for the next several hours while we get in touch with your father or we can do this in the next thirty seconds and you walk on out of here. What do you say?"

"A quick cheek swab and it's done," the tech says. "Not

150

even painful." She flips the cap off the Q-tip and leans in toward me. "Open up."

I can't think of any more excuses, so I open my mouth and she rubs the swab quickly along the inside of my cheek.

"See?" she says as she caps the swab and then strips her gloves off. "Couldn't be easier."

I watch her walk out of the room, and I feel strangely violated. "Can I go now?" I ask Detective Naito.

"Sure," he says, standing up and pushing his chair back. "But don't go far. We might have some more questions for you."

Ava's car isn't in the driveway when I get home, and I can feel my agitation starting up again. I must have gone through the conversation twenty times in my head but I can't figure it out. Yes, the person in the photo looked like Ava, but the quality of the picture wasn't that good. I even thought I saw Ava at the food trucks that night. There must be thousands of girls who look like us in the dark and from far away. To think anything else is just crazy.

I sit in the car and dial Ava's number, but it goes straight to voice mail, so I hang up without leaving a message. I text her to call me, and then climb out of the car and go into the house. I can hear Cecilia's TV on in the kitchen, so I quietly walk down the long hallway toward our bedrooms. I open Ava's door, not even sure what I'm looking for in the messy room, until I spot the speeding ticket on top of a pile of papers on her desk. I fold it up, put it in my pocket, and pick my way through the mounds of discarded clothes to the closet. She has no organizational system at all, so I flip casually through the rack. My fingers touch the soft leather before it even registers, and I pull the jacket slowly out of the closet, glancing toward the open door to make sure nobody's watching me. I pull it toward me and get a faint whiff of Ava's perfume over the smell of new leather. Just holding it freaks me out, so I shove it back into the closet and smooth the clothes around it until I'm satisfied that it looks like it hasn't been disturbed.

I try to calm down. Ava buys new stuff all the time. It's no big deal. It's just a coincidence that she has a new red leather jacket. And that it looks just like the one that the mystery girl was wearing in the photo right after Casey was killed.

"What are you looking for?" Ava asks from the doorway.

I jump back like I've been shocked. "Jeez, you scared me." I was going to tell her everything—about what the cops know and the photo, but now I'm not so sure. "I was looking for those jeans I borrowed last week. I think I might have left five bucks in the pocket." I casually reach in and pull the jacket out, like it's no big deal. "This is nice. When did you get it?"

"I don't know. A couple of weeks ago, I guess. There was an end-of-season sale at the mall." She looks up at me, but I don't see anything in her eyes that's giving her away. "You want to borrow it? I haven't even worn it yet."

I look down and see that the tags are still hanging from the sleeve. Has she really not worn it? If she did wear it that night, why would she lie about it? "Maybe," I say, putting it back in the closet.

"So, what happened?" she asks, flopping down onto her bed.

"Well, they didn't arrest me. Yet. And it has nothing to

do with the fake ID." I watch her face closely. The face I've trusted as much as my own all my life. Until now. "They wanted to ask me some questions about Casey."

Ava picks some of the polish off her fingernails, putting the scraps of color in a little pile on her bed. She doesn't meet my eyes. Is that a sign of guilt? "Yeah?" I'm searching her face for clues, but she looks totally unconcerned. "Good thing you have nothing to hide, right?"

"That's what they're trying to find out. I even gave them a DNA sample. To eliminate me. Us."

Her eyes go wide, but now I can't tell if it's all just an act. "So what do we do now?"

I'm about to answer when we hear the front door open and a booming voice calling our names.

"Daddy's home!" Ava shouts, scrambling off her bed to greet him.

I glance at her open closet and catch a glimpse of the red jacket pushed way to the back, which gives me an ache in the pit of my stomach. Dad's home, but I'm not sure I've done enough. We're keeping secrets from each other, and I've never felt so alone.

CHAPTER 14

"I'm sorry," the woman on the phone says, her voice wary and a little suspicious. "We don't give out that kind of information. License plate lookups are done only for law enforcement or licensed private investigators." She pauses. "What did you say you need it for?"

I can feel my heart pounding, even though it's what I expected her to say. The speeding ticket was sent to us, which means the driver must have a copy of the fake ID—but the car might be registered to someone else. Someone who might help me figure this out. There's no way that all of these random Alicia sightings are coincidence—someone is doing this on purpose. "There's a car blocking my driveway, and I wanted to see if I could get in touch with the person who owns it before I have it towed." I'm surprised at how smoothly this comes out. Almost like I didn't practice it for an hour this morning.

"Have you tried leaving a note?"

"No. I haven't," I say. "Thank you for the advice." I hang up the phone and stare at the screen. Now what? Aside from Detective Naito, I don't know anyone in law enforcement. I open my desk drawer and pull out his card. As I stare at the phone numbers, an idea starts to form. I pick up the diamond *A* pendant that's sitting on my desk and fold my hand around it. Alicia would do it. The worst they can do is say no.

My hand is shaking as I call the DMV's number again and pray someone else answers this time. I say a silent thank-you when a gruff male voice answers the phone.

"Hi," I say, pitching my voice higher than normal. "I really hope you can help me. I'm the assistant to Detective Jim Naito in San Diego County, and our computer system has totally gone down. He needs me to get some information on a license plate number right away, and until the computers come back up, there's no way I can get it for him."

"I'm sorry," he says, exactly like the first woman. "We don't give out that kind of information."

"I know," I say as sweetly as I can. "As someone in law enforcement, I'd never ask you to break the rules, but I'm seriously in trouble here." I give a quiet sniff into the phone and let my voice waver a bit. "I just got this job, see, and I've got a baby girl at home to take care of, and my no-good husband ran off with his receptionist, so she's all I got. If I can't get this one little thing for the detective in the next five minutes, I'm pretty sure he'll fire me." I pause and can tell that he's still listening. "I knew you wouldn't be able to help me," I say. "It's just that I'm so desperate to save my job—"

"Hang on," he says wearily, and the hold music comes on.

I let out a deep sigh and relax a tiny bit. He might actually do this. "Look," he says, coming back on the phone, "they could have my ass for this, but I've been where you are, so I get it. What's the license plate number?"

I tell him, and he clicks back off the line. I can feel my heart pounding as I hold the phone to my ear and wait through the hold music.

"Okay, here's what I can do," the guy says. "I can't give you an address, but I can get you a phone number. Will that help?"

"That would be great! Thank you so much. I really, really appreciate this, and so does my daughter, Katie." I wince at that last part. I might be going a little too far with this.

He reads off the numbers, and I write them down on a scrap piece of paper. "You're the best!" I say, as bubbly as possible.

"No problem," he says. "You stay safe out there."

"You too."

It doesn't take long to do a reverse lookup on the Internet to get that answer and more questions: Who does Ava know in Oceanside, and why is she using that address?

———

"Oh. My. God!" Ava screams just before the front door slams so hard that my window rattles.

I stick my head out of my room in time to hear Cecilia yell about not slamming the door. Ava pounds on the wall as she walks down the hallway, with Maya right behind her.

"What's going on?" I ask.

"Asshole!" I hear, followed by a sharp bang, and I reach the doorway to her room in time to see her throw the second of a pair of stilettos hard at the wall.

"What is it?" I ask. Cecilia is right behind me, looking concerned.

"Dylan Harrington, that's what! He cheated on me—can you believe that? With a junior from Claremont! She's not even that cute!" Ava's hair is messy, and her face is red as she looks for something else to throw.

"I knew he was trouble," Maya says from the corner of Ava's bed.

Ava whirls on her. "You thought he was hot!"

"Hot, but trouble," she insists.

I glance pointedly at Cecilia, but Ava doesn't take the hint. Cecilia's not supposed to know about Dylan because Ava didn't go out with him. Alicia did.

"One of his friends posted that he was up in Cardiff with some girl, and sure enough, we went there, and they were totally making out under lifeguard tower number four."

Cecilia shakes her head, a scowl in her eyes. "Seriously, Ava, again with the boys. When are you going to learn they're not worth it?" I relax a little. I'm sure Cecilia can't keep up with who Ava's seeing.

"Dylan sure wasn't." The anger seems to seep out of her, and now Ava's eyes are shining with tears.

Cecilia visibly softens when she sees that Ava is really upset. "You're a smart, beautiful, kind girl. In a few days this

Dylan person will be just a memory." Ava seems to sink into Cecilia's hug.

"I doubt it," she says, wiping a stray tear off her cheek.

"I promise," Cecilia says, pulling back and patting her on the cheek. "I'm going to go start dinner." She gives her hand a squeeze. "Don't let the bastards get you down."

Ava can't help but laugh at that. Cecilia never swears. "Okay. If you say so."

"I say so."

None of us says a word until Cecilia is safely down the hall. "Did anyone else see you?" I ask.

Ava shrugs. "I don't know. Why does it matter?"

"It doesn't."

"It was really hideous," Maya says. "Dylan didn't even look sorry. Almost like he was enjoying the fight."

"Fight?" I watch Ava carefully. "What did you do?"

She turns to me, her hands on her hips. "I wished them the best and walked away. What do you think I did? I told both of them exactly what I thought."

"And that's it? Nothing physical?"

"I may have pushed that bitch a couple of times. But she totally deserved it. And more."

"Okay," I say. Even in the midst of all this anger, it's hard to believe that Ava would do anything else. One minute I'd never believe she'd do something to Casey (or more realistically, get someone to do it for her), and the next I'm holding a red leather jacket that puts her at the scene and we're getting speeding tickets that belong to somebody who really lives in Oceanside. What else isn't she telling me?

"Well, I'm taking care of Dylan right now," Maya says, tapping on her phone. "One more second . . . and there." She flips her phone around to us, and I see a photo of Dylan and a girl who's definitely not Ava clearly making out on the beach. "I posted it on my wall and then tagged everyone who knows Alicia."

Ava kneels on the bed and puts her arm around Maya. "You're the best."

"I know."

"So we're still going out tonight, right?" Ava asks me, glancing at her closet.

I can't believe she really wants to get out there and do it all over again. "I'm not going out," I say.

"Oh, come on. There's only a few days left of spring break," Ava says. "Don't let one little incident spoil everything. We were just starting to have some fun."

"I don't really count getting attacked at a party as a little incident. And I meant it when I said that I was done as Alicia. Now that Dylan's over, you should be too."

"Do whatever you want, but I'm going." Ava walks to her closet and starts pawing through outfits. "This will be a good time to get Dylan out of my system." She holds up a dress that looks more like a tunic, it's so short. "What about this for drowning my sorrows?"

"That'll work," Maya says with a grin.

"Lex, you really need to learn how to live a little." She holds up the dress and looks at herself in the reflection of the window.

I reach over and quickly pull her curtains closed. It's not

totally dark yet, but it's creepy even thinking about someone sitting out there watching us.

"Hey! I wasn't done."

"Use your mirror," I say. "The whole world can see you out there."

"Like anybody even cares," she protests, but turns to the mirror. "I told you those seeds don't mean anything. You're being paranoid."

"Someone out there might be stalking us," I say. "I don't consider that paranoid."

"You guys are like an old married couple." Maya grins and then goes back to tapping on her phone. "Hey—when were you at the reggae festival?"

Ava's busy looking in the mirror over her desk. "Never. Why?"

"Because someone named Nancy tagged Alicia in a photo from last week." She hands her phone to Ava.

"That's not me," Ava says, handing the phone back.

"Let me see it," I say. The photo is a picture of Ava holding a beer with a stage in the background. She's standing next to a girl with blond hair and a guy with dreads. It's taken from pretty far away, but it sure looks like her. "Are you sure that isn't you?"

"I'd know if I accidentally stumbled into a reggae festival," Ava says. "Must be you."

"Come on," I say. "That's not me." I scroll down. There are tons of photos on Alicia's feed that I haven't seen before.

"Give it," Maya says, her hand out. She zooms in on the

first image. "Probably Photoshopped," she says. "Someone got a picture of one of you and cropped the head onto someone else's body. Do you guys know this Nancy person?"

We both shake our heads.

"I'm sure it's some kind of joke. Maybe someone found out about Alicia," Maya says.

"I thought you locked this page," I say to Ava. "So that people we actually know won't find it." The last thing we need is to have to explain Alicia's page to people at school.

"We did," Ava says. "I haven't even looked at it in forever."

Maya taps on her phone. "Uh-oh," she says, using her finger to scroll down.

"What?" I ask, trying to see over her shoulder.

"You haven't been posting as Alicia, have you?" she asks me.

"No. I told you—I totally forgot about it."

"Well, someone has. Alicia Rios has been a very busy girl lately." She scrolls down some more. "The page must have been hacked. There's a trip to Tijuana . . . a beach party that looks like it's in Mission Bay somewhere."

Ava grabs the phone. "Let me see that." She studies the photos on the page. "I didn't take this profile shot—did you?"

She turns the phone to me, and I see a selfie, obviously taken in a bathroom mirror that shows part of an eye and some hair. "No. You can't even see who that is."

"Shit." Maya taps her phone hard. "I can't get into the account anymore. Someone changed the password."

"That's crazy," Ava says. "Give it here." She taps on the

phone with an increasingly frustrated look on her face. "Call them or something. Tell them that someone stole our page."

"It's not that easy," I say, looking at the phone. I try all of our usual passwords, but none of them will get us in.

Maya takes her phone back. "You know who can figure this out, don't you?"

I stand up. "No way. I don't want Zane getting involved in this."

Ava leans against her desk. "Maya's right. Zane could figure out if the pictures were Photoshopped. He might even be able to figure out how to get back into Alicia's page. Quicker than the stupid people who run the site, anyway."

"I don't want anyone else involved in this. I already told him that we weren't doing Alicia anymore."

"Whatever." Maya hands me the phone so that I can see the photos again. "If you go through the Internet, it might take weeks. Zane could have it done in an hour."

I'm outnumbered. And they're right. Zane was setting up our wireless system back in elementary school. If anyone can figure this out, he can, but I don't want any of his I-told-you-so attitude. "Fine. But I'm not calling him."

Maya takes the phone back and continues scrolling. "Hey." She looks up at me. "When did Casey die?"

"March thirtieth. Sometime around midnight." I know I'll never forget the date. It looked so official on the paperwork Detective Naito had.

"And you definitely didn't see him that day?" Maya is starting to sound exactly like a cop.

"No. Why?"

"You're not going to like this," Maya says, handing the phone back to me. I look on Alicia's time line and see a one-line posting from March twenty-ninth at eight-thirty p.m.—four hours before he died. A line that neither Ava nor I put there.

Going to see Casey after he gets off work—wish me luck!

CHAPTER 15

I click Alicia's page off my phone just as Dad walks into the kitchen.

"Hey, gorgeous," he says, giving me a kiss on the cheek.

"Hey, Dad," I answer, shoving the phone back into my pocket.

He places a tissue-paper-wrapped lump in front of me on the counter. "I forgot to give this to you when I got home yesterday."

I pick it up and feel the liquid sloshing around. "You don't have to keep bringing me snow globes. I'm not a kid anymore."

"Don't remind me." He's smiling, but he still looks sad. "Aren't you going to open it?"

I pull the tissue paper away to see a glass globe with the South African flag inside.

"I know it's not the tacky plastic ones that you like, but

you'd be amazed how hard it is to find a snow globe in South Africa."

I shake it up so that the glitter fills the water. "It's perfect. Thanks."

"Listen, I was thinking that this spring break must have been pretty boring. How about we pick a week right after school gets out and go on vacation, just the three of us? Anywhere you guys want—Hawaii, Mexico, Paris . . . anywhere."

As long as we're not in jail by then. "Sure. That would be great."

Dad pours himself a cup of coffee and leans his elbows on the counter next to mine. "Stop sulking, okay? I already told you that we're going to fix this Stanford mess. I'm sure it was just a big mistake. I've got a call in to a buddy of mine who has some pull, to see what he can do."

I can feel tears pricking the backs of my eyes. Dad's been so nice about it since he got home, like it was Stanford's mistake, not mine. "Once you get rejected from Stanford, that's it. No reconsiderations."

Dad winces at the word "rejected."

"Probably just some overzealous administrator who didn't know what they were doing." He kisses me on the forehead. "Stanford is where you belong. We'll get you there, don't worry."

"Hmm," I say. Is it really where I belong?

I wait until he's shut the front door behind him before I pick up the house phone. It beeps as I scroll through the call history on the handset, trying to remember what day the salon called. Just as I'm getting impatient, I see the call from Leon's and a number. It doesn't take more than a few seconds to look up the salon on the Internet and get an address. I have only an hour to get there before Alicia's appointment. Someone is pretending to be Alicia, and I have to find out who it is. Even if I find out that it's Ava.

I follow the directions to a small strip mall in Solana Beach. Leon's is wedged between a taqueria and a dry cleaner's, and it's easy to spot because of the blown-up photos of slightly out-of-date haircuts posted in the window. Ava usually gets her hair cut in the city at two hundred dollars a pop, and I can't imagine her coming all the way out here, even if she's trying to be incognito.

I sit in my car with a good view of the front door, watching people come and go. My stomach is in knots, and I'm not sure if I'm hoping that Ava will show up or that she won't. Her car is nowhere in sight, but I'm not surprised—if she's coming out here as Alicia, she's not going to park her car right out front. Maybe she won't drive her car at all. I put the speeding ticket in the top drawer of my desk. It was for a 2011 Honda. What would Ava be doing in someone else's Honda? None of this makes any sense.

Watching the numbers on the clock change makes time drag, and I get to 4:20 before I've had enough. Nobody even remotely matching Alicia's description has gone through the salon door. What if I missed her? Even though Ava is never early for anything, what if she beat me here?

I get out of the car and walk toward the salon. Having a confrontation here in front of all these people is better than not having a clue what she's up to. I pull open the door, and the uniquely salon smell of hair dye and perm solution hits me right in the face.

"Excuse me." A woman with a clipboard pushes past me to the reception desk. "Here's my client card with all the info."

"Thanks," says the bored-looking receptionist. "Take a seat, and someone will be right with you."

There are six chairs lining the styling area of the room, three on either side. Four of them are occupied by women in various stages of cut or dye jobs, but none of the women is Ava. Maybe she was right and it was a different Alicia Rios. I'm almost disappointed as I turn to go.

"Alicia!" says a woman who's holding a blow-dryer to an older woman's head. "Hold on one second." She snaps the dryer off and leans over to tell the woman something, handing her a magazine off the counter in front of her. The stylist's hair is a red color that is found nowhere in nature, and it's piled on her head in stiff, messy curls. I wonder if she did this to herself or if it was a training exercise by a new employee.

She smiles at me as she approaches the front of the salon. "I'm sorry, hon, but when you didn't show up today, I gave your time slot away." She walks up to a big appointment book that's spread out on a desk in the front. "Let's see," she says, flipping pages. "I'm booked up for the beginning of next week, but things free up starting on Wednesday."

I'm totally caught off guard. I don't know what to say. Has Ava been coming here in secret? "Um—"

The woman looks up and runs her fingers through the ends of my hair. "We'd better make it Wednesday. I can't believe your hair has gotten this out of control in six short weeks. Looks like rats have been nesting in there. So Wednesday? At the same time?"

"Sure," I say. "Thanks." I grab a business card from the counter in case I need it later. I have one hand on the door when an idea hits me. "Hey, could I get a look at my client card? I got a new cell number, and I'm not sure you have it."

"That's right. I had to look it up on the Internet because the one we had wasn't working," the woman says, reaching for a small box that looks like it once held recipes. So much for high-tech. She turns it toward me and flips it open. "Alphabetical under *R*. Put your new address in there while you're at it, okay?" She walks back to the woman in the chair.

I flip through the cards casually, in case anyone is watching me, and pull out the one with Alicia's name on it. I don't recognize the handwriting, but that doesn't mean anything. It might have been filled out by someone who works here. It has a phone number written on it and scratched out, with our home number written over it, and an address in Oceanside. As far as I remember, we don't even know anyone in Oceanside. Why would Ava use such a random address? I quickly punch the information into my phone and put the card back in the box. "Nope," I call out. "It's fine. I'll see you next week."

"Okay, Alicia." She waves with her free hand. "See you Wednesday."

CHAPTER 16

The echo of the bell has barely faded when the room fills with the sounds of chairs scraping the floor.

"Alexa, can I see you for a moment?" Ms. Campbell calls just as I reach the door.

"Sure," I say, hiking my backpack up and walking toward her desk. Ever since the email from Stanford, I've been letting things slip a little. . . . Fine—maybe a lot. I square my shoulders and look straight ahead. It's not like I don't know what this is about.

She pretends to look busy, straightening some papers on her desk. "I didn't see your paper on *Brave New World*."

I can feel my face get red, but I refuse to look away. "That's because I didn't turn it in."

That gets her attention. She looks up at me. "Didn't turn it in?" She repeats. "Have you been sick? Are there problems at home?"

I shake my head. I know what Dad keeps saying, but I'm not sure even he can change the collective Stanford mind. And if I'm not going to Stanford, AP English is feeling a lot less important. Once I got past the guilt, it's actually been kind of freeing not to slave over seven hours of homework every night. "No. I just didn't see the point."

I try not to smile at the fact that Ms. Campbell is at a total loss for words. "The point? The point is to teach you how to think critically while you read, and how to consolidate those thoughts into a coherent essay, all things you're going to need next year at Stanford—"

"I didn't get in," I say. You'd think it would get easier each time I say those words, but it doesn't. "I'm not going to Stanford."

Immediately the annoyance in her eyes turns to pity. She wrote one of my recommendations, so she had a stake in it too. "I'm so sorry. But any other university is going to require this level of analysis as well."

"Even if I can get in, I don't want to go anywhere else," I say. "Come September maybe I'll get a job. Or maybe I'll travel. Or maybe I'll sit around at home doing nothing. Which is why I didn't see the point of wasting my time with an essay." I look away as tears fill my eyes.

"There are still so many options—" Ms. Campbell begins.

"Not for me," I say, angrily wiping my tears on my sleeve. I've never missed an assignment, never failed a test, and being a crappy student is harder than I thought it would be. Not only am I a total loser academically, but I can't help standing here and bawling like a baby about it. "Look, I appreciate what you're trying to do, but I might as well not waste my time with papers and tests that aren't going to do me any good."

"You can still turn it in late," she says, clearly not listening to me. "I'll mark it down a grade, but it will still count."

"Thanks," I say, turning toward the door, knowing that missing this first paper was hard but the rest will come easy. "But I'll be fine."

I rush to AP Spanish but have barely taken my seat when I think I hear my name over the loudspeaker.

"Was that for me?" I ask the girl in the next chair.

She shrugs, but Zane slides into the seat on the other side of me and says, "Yeah. They called you to the front office."

"What now?"

"Want me to come with you?" he asks, handing me my backpack, which was on the floor next to his feet.

"No—I'm sure it's no big deal." I shove my books into my bag and head into the quickly emptying hallway. I don't see the cops until I'm about to open the office door. In that split second I start to panic, but I see Principal Forrester recognize me and say something from behind the glass. The rest of the room turns to look, so I take a deep breath and step inside.

"What's going on?" I ask, trying not to sound as freaked out as I really am.

The men turn, and I see Detective Naito and two cops I don't know. I hear a radio squawk and see a female cop sitting in one of the plastic chairs, talking into a radio that's attached to her shoulder. Ava is standing next to the front-office lady, looking shaky and pale.

"They found Dylan," she says, her eyes filling with tears. "Outside the gym at the university."

I look at all the serious faces, not totally understanding what she's saying. "What do you mean, they *found* him?"

"Dead. Someone killed him, just like Casey," she says, tears streaming down her face, and a look of fear in her eyes that I've never seen before.

"Alicia?" one of the men asks, turning toward us. He's not dressed in a uniform but is wearing a black Windbreaker with a badge embroidered on the front.

"I already told you, there's no Alicia Rios," Principal Forrester says. "I told them they had the wrong girls," she says to me, and I smile at her gratefully. "Alexa and Ava are two of our best students."

Detective Naito steps forward. "If there is no Alicia Rios, then we have even more to talk about than I thought."

I look at Principal Forrester and have no idea what to say. It feels like we're in it deep. "It's true. It was all a joke." I go for a small smile, but nobody in the room smiles back.

Detective Naito's eyes have lost all their friendliness as he looks from me to Ava. "There have been some further developments, I'm afraid." He glances down at the screen in his hand and then back at me. "If you're not Alicia, then what is your name?"

"I'm Lexi. Alexa." The cops' faces are serious. I force a small laugh. "All of this is a total misunderstanding."

"That's right!" Ava jumps in, wiping her cheeks with the palm of her hand. I can't tell if she's just acting or if she's really this upset. "Just a misunderstanding."

"There really isn't an Alicia Rios. We made her up. And then we got her a fake ID," I say, and then glance at the principal, who frowns. "Not for drinking or anything. Just so it would look more authentic." I feel like I'm talking too fast, trying to cover too much ground in one sentence.

"And we didn't want to get busted for that," Ava jumps in. "So when you came to the house before, we just said Alicia was out so we wouldn't get in trouble."

One of the other cops looks at us. "I'm afraid you're in a lot more trouble than just a fake ID." He turns to the others. "What should we do here? Any ideas?"

Detective Naito looks down at his computer. "The warrant is for Alicia Rios." He looks back at us. "I guess we should take them both in until we can get to the bottom of this."

"Warrant?" I ask. I can feel this situation getting more serious. "What do you need a warrant for?"

The woman cop takes a step toward us. "We have a warrant for the arrest of Alicia Rios on suspicion of murder." She puts her hand on her belt and fingers the shining handcuffs that are hanging there.

"Are you kidding me?" Ava says, putting her hands up and taking a step backward. I can see her whole body shaking. "I'm sorry Dylan's dead, but we didn't do anything wrong."

"Maybe we should take a trip down to the station to try to figure that out," the tall cop with the glasses says.

"You can't arrest me," Ava says, her voice barely audible and tears streaming down her face. She isn't even trying to stop her tears anymore. I follow her glance to the hallway, where people are starting to gather, looking in the windows like it's some kind of show. "Not in front of everyone." The last few words are reduced to a whisper as she chokes back sobs.

I see that Ava's teetering on the brink of hysteria as the woman pulls the handcuffs off her belt and moves toward her. Ava's breath comes in ragged bursts, and her face has gone completely white. I watch her hands tremble as the cop pulls one arm behind her back.

At this moment I see how vulnerable Ava is. Technically it's her fault we're in this mess at all, but I should have told the truth at the station that day. The only thing I know for sure is that I didn't kill anybody, and that's the best defense I have right now. I wish I could say the same for Ava.

"I didn't do anything wrong," Ava insists as the cops look at each other, obviously unsure about what to do next.

"She's right." I step in between her and the cops. "This doesn't have anything to do with Ava. I was with Casey that night. We went out to dinner and then down to the beach, but he was very much alive the last time I saw him. And I don't have any idea what happened to Dylan."

The detective puts out a hand to stop the cop from handcuffing Ava. "So it was you down at the police station the other day?"

"Yes. You took me into the room and showed me the surveillance photo of the girl in the red leather jacket." I glance at Ava, but I can't tell if she realizes what I'm saying. I'm not sure she even remembers the red jacket at this point, but I silently beg her to keep her mouth shut. The only way to keep us both out of trouble is to get the cops to take me. They can't convict me if I didn't have anything to do with the deaths. I know that the suspicion is mounting, but I need to find out if Ava's involved before throwing her to the system. This is the last little bit of control I have. I concentrate on breathing slowly, trying everything I can to stay calm and in control. "I'm the one you want, not Ava. I'll go with you."

The woman cop hesitates, and I can see she's not sure what to do. I turn to her. "Take me," I repeat.

"But you're not Alicia Rios," the cop says, looking at me.

"And neither is she." I point to Ava. "You don't get it. Alicia doesn't exist." I feel my frustration rising as nobody seems to be listening.

"Give him your IDs," Principal Forrester says, nodding at the school tags that are hanging around our necks.

Detective Naito takes both of them and compares them side by side. "So you really are twins?"

"Yes!" Ava says, and I can hear the relief in her voice. "Twins. Not triplets."

He holds my ID up. "And this is you?" he asks me. "Alexa? And you were with Casey the night before he died?"

"Yes." I glance outside the doors to where the crowd is getting bigger, and I start to panic. "Let's just go."

Principal Forrester steps between me and the cop. "I can't do anything to stop them from taking you. But I'll get in touch with your father right away—have him meet you down at the station."

"Thanks," I say, glad at least that I don't have to be the

one to call Dad. I make a move toward the door, but the woman cop stops me. "You have to be handcuffed," she says. "For everyone's safety."

I'm operating on autopilot as I turn around and feel the heavy metallic cuffs snap onto my wrists. I suddenly feel claustrophobic, like I can't breathe.

"Lexi!" Ava cries. "What are you doing? This is crazy!"

I look her straight in the eye, relieved for the moment that it's me and not her. I have to hold on to this one tiny victory. "It's going to be fine. We didn't do anything wrong, so there's nothing to worry about." I hope she knows enough to shut up and keep herself out of trouble.

Ava's eyes fill with tears again as she searches for something else to say.

"Calm down. It's going to be fine," I repeat.

One of the cops holds up my backpack and turns to me. "May I?"

"Whatever," I say impatiently. There's nothing in there except my books and the lunch Cecilia packed me this morning.

Ava steps forward. "I'll take it home for her."

"We have to take it into evidence," the cop says, opening it and rifling through the contents.

Escorted by all the cops, I walk through the silent hallway with my head up, looking straight ahead, fully aware of the eyes that are on me as we pass several open classroom doors. As we get to the large circular driveway out front, I see a big yellow tow truck with a white car attached to the back of it.

"My car!" I say, watching the truck pull it around the corner and out of sight. It feels like it's being stolen from me right in front of everyone.

"Part of the warrant," Detective Naito says.

I hesitate, feeling like I'm surrendering everything right now. "But Casey was never in my car."

"Then you don't have anything to worry about," he says.

"Watch your head," the woman cop says as she opens the back door and lets me slide awkwardly into the squad car that's parked at the curb.

Detective Naito sticks his head into the backseat. "You have the right to remain silent. Anything you say can and will be used against you in a court of law. . . ." I tune out the rest of it. I've heard it recited countless times on TV shows and in movies. I never thought I'd hear it in real life.

I feel a sense of expectation, and I focus on him again.

"Do you understand these rights?"

"Yes," I say, even though I haven't heard a word he's said in the past couple of minutes. I look beyond the front of the cop car and see crowds at every window, and Ava, Principal Forrester, and a small knot of people at the top of the steps. Slater leans over and says something to Ava, but she just shakes her head frantically.

"Let's just go," I beg the detective.

"I'm calling Dad too!" Ava shouts, already tapping her phone. "He'll know what to do."

I allow myself a small feeling of relief as the car door is shut and I can't hear anything else from outside. Dad will work it out. He'll be pissed, but he'll get this all figured out. Ava's on the phone, one hand waving in the air as she tries to explain what's going on to Dad. I can only imagine what's happening at the other end, but I really don't care. All I want is for him to hurry. As I shift in my seat and look behind me, I catch sight of Zane in the side doorway, his eyes full of concern as they lock on mine.

For once, Zane is right—I'm in way over my head.

CHAPTER 17

I rest my forehead against the front seat for the entire drive. I don't want to look out the window and see anyone I know. Just being in the back of a cop car with handcuffs on makes me feel a guilt that's hard to shake, no matter how many times I protest that I'm innocent.

The car stops, and I look up to see the brick building from last week, only this time things are so different. That day, I could turn around and walk out anytime. The heavy, warm metal around my wrists reminds me that this is no longer true. I'm silently grateful that there's nobody waiting out front as the woman cop opens the back door and walks with me into the side entrance of the station. No orange plastic chairs this time, no slightly surly greeting by the desk cop. Just harsh fluorescent lighting and what looks like miles of shiny linoleum leading down a long hallway. There are no sounds but the clanking of keys and the occasional squawk of noise from the cop's radio. I look around, but I don't see Detective Naito and the others anywhere, and I wonder if we beat them here.

I expect to get fingerprinted and have my mug shot taken, but to my surprise we take a right at the end of the long hallway and stop outside another interrogation room. The cop unlocks it and ushers me inside. It looks just like the one I was in the other day, right down to the hard plastic chair, which she now motions me into. As soon as I sit, she unlocks the handcuffs and pops them off my wrists. I suddenly feel like I can breathe again.

"We don't have to worry about you, right?" she says, tucking them back into her belt.

"No," I say. "Ma'am," I add quickly, because it seems like the right thing to do. I shake my hands out to get rid of the feeling of heaviness that's still on my wrists.

"Sit tight. Someone will be with you in a moment," she says, and heads for the door.

I think about asking her about the booking and the mug shots, but then I decide that it's probably better to just sit here and shut up. No use reminding them of the technicalities if somehow they forgot. I sit back in the chair and wait, staring at the ceiling and at the clock over the door—everywhere but at the big mirror on the wall in front of me. I don't have to see behind it to know I'm being watched.

After what seems like an eternity, Detective Naito walks in, followed by another, slightly taller cop. "This is Detective Richardson," Naito says as he sits down next to me and the other detective takes his place at the other end of the table.

I nod, guessing correctly that handshakes aren't really part of the arrest process. "Am I under arrest?" I ask.

The two detectives exchange a glance. "That depends," Detective Naito says. He leans forward on his elbows across the small white table. "Why don't you start by telling us about Alicia."

I sit back and relax just a little. If I were seriously in trouble, I'd be backed up to a yardstick on the wall getting my picture taken right about now. I just have to explain it so they understand. "There is no Alicia. Ava and I made her up." I smile a little but get no reaction from either man. "It started out as just something fun. You know, we'd take turns being Alicia and go out with different guys. Well, Ava mostly went out with them. I . . . filled in for her sometimes."

"So you lied to me the last time you were here," Detective Naito says, his eyes crinkling with concern.

I have no good excuse at this point. "I did—about my name. But everything else was the truth. I went out with Casey the night before he died. I didn't see him after that."

The other cop flips through a manila folder. "We have eyewitnesses that put you on the beach last Thursday when an altercation broke out with Dylan Harrington and a young woman named Selena Lee."

I feel an icy shiver work down the length of my spine. I don't know how to get out of this without implicating Ava. If they find she was out with Dylan, they'll haul her in here for sure. If she is involved in this, I can't be the one who sells her out. I take a deep breath and dive in. "He was cheating on me," I say quickly, before I have time to think about it.

Now I'm in too deep to turn back. "I caught him, we had an argument, and we broke up. But that's it. He was alive the last time I saw him." I pause, but I have to know. "What happened to him?"

I can feel Detective Naito watching me carefully. "Preliminary reports say that he was stabbed in the back of the neck." He tilts his head. "Exactly the same as Casey Stewart."

Bloody images flash through my mind. "That's awful," I say, the emotion behind it genuine. Neither of those guys deserved to die.

Detective Naito brings out the photo of the girl with the red jacket. "So you were with Casey Stewart the night he was killed?"

I stare at him. They're trying to trick me. "No—it was the night before. In the parking lot of the Cheesecake Factory." I point to the photo. "But I don't know who that is, because it's not me. I was telling the complete truth about that." I hesitate, but I have to account for any of my DNA that they might have found on his body. "Look. I didn't tell you everything about that night." They don't say anything, so I continue. "I met him there after he got off work at ten. We walked on the beach and had some ice cream. It got cold, so we went back to his car to talk some more. The restaurant had closed by then, so the parking lot was pretty empty." I hesitate, but then continue, knowing I'm already in this far. "Things . . . um . . . things got a little bit crazy. I tried to get out of the car, and he . . . he . . ." I can't bring myself to say it. Even bringing it up makes scenes from that night flash through my mind.

The two detectives are leaning forward, listening intently. "He what?" Detective Naito finally asks.

"He wouldn't let me go," I say, squeezing my eyes shut as the images from that night replay in my brain. "He wouldn't stop when I told him to. . . . He held me down against the seat." I stop here to catch my breath. The image of Casey looming over me, the feel of his teeth on my skin, the sound of his laugh are all too vivid.

"But you got away?" Detective Naito asks.

"Yes." I nod. "My dad is big into self-defense. He made us take classes to learn what to do if we were ever in a situation like that."

"What did you use?" Detective Richardson asks.

"My keys," I say.

Detective Naito's head snaps up, and he glances at the big mirror on the opposite wall. "Your keys?"

"Yes." I hold up one fist. "You put them in between your fingers like this. I knew I only had one shot at him, so I took it. Right across his cheek." I look at the two of them. "Not enough to make him stop, but enough to slow him down so I could get the hell out of there and back to my car."

"And that's it?" Detective Naito asks.

"That's it," I say.

They glance at each other. "Starting to sound like motive to me," Detective Richardson says quietly.

What I've just done starts to sink in. I've handed them the one thing they were missing. "Motive?" I say. "There's no motive, because nothing else happened. I started the car and got out of there as fast as I could. The last time I saw him, he was leaning against his car in the parking lot. Alive."

Detective Naito flips through the folder. "And what time was this?"

"About eleven o'clock," I say.

"And then you went straight home?"

"Yes." I look him right in the eye. "I don't know who that is in the picture you have, but it wasn't me. Or Ava."

"And you still maintain that Casey didn't scratch you? Even if evidence says otherwise?"

I remember the DNA they took from my cheek the last time I was here, and I feel set up. "The DNA you found under his fingernails matches mine?"

The two detectives exchange wary looks. "It does," Detective Richardson says. He leans forward and puts his elbows on the table. "And from the looks of it, it would have been a fairly large scratch."

The only thing I know is that Casey didn't scratch me that night. And that Ava and I have basically the same DNA. I pull up my sleeves and show them my arms. "See? No scratches. I already told you that I was in Casey's car that night, so even if my DNA is in the car, it doesn't prove anything."

Detective Naito flips through the folder. "Where were you around five o'clock this morning?"

"Why? Is that when Dylan was killed?"

He glances at Detective Richardson. "Approximately."

"Sleeping. At home."

"Can anyone verify that?"

I shrug. "Cecilia was in the kitchen packing our lunches

184

when I got up at six-thirty. She'll tell you that I was home, asleep."

The detectives share a glance, and I know I'm in trouble. The university is only about twenty minutes from the house—plenty of time to get there, kill Dylan and get back before anyone else got up.

"It says here that you're taking AP Biology. And that you've applied to some prestigious schools next year," Detective Richardson says. "What's your major going to be? Premed?"

I look at him but have no idea where he's going with this. It seems like every time I open my mouth, I get into bigger trouble. "No. Business."

"But you've taken a lot of science courses?"

"Yeah. I like science. So?"

"Interesting," Detective Naito says. He pulls some photos from the folder and hands them to me.

I glance at Dylan's deathly white profile and the spreading pool of black blood next to him and push the photo away. This corpse doesn't look anything like the guy I met outside Ava's room that night. "I don't want to see that!"

Detective Naito pulls the photo back and looks at it as if studying it for the first time. "What's interesting is that we're thinking that whoever did this has some sort of a medical or science background." He turns in his chair and puts one finger on the back of his head, just below his skull. "Because you'd have to know the exact spot to slip the knife into so that severing the spine makes the victim immediately helpless." He turns back around. "Not to mention dead." He leans forward on the table again. "It's how they kill livestock on small farms. Knowing a trick like that would be the great equalizer, wouldn't it? All it would take is a small knife and a little knowledge of the human body, and someone who is much smaller"—he looks me up and down—"say five foot two, could disable a much larger person."

It feels like Detective Naito has already convicted me. I look at him, but there's no sympathy in his eyes. This is all slipping out of control. "Look, there's no way I could do that to an animal, much less a person. And maybe your sample was contaminated or your tests were wrong, but I didn't have anything to do with Casey's death. Or Dylan's."

Detective Naito puts both palms faceup on the table. "That's what you keep saying. We're just doing our job, tracking down leads." He looks directly at me and takes a theatrical pause. "The only problem is that all the leads keep pointing to you."

I can feel the panic rising in my throat as I look around the bare room. What the hell is going on here? I told them the truth. At least, most of it—I should be walking out of here by now. "I didn't do anything wrong," I say, my voice echoing off the blank walls. "Yes, I went out with Casey, but that's it. No way could I ever kill anyone." I can feel my brain grasping at anything that might make this all go away. "What about the sunflower seeds? I told you, some strange things have been going on lately. I think someone's been following us. Trying to set us up."

Detective Richardson leans forward on the chair. "Funny

thing about the seeds," he says, flipping through the papers in the file. "We did get a DNA hit on them. An Alicia Rios." He pauses. "At least, one Alicia Rios who appeared down at the police station last week."

I look at the two of them, but neither of them smiles. "What do you mean? *My* DNA was on them? That's impossible!"

"Science doesn't lie," the detective says.

"Maybe that was from when I picked them up off the ground. But there was nothing else?"

The door opens, and a woman I don't recognize walks in.

"The steering wheel tested positive for blood," she says to the detectives. "We're getting trace on it right away."

Frustration is flooding my body as my mind races. "I already told you—"

"In light of what you've told us, we're going to need your keys too."

"They're in my backpack," I say, my frustration rising. It feels like this is all an insane nightmare. "Which you already have. How long—" I'm interrupted by the door being flung open.

"Don't say another word," a tall woman in jeans and an off-white sweater says to me as she surveys the room. She's not wearing any makeup, and her straight blond hair is pulled back into a low ponytail. She looks more like an elementary school teacher than a cop.

Detective Naito closes the file and leans back in his chair. "That was fast."

"Why are you even bothering to question her?" the woman asks. "You know I'll get all of this thrown out of court. She's a minor, for God's sake."

"She's seventeen," Detective Richardson says. "And under suspicion of murder. When it goes to court, they're going to request to try her as an adult anyway."

Fear grips my chest as I hear those last words. Tried as an adult? How in the world could it ever get that far? This is all so crazy. I look from the woman back to the detectives. "What's going on?"

"Sorry," the woman says, walking over and extending her hand. "Elisa Alvarez, defense attorney." She looks at me intently. "*Your* defense attorney."

"I don't need an attorney," I say. "I didn't do anything wrong."

"Actually," says Detective Naito, pushing himself away from the table, "you probably do need one. And as Ms. Alvarez here is one of the best defense attorneys in the state, you might want to listen to her."

"Did my dad send you?" The thought of Dad knowing that I'm sitting in jail makes me a little sick to my stomach. "Because this whole thing is crazy."

She glances at the mirror across the room. "Let's talk about this once we get outside." She extends her hand to help me out of my chair. "I'm assuming we're done here," she says to the room in general.

"We do have a warrant," Detective Naito says, handing her a piece of paper.

Ms. Alvarez lifts her eyebrows. "And what's the name on that warrant?"

"Irrelevant," he says.

"Highly relevant," she says, tucking the paper into her bag. "You have a warrant for someone who is not my client, yet you insist on illegally detaining and questioning her."

"We don't need a warrant on a felony. As you well know," Detective Naito says. "And nothing that was done here was illegal."

"Let's go," she says to me, turning on her heel.

I glance at the detectives. "What about my car?"

"What about it?" the lawyer asks.

"They have it," I say. "My backpack too."

She shakes her head. "You guys don't know when to quit, do you?"

"The car tested positive for blood," Detective Naito says, the hint of a smile on his face. "And Casey Stewart had an antemortem gash on his cheek made by a set of keys like the ones Alexa has. We're sure the DNA in her car is going to be his."

"I already told you why!" I say. I turn to Ms. Alvarez. "I did scratch Casey with the keys, but only to get him off me. That's it!"

She looks at the two detectives and then beyond them toward the mirror. "We're going to need some privacy for a few moments."

"You can use my office," Detective Naito says.

"This way," Ms. Alvarez says, leading me into the hallway.

She heads straight for a door on the left and ushers me into it. Apparently she knows her way around the police station. "So how about you tell me what's going on," she says after closing the door behind us. "There are no recording devices in this office, so whatever you tell me is in strictest confidence. What have you told them?"

"I've been telling the truth!" I say. "But nobody believes me."

She leans against the door. "I need to know what you've said so that I'll know where to begin your defense."

Her gaze stays on me as I quickly recount how Ava and I work Alicia, and what happened that night, from the time when Casey and I left the restaurant until I drove away. "And then the cops showed me pictures of some girl who was nearby right around the time he was killed, but it wasn't me." I can feel hot tears pressing against the backs of my eyes. "I swear it wasn't me."

The display of emotion seems to have no effect on her. "Okay. So you say that Casey was never in your car?"

"No." I shake my head. "Never."

She lifts her eyebrows but otherwise doesn't react. "So there would be no reason why his fingerprints would be there?"

I sniff a little bit. "No. I'm sure of it."

"Okay," she says. "You might not like this, but I'm going to suggest that you let them keep your car. You already gave them an explanation about the keys, and it's fairly believable."

"It's believable because it's true!" I say.

She waves that comment away as if the truth has nothing to do with it. "If we let them have the car now, it'll save us time later." She glances at me. "They'll only get another warrant and tow it down here in a few days. This way, it will look like we're cooperating with them, and we can get your car back to you by tomorrow. Hopefully your backpack too."

Ms. Alvarez makes it look like she's in control, and for the first time all afternoon I feel a little bit relieved. "Okay. I swear this is all a big misunderstanding." I hesitate but decide that I have to trust her. I don't really have much of a choice. "Listen . . . I have to tell you the truth. Ava went out with Dylan. Not me."

She looks puzzled. "Who's Dylan?"

I stop, my heart in my throat. She doesn't know about Dylan. "A guy who was killed this morning." I can't even look at her when I say the next part, it sounds so bad. "Another guy who went out with Alicia Rios."

She lets out a deep sigh. "Apparently we have some more talking to do," she says, looking around the room. "But not here." She sits down on the corner of the desk. "I have to tell you, the detective was right. They don't need a warrant for a felony, and from what I can tell, they're going to arrest you today."

I start to panic at her words, my eyes filling with tears. All I can picture is a cold jail cell with a toilet in the corner. I can't go to jail.

"Don't worry." She leans forward and puts one hand on my shoulder. "They're just going to fingerprint you and take some photos, and I'll have you released in an hour under an 849(b) into my custody. You won't go to jail today."

I nod as the words sink in, and I wipe my eyes on my sleeve. "Thanks."

She looks down at her jeans. "I was volunteering at the shelter when I was called away, and I need some time to get the details of the case. We can meet in my office in a couple of days. I'll answer any charges for you, and I'll make sure there are no more surprises." She opens the door. "Let's go."

I like that it feels that someone is on my side, even if she doesn't totally believe my story. "Was my dad mad?" I ask as I follow her out the door. "When he called you?"

She turns back to look at me, a slightly confused look on her face. "Your dad? I don't know if he's angry or not." She shrugs. "I was sent by Zane Romero."

CHAPTER 18

Dad's driving so fast, I'm pressed against the soft leather seat of his car as he accelerates up the hill. Neither of us has said a word since we left the police station. I wish he'd get mad or yell or something. Staring straight ahead in silence is killing me.

"I'm sorry." My voice cracks and seems to evaporate into the air.

Dad chews his bottom lip and glances out his window. "I know."

Those two words give me some courage. "I didn't do anything wrong."

He stares straight ahead. "You didn't pull an Alicia on anyone? You didn't lie to me about it? Or to the police?"

"Okay—"

"For God's sake, Lexi—I had to come and pick you up

at a police station!" I can feel him ramping up. "All this crap has been going on while I was away, and you didn't even tell me? I'm your father. What if you'd been hurt . . . or killed? All because you didn't want to tell me what kind of trouble the two of you were in!"

"I'm fine," I say quietly, facing the side window. "Thanks for asking."

I see him flinch at my words, and I'm glad. He glances at me. "Good," he says, the harsh edge to his voice softened somewhat. "That's good. As soon as we get home, I'll get in touch with a few lawyers I know, and we can get rid of that two-bit ambulance chaser you met with down at the station."

"Ms. Alvarez?" I ask. "I like her. And Detective Naito said that she's one of the best defense attorneys in the state."

Dad winces as I say the detective's name. "I'll tell you one thing, young lady. From now on, I'm in charge. I say who you talk to and who you don't. Keeping this to yourselves is what let it get so far out of control in the first place."

I wish I could just hand everything over to him and Ms. Alvarez in a neat little package. There's nothing I'd like more than to take myself out of the equation. But I know I can't. "I was only trying to help," I say, figuring this is what he wants to hear right now. "I thought I could fix it before anyone found out."

"And how's that working for you?" he asks, pulling into the circular driveway. "You're busy fixing it while I get a frantic phone call from your sister that the cops have taken you away in handcuffs." Dad shakes his head as he reaches for the door handle. "I don't want you talking about this with anyone. Not even Cecilia. She's already upset enough."

I walk toward the stone steps that lead down to the patio, glancing once at the space in the driveway where my car should be. I hope Ms. Alvarez is right and I'll get it back tomorrow. I feel trapped not having any way to get around. Not that Dad's going to let me out of his sight.

"Lexi!" Ava shouts as soon as I walk in the door. She runs up and throws her arms around me like I've been gone for months. "Thank God you're okay."

"You wouldn't have to thank anyone if the two of you hadn't been screwing around in the first place," Dad says, glaring at us.

Anger wells up inside me. "We weren't screwing around. I've been trying to deal with this since the first time the cops came to the door."

He looks surprised. "Which is right when you should have called me! I could have fixed this in two minutes, but now I'm going to spend money on lawyers and have to take time off work."

And there it is. "You can't fix everything, Dad," I say, my voice surprisingly cold. "Even with all the money you have to throw at the problem, you can't get me into Stanford and you can't make this problem disappear."

Dad looks around, and for a split second it feels like he's going to throw something at me. I've never talked back to him like this before, and I feel a weight lift off my chest. I recognize the look on his face as he struggles to speak—it's powerlessness. Ava just stares at us.

"This isn't about money," he says, his voice gruff and low. "This is about trust. And apparently you don't have any in me."

Cecilia appears from the kitchen, but she won't even look at me. Her face is drawn and pale, and I know it's not all just worry about her sister and the mysterious Rubi. For the first time since Dad picked me up, I feel ashamed of what we've done and the lies we've told to get here. I wonder if she thinks I really did it, if she thinks that someone she knows as well as she knows herself really is capable of murder. I know the sick feeling those thoughts leave in your stomach.

"There's some food on the counter," she says—her version of a peace offering to try to get things back to normal.

"Like I could eat," Dad says, brushing past her. He turns to me and Ava. "You're grounded until I say you're not." He storms out of the room and we hear his door slam at the other end of the house.

"What happened?" Ava finally asks. "I was so freaked out when I saw all those cops in the office. I totally can't believe they took you to the station—in handcuffs." I watch her hands as she talks, punctuating the air with fingers wearing chipped pink polish. Could they really have held a knife? Could she really kill someone in cold blood?

I pull myself away from these thoughts. "Seriously, Ava," I say, walking back toward the kitchen. "Calm down."

"Zane totally had everything under control," Ava continues, ignoring me. "He talked to one of the detectives after he saw your car on the tow truck, and in two seconds he was on the phone—said he was talking to some kind of family friend."

"He got the lawyer for me," I say, wondering why he'd go to all that trouble. "She's cool, even though she let the police keep the car."

She puts one hand to her mouth. "Oh my God! They took your car."

"It's going to be okay." At this point, it seems like the least of my problems. "My lawyer said I should be able to get it back tomorrow." My lawyer. So weird saying those words.

"Are you hungry?" Cecilia asks, lifting the lid on a pot on the stove. Her hand is shaking.

"Starving," I answer honestly. Usually my stomach rejects food in the middle of trouble, but it feels like I haven't eaten in a year.

Cecilia carries a bunch of parsley to the cutting board. "Let me just get some of this— Dammit!" The knife clatters to the cutting board as she sticks her finger in her mouth.

"What happened?" I ask.

"Cut myself. It's no big deal." She grabs a paper towel off the roll and wraps it around her finger.

I nod, but I know she's lying. It is a big deal. In all the years I've known her, she's never once cut herself in the kitchen. Maybe Dad's blaming her for not watching us carefully—no wonder she's upset. Now I feel even worse that I dragged her into this mess. No way can he fire her. I can't imagine not having her around.

Cecilia dishes out some chicken and rice with her good

hand, and I take my place at the counter, with Ava right beside me. I'm not sure if it's excitement or guilt that's got her so wound up. She's still talking about this afternoon while I take a few bites of dinner.

"So what did they say about Dylan?" she asks. "Did they give you any details?"

I watch her, alert for anything in her voice that might give her away. "Not really. Just that he was killed sometime around dawn by the gym. The same way Casey was killed." I wonder where she was early this morning. She came into the kitchen and got coffee right after I did, but that doesn't mean anything. Her alibi is as good as mine. Which means it sucks.

Ava's biting her lip, and she looks lost in thought. "You mean stabbed?"

"In the back of the neck," I confirm. I watch her face carefully.

She looks at me. "What's going on?"

"That's what I need to figure out. One dead ex-boyfriend might be a coincidence. The cops think two means there's a serial killer."

Cecilia drops a plate in the sink with a clatter and turns around to face us. I can see she's rattled. "There are two dead boys? And they think you had something to do with it?"

I look over at Ava, but she's not giving anything away. "They think Alicia did. All I know is that it wasn't me."

Ava's eyes narrow. "So what are you saying? That I'm involved somehow? Go on—say it."

I want to believe she had nothing to do with all this. I mean, come on, this is Ava we're talking about, not some as-

198

sassin. But there's a tiny nugget of doubt that isn't sure what to think anymore. All clues seem to lead to Alicia, and there are only a few things that I know for sure, and the main one is that I didn't do it. "No," I finally say, although I'm not sure I believe it. "But there are a bunch of cops in a brightly lit building that think that one of us might."

"That's ridiculous," Ava says, turning away from me.

I reach over and grab her arm, spinning her around. After all I've been through, she doesn't have the right to walk away from me. Not now. "Then explain it to me, will you? Why do the cops have a photo of a girl who looks suspiciously like you in that neighborhood right around when Casey died? Wearing a red leather jacket that just happens to be hanging in your closet?" I look into her face, a face that's more familiar to me than my own, and realize that it's not the deaths that have me so upset. It's the fact that she could hide something from me so well. She has to know how our DNA got onto Casey.

"That's not evidence," Ava says, angrily shaking my hand off her arm. "At most it's a coincidence. Look, I had issues with Dylan, and whatever happened to him and Casey sucks, but I had nothing to do with it." She takes a step toward me. "And what about you? You act all innocent, but how do I know it wasn't you in that surveillance photo?" Her voice is getting louder with every word. "Maybe instead of just scratching Casey with the keys, you took it a step further?"

Anger boils up inside me. I could have let them take Ava down to the station in handcuffs, but instead I volunteered, and this is the thanks I get? "How dare you—"

Cecilia steps between us. "Girls! Stop it this instant!" She pushes us apart roughly, looking from me to Ava in a way that suddenly makes me feel guilty. "This is no way to act. Whenever one of you is in the tiniest bit of trouble, you always pull together, and now you're out here screaming just when you need each other the most."

Ava is shaking. "I don't have to stand here and take Lexi's crap," she says.

My crap? Doing her a favor is what got me into this in the first place.

Cecilia puts Ava's hand in mine and clasps ours with her own. She doesn't say a word, but looks us both in the eyes and then turns to open the refrigerator. The feel of my sister's hand in mine makes the hard lump inside soften a little bit. That is, until she yanks her hand away.

"So the only piece of evidence you have is some stupid jacket that's hanging in my closet? I bought it at the mall a couple of weeks ago. Like hundreds of other girls."

"Show me your arms," I say evenly.

"My what? What for?"

"Somehow our DNA got under Casey's fingernails. The cops think he scratched one of us just before he died."

"You've seen my arms a million times!" she shouts. "We were just at the beach together, for God's sake."

"I wasn't looking for anything then."

Ava pulls up the sleeves of her sweater to show me her unbroken skin. When I don't say anything, she pulls her shirt over her head and twirls around in front of me in her bra. "Look closely," she says. "You won't find anything because

I wasn't there." She grabs her phone off the counter and throws it at me. "Take my phone. Go ahead. Check the texts, the call history, anything you want. The only thing I know for sure is that I was here, asleep in my bed, when Dylan was killed this morning." I see tears glistening in the corners of her eyes. "But apparently my word isn't good enough for you anymore."

And that's the sentence that hurts. Since we were born, it has been the two of us against the world, and I've been more alone these past few days than I've ever been before. The reality of it is that I don't think Ava could hurt anyone. Drive them crazy, maybe. Talk behind their back about their fashion sense, definitely. But kill someone? "Sorry," I say quietly.

"You bet you're sorry!" Ava continues, the heaviness of the moment obviously lost on her. "You come home, accusing me of—"

"Ava!" Cecilia says sharply.

Ava's mouth shuts abruptly, and she pulls her shirt back over her head. "Fine. Whatever."

"Don't be such a poonch," I say quietly.

The edges of a smile appear on her face for a quick second. She looks at my plate. "Are you going to finish that drumstick?"

"No," I say, pushing my plate toward her.

"You sure you don't want it?"

"I'm sure," I say, watching her take a bite.

Maybe if we say normal things to each other for long enough, it will all get back to normal.

CHAPTER 19

Maya gives me a sad smile as she walks me to my locker. All I can see of Ava is the back of her head as she rushes in front of me. So much for getting back to normal. "Are you going to be okay today?" Maya asks me.

I try to focus on getting my books into the backpack I borrowed from Ava, and not at the way everyone's staring at me. "I guess," I answer. "It's better than sitting around at home waiting for the lawyer to call. Plus, Dad thinks that going to school is some kind of punishment. But it's good to get out of there. It's like everyone at home is just holding their breath waiting for the next bad thing to happen. School can't be worse than that." At least, I hope not. I need something to get me through the next eight hours until we meet with Ms. Alvarez.

Maya glances over her shoulder. "You should know what you're walking into. . . . People are talking."

I wince, although I'm not surprised. It's not like yesterday's events went unnoticed. "I figured," I say. "It's not every day that someone gets led out of the school in handcuffs."

"Not our school, anyway." She smiles but doesn't look happy. "But most people say they don't believe you did it."

"Well, that's comforting," I say, watching people swarm the hallway. A girl I don't know in a swim team hoodie glances at me and then grabs the girl in front of her so she can look too. I wonder if they actually think I did it.

"I'm sure it will all get fixed soon," Maya says. "The cops know what they're doing."

I can barely manage a grunt in reply. As we walk away from my locker, I see people whispering and turning away. Everyone tries to be casual, but I can feel the glances like ice on my skin as we head toward the quad.

Maya squeezes my hand as she turns toward Building A. "It's going to be okay. I'll meet you for lunch, all right?"

I nod, not trusting my voice, feeling like a kindergartner on the first day of school.

It's like the cops have given me a magic power that renders people completely silent the minute I come within three feet of them. Everyone's talking at a normal volume until they see me; then it's dead silence. Pun intended.

I make it through the first three periods by staring either straight ahead or down at my books. Apparently I was wrong—the only thing worse than sitting at home and waiting for bad things to happen is being at school and waiting for bad things to happen, knowing that half the people around you are looking forward to the show.

"Hey," Zane says, pulling me toward him with one arm around my shoulder as I walk to Spanish. Twenty-four hours ago, things were so different. I feel so much bottled-up energy, I'm not sure how I'm going to sit at my desk and conjugate verbs for an hour.

"Hey yourself," I say, trying to pretend that I'm not on the verge of losing it. "Thanks again for calling Ms. Alvarez. She's been cool."

"Any time. Glad to see she got you out of the joint." He looks around at the people in the quad. "No Ava?"

I shrug. "I haven't seen her since she bolted out of the car this morning. She's not exactly helping things, anyway."

Zane looks concerned. "Did you guys have a fight?"

"Sort of. Not really." I try to put it into words, but I can't. "She's just been . . . different lately." I look away from him. "I don't know."

Zane is silent for a moment. "You don't really think Ava had something to do with this?" he finally asks.

I don't want to think about it right now. I don't want to try to come up with reasonable explanations for all the clues that seem to be pointing right at us.

Zane touches my arm. "Because whatever's going on, she'd never do something like that to you. She was a wreck when they took you away yesterday. And I saw her in *Annie* in ninth grade. She's not that good an actress."

I don't answer. I want to believe him, I really do. I want to know that Ava would never betray me like that. She's been part of me since before we were born, and while there's none of that mystical twin crap with us—no private languages, no feelings of pain when she gets hurt, no telepathy—I can't imagine not having her next to me.

"You think I don't see it, but I do," Zane continues. "You pretend she drives you crazy, that you don't have anything in common, that you've carved out these specific roles for yourselves over the years." He pauses. "But I know that's all bullshit. She'd do anything for you, and you know it."

I turn to face him. "So how do you explain the jacket that mysteriously shows up both in the surveillance photo and her closet? The speeding ticket, the hair salon—even the bartender at the club that night. Only two of us can pretend to be Alicia, and the only thing I know for sure is that none of those have been me."

"How many girls have bought red leather jackets recently? And what if it is her in that photo? So she went out that night—doesn't mean she had anything to do with Casey's death."

"But why wouldn't she tell me the truth about where she was the night Casey was killed? Why would she just let me get ambushed at the police station like that?" It feels like we're playing tennis—every excuse he can volley at me, I have an answer I can smack back at him. There's one answer I haven't wanted to look at too closely. One that makes so much sense, it scares me. "Maybe . . . ," I say, hesitating, because once I say it, it might become real. "Maybe Dylan broke up with Ava because he knew too much, didn't want to get implicated. And maybe that's what got him killed."

Zane glances at me. "You watch too much crime TV."

He doesn't believe me. Nobody will believe me. "And your opinion of the average person is way too high," I reply.

"You and Ava are not exactly average people," he says.

———

"So," Ms. Alvarez says, flipping back through the papers in the large folder on her big wooden desk. "It looks like we have some decisions to make."

"I don't like any of the options," Dad grumbles from his seat next to me. "Are you trying to tell me that there's no easy way to make this whole mess disappear?"

Ms. Alvarez puts her palms together. She looks so different today with her hair pulled back in a severe bun and a dark brown lawyer suit on. Less *I'm here to help* and more *Don't screw with me.* Which is basically what you want in someone whose job it is to save your life. "I'm afraid not. There's just too much evidence for an easy dismissal. I can help her avoid actual jail time at this point, but she's going to have to be arraigned, and my guess is it will be sometime in the next two to three days."

"Arraigned." "Jail." Words I never thought would be said about me. Everything still feels so surreal, like someone's going to call off this practical joke any minute.

"What are the charges exactly?" Dad asks Ms. Alvarez. I know he agreed to keep her as my lawyer only because the lawyers he knows said that she's the best criminal defense attorney around. He hates that she wasn't his choice, and the creeping tone of impatience in his voice gives that away.

Ms. Alvarez's face is impassive. "Two counts of first-degree murder, with a possible additional charge of lying in wait for Dylan Harrington."

Hearing the charges out loud suddenly makes it all real. "So . . . what?" I breathe rapidly to keep from crying. "The cops aren't even out looking for the real killer?"

"They did look for the real killer," Ms. Alvarez says, her eyes steady on me. "They found you."

I feel like I've been punched in the stomach. "But I didn't do anything!" I say quickly. "This is crazy! I get assaulted by some asshole, and the next thing I know, *I'm* the one in trouble. I only met Dylan once when he was with Ava."

She glances at Dad. "Which is where some of the decisions have to come in." Ms. Alvarez taps the front of the file folder with the end of her glasses. "Listen, they have evidence that puts you in the vicinity right before Casey's death." She pulls out a paper and glances at it. "They have the sweater covered in blood that they found at the scene, Casey's DNA on your keys, and traces of his blood on your steering wheel."

"But I already explained all that! Over and over! I must have had blood on my hands from scratching him when he attacked me. That's how it got on my steering wheel."

"I know," she says. "And that's the story we're going to build for your defense." She leans forward on the desk. "They have nothing but theories for Dylan Harrington's death at this point. Most of what they have is hearsay. The DNA evidence they found on Casey is shaky at best. From what I can see, we've got enough wiggle room to get out of it."

"So the DNA they got from Casey didn't match the girls'?" Dad asks. I can tell from the eagerness in his voice that he's looking for any bit of good news.

Ms. Alvarez shrugs. "It did, but there's no evidence that it happened right before his death. There is some newer genetic testing they can do that might be able to separate each girl's DNA, but it has to be sent out and takes a long time. And there are no guarantees that the differences will be enough to tell which girl's DNA was actually under his fingernails. Right now, we can make the argument that Lexi's DNA got there during the struggle in the car the previous night. In any case, it's a hole in the case big enough to drive a truck through." Her eyes narrow as she looks through the notes in her files. "There's no fingerprint evidence at either scene, at least none that can't be easily explained."

"What do you mean 'easily explained'?" Dad asks.

She looks pointedly at me. "It means that there aren't any of Alexa's fingerprints in Casey's blood. *That* would be difficult to explain."

"There aren't any because I wasn't there when he was killed," I say again. I think about the girl in the red jacket. "Neither of us was."

Ms. Alvarez closes the folder. "Which is where our decisions come in." She turns to Dad. "Nobody has asked for a sample of Ava's DNA or fingerprints. Right now, there's nothing concrete linking either girl directly to the deaths, and I don't think there's a jury in the world who will convict Alexa on such flimsy evidence, despite the seeming coincidences. We need to decide if we're going to offer up Ava to the prosecution or try to keep her out of the proceedings altogether."

Dad hesitates, then takes a deep breath and turns to me. "I agree. They'll never convict you. If what you're saying is true, there's no way to prove that you had anything to do with the deaths of those boys. No sense in throwing your sister under the bus if we don't have to."

"So, what? I get to deal with all this while Ava just sits home and watches TV?" I can't get the image of the girl in the red jacket out of my head. My resolve to keep Ava out of this is slipping.

"As long as you're telling us the truth, you can both sit and watch entire seasons of the Kardashians, for all I care. They won't convict you." Dad sounds so sure of what he's saying.

"Everything I'm telling you is true! I didn't have anything to do with any of this."

"So the only other answer is that someone is setting you up," Dad says. "Who would do that?"

Ms. Alvarez shakes her head. "Doesn't matter. It's not our job to prove who committed these crimes. My only job is to convince a judge that Alexa didn't."

I glance at her. If we can find out who really did all this, then Ava and I are both off the hook. "Someone hacked the online page." I turn away from Dad. He's going to be pissed. "The one we set up for Alicia."

"You set up a *page* for her?" Dad practically shouts. "How far did you two take this thing?"

Ms. Alvarez ignores him and sits forward, interested. "Hacked? What do you mean?"

I glance down at the floor. "I mean that we set up a page for her—you know, in case someone went looking. We wanted to make it feel like Alicia was real. Anyway, we found out that someone else got into it and has been posting Photoshopped pictures of Alicia in places we've never been." I hesitate. "There was even a message that we didn't put there. One from the night that Casey was killed."

"Why didn't you tell me this in the first place?" She turns to her computer. "What's the address?" Ms. Alvarez types quickly, her short nails clicking on the keyboard. She turns the monitor so that we can see it. "Is this it?"

There's the same bad selfie from the other day. "Yeah, that's it."

Dad leans forward but doesn't say anything to me. I can feel the disappointment flowing off him.

"What parts were hacked?" she asks.

"Scroll up. The new stuff is at the top."

She passes the photos of Tijuana and the reggae festival. "Right there," I say, spotting the message from the night Casey was killed. "We didn't write that."

"Hmm," she grunts, taking a closer look. "Has anyone else seen this?"

"I don't know. We originally locked Alicia's page so that only people we wanted to could see it, but now it's open so anyone can search it. The password's been changed, and we can't get into it now to change anything." Ms. Alvarez scrolls up faster and passes some new pictures that weren't there the other day. "Wait! Stop."

"What?" Dad asks.

"That one," I say, pointing to the screen. "It wasn't there before." I put my hand to my mouth and take a quick breath as I realize what I'm seeing. "Jesus. It's me and Casey in the parking lot." My stomach lurches as I recognize the moment when he was pounding on my car window. You can't see my face in the shadows of the car, but I remember the feeling of fear all too well. "Go up more." Ms. Alvarez scrolls up to the next photo in the feed. "That's Dylan," I say, pointing to a photo of Ava and Dylan at the lifeguard tower. His face is a mask of fury as he shouts and gestures in her direction. "That must have been when Ava caught him cheating on her." I feel sick and back away from the desk. "Oh my God. Someone's been following us around and documenting everything. But why?"

I hear Ms. Alvarez tapping on the keyboard. "There's more," she says.

I shake my head—it already feels like my reality is splitting into two. "I don't want to see any more." I collapse back into my chair and put my head in my hands.

"Who's that?" Dad asks. "I don't recognize that boy."

I lift my head toward Ms. Alvarez and see a photo of Eli and me standing on the lawn at the apartment party just seconds after he figured out Alicia. There's hurt behind the anger in his eyes in the picture. I can't believe somebody put it up there for everyone to see.

"That's Eli. A boy Alicia went out with a few times." That's as much as I can manage to explain right this minute. "What are we going to do?" I ask. I feel helpless and alone.

"I'll get some people on these," she says. "And hope that nobody else finds them first."

I'm grasping at ideas as they flash through my brain. "But if both Ava and I are in them, then it proves that someone else was there. Someone else was watching us."

Ms. Alvarez turns away from the screen. "All these prove is that you had motive and opportunity. Showing a jury photos of you and your sister with boys who were murdered shortly after they were taken would definitely change the case, and not in your favor."

I glance back at the image on her computer, and my heart races as the reality hits me. She's right—all of these guys were killed after these photos were taken. All except one. Eli.

CHAPTER 20

I fasten the pendant around my neck and look in the mirror. I can tell that I put the makeup on in a hurry, but I hope that no one else can. Eli knows I'm not Alicia now, but a small part of me thinks he might change his mind when he sees me. Going to the club in full-on Lexi sweats and Uggs isn't going to help that at all.

I look down at my cell. Eli still hasn't answered any of my texts, and his phone is going straight to voice mail. I try not to think about what that might mean. I just have to get out of here and fix this before it's too late.

The house is quiet as I open my bedroom door. If Dad catches me sneaking out, he's going to kill me, but if I don't, Eli's life could be in danger. I have to make him believe me, even if nobody else does.

I slip down the hallway with the heels I swiped from Ava in my hand to avoid making too much noise on the imported terra-cotta tiles. My prayers are answered when I see Ava's bag sitting on top of the kitchen island next to her jacket. Thank God. If she'd put it in her room, I don't know what I'd do.

I reach in and fish around quietly until my hand closes on her key ring. I'm focused so hard on staying quiet that I don't hear anyone else in the room.

I stifle a squeal as her hand darts out to grab my wrist. "What do you think you're doing?" Ava asks, pulling my hand out of her bag, her keys dangling from my fingers.

I hesitate, feeling my heart pound in my chest. I can't tell her what I know—not if there's even a tiny chance she's in on it. "I need to borrow your car. To go see Eli." Lies are always easier if you make them close to the truth.

She smiles. "Eli? What for?"

"I need to talk to him again—maybe see if we can work this out. Tonight might be the only chance I have to apologize. You know, before the arraignment." I force myself to stop talking before I start babbling.

She looks at me strangely. "Dad said that they're not going to let you see the inside of a jail cell."

"That's what he thinks. Ms. Alvarez can't guarantee anything. I have to at least try to apologize."

Ava seems to consider this for a moment. If there's one thing she's a sucker for, it's doomed true love.

I close my hand around her keys. "So can I borrow your car?"

Ava tilts her head and looks at me. "No." Neither of us says anything for a brief moment. "But I'll drive you."

My heart races. I have to tell Eli that he's in danger, but I don't want her anywhere near him. On the other hand, if Ava's with me, then at least I'll be able to keep an eye on her. Besides, she's caught me. If I want to see Eli tonight, I don't have any other choice. "Okay. He's playing at a club downtown." I glance at the clock over the oven. "They go on in half an hour."

In a quick motion, Ava snatches the keys from my hand. "Let me grab a couple of things and we'll get out of here."

————

"*You have reached your destination,*" the mechanical voice says from the dashboard of Ava's car.

"Where?" Ava asks, peering through the windshield at the grimy storefronts and flickering neon signs in the windows.

"Over there, I think," I say, pointing to a doorway where a few people are spilling out into the street.

"Not exactly uptown." Ava fixes her lipstick in the rearview mirror. "Let's do this," she says, pouting at her reflection.

As we approach the club, I see a couple of girls in heavy eye makeup and torn black leggings, and I'm suddenly glad that I put on skinny jeans and a silver top. This is a rougher crowd than I'm used to.

"Why the Aliciafication anyway?" Ava asks, glancing at me.

I shrug, a little embarrassed that I'm thinking about Eli when there's so much else going on. "I don't know. I guess I just wanted to look the part."

Ava steps back and looks me over. "You look good, but

I can do a little better." She reaches behind me and pulls my shirt tighter, tucking it into the back of my jeans. She motions to me to come closer as she rummages in her bag. Pulling out a couple of pencils, she drags me into the light of the one hardworking streetlamp on this block. "Look up," she says, bringing my face close to hers. I feel something cold on my eyes as she lines them, and then she smears some of her lipstick onto my mouth. "There," she says after pulling my hair out of the loose bun and combing it with her fingers.

There are no mirrors around, and not enough light to see my reflection in the windows. "I'll have to take your word for it."

"I have to admit, it's pretty badass to sneak all the way down here in the middle of the night. I wasn't sure you had it in you," she says, stepping back to take one last look at her work. "Maybe Alicia isn't as imaginary as you think."

The swagger in her step gets more pronounced the closer we get to the door of the club, and I'm amazed as always at the confidence she has in any situation. Ava glances toward the cashier. "I drove. You owe me one cover charge."

"Fine," I say, digging in my pockets for some cash.

The sound of the band gets louder as we turn the corner into the main room of the club, the drums keeping perfect time to the pounding of my heart. The club is in what looks like an old theater. Even in the dark I can see that the ceilings are flecked with gold and the stage is draped in heavy, blood-red velvet curtains. It's the perfect frame for Eli as he rakes his hand over his guitar, sweat glistening on his forehead as he sings into the microphone like it's any other night. The feeling of relief that he's okay is stronger than any emotion I remember. He's fine. Oblivious. I only hope I can keep it that way.

The floor is crowded with girls pressed up against the front of the stage, and I get a sick feeling in my stomach as I realize that I'm not with him anymore. He won't jump down from the stage after their set and walk toward me, the ends of his hair damp from the heat. I shake my head because there's no room for that kind of sentiment right now. Now is about keeping Eli alive, not about keeping him with me. I know he can't see me in the back of the club, but I suddenly feel very exposed.

"They're good, aren't they?" Someone shouts into my ear, and I jump back, my skin tingling from his hand on my arm.

"Jesus, Slater, you scared me half to death," I say once I can speak again. "What are you doing here?"

He smiles, the stage reflected in the sunglasses he's wearing even though we're inside. At night. "Zane dragged me to that party where they played last week, and they rocked."

"Zane's here?" I feel a little less anxious. It would be good to talk to Zane.

"No. Has to get up at the crack of dawn tomorrow." He shrugs, taking in the makeup and giving me an approving smile. "You look nice."

"Thank you." I grin at him.

Slater glances at Ava. "I'm a little surprised to see you guys here. What with everything going on and all."

I try to look casual. "Dad would kill us both if he knew. We sort of snuck out."

"Nice," he says, nodding.

I look around to see if I can spot Melissa or any of the girls. I feel eyes on me, and scan the crowd until I find Rebecca staring at the two of us from the front of the stage. She glares at me and then goes on dancing in front of Eli. I wonder if she went to Seattle with them.

My eyes linger on Eli as he dominates the crowded room. The lights from above the stage make his dimples stand out even more than usual, and as he gestures and sways with the rhythm of the music, the movements are mimicked in the ripples of the packed dance floor. Somehow, I have to pull him back to earth. I have to get him to talk to me so I can let him know what's going on.

I look over and realize Slater's been talking to me. "I didn't hear that," I say, pretending the club is too loud. "What did you say?"

"I asked if you wanted a drink. I'll get you one," he shouts.

I don't want to be mean, but I so don't have time to hang out with Slater right now. "Maybe in a little bit," I shout. I spot Linzey behind us near the bar. "I need to go talk to someone."

Disappointment is written all over his face, but he gives me a quick nod.

I take a deep breath as I approach, but the minute Linzey sees me, she turns away. I can't let that stop me.

"Linzey," I say, tapping her on the shoulder. "Come on, I need to talk to you."

She spins around, anger written all over her face. "None of us want to talk to you, whatever name you're going by these days."

"I'm sorry about that!" I say. "I never meant to hurt anyone."

Linzey shakes her head in disgust. "You shouldn't even be here. You don't belong anymore." She glances away from me. "He's going out with Rebecca again. Things are back to the way they should be."

"Good," I say, somehow squeezing the words around the giant lump in my throat. Eli has already moved on. "I'm glad he's happy."

"Don't fuck with it," she says. "You should go."

"I just need to talk to him for a minute," I say. "He could be in trouble." I glance over at the stage and realize it's empty, the music that's coming over the loudspeakers not Eli's band but an old Green Day song. The space around us has cleared a little, with everyone making their way to the bar. "Where did they go?"

Linzey follows my gaze. "On a break, I guess," she says. "They still have about half the set left."

I look around but don't see Eli anywhere. Or Ava. "I have to find him," I say quickly.

"No!" Linzey says, grabbing my arm with surprising force. "Leave them alone."

"Let me go." I wrench my arm out of her grip and push through what's left of the crowd until I find Melissa messing around with some cords on the edge of the stage. Rebecca is standing just to the left but turns away as I approach them.

"Melissa!" I say just before I reach her.

Her face brightens when she hears her name, but a shadow falls across it when she sees that it's me.

None of the band guys are in sight—I have to risk asking for her help. "Have you seen Eli?"

"No," she says, her voice icy.

"Come on, please," I beg. "I'm not trying to get back with him. But there's something I need to tell him—something important. I just need two minutes and then I'll go."

She looks toward the stage, deciding something. "I think the guys went to kick it in the back room for a few minutes," she says flatly. "Oh, wait," she says, snapping her fingers. "Eli had to get a new strap out of the van." She points to his guitar in its stand on the stage, the black leather strap hanging loose and unfastened at the back. "That one's been dying a slow death for weeks."

"Where's the van?" I ask, trying to keep the desperation I feel out of my voice.

Melissa nods to a door on my right with a green Exit sign above it. "In the alley just there. I'm sure he'll be right back."

"I'll go meet him," I say, relieved that I'm not going to have to have this conversation in front of everyone. This couldn't have worked out better. The door is closed but not latched when I reach it, and as I open it, I feel a blast of cold air that's in sharp contrast to the warm, muggy feeling inside the club.

The white band van is parked halfway down the alley near a tall wire fence that turns it into a dead end.

"Eli?" I call as I head toward it, my heart pounding with anxiety.

His head pops out the open door of the van, but he scowls when he sees me. "What are you doing here?"

"I need to talk to you."

He pretends to look thoughtful. "It's hard to care when I don't even know who I'm talking to." He waves his arms around as if he's doing a magic trick. "Lexi? Ava? Alicia?"

I hold both hands up in surrender. "Look, I don't blame you for being mad. But I didn't come here to talk about us." I'm talking quickly, knowing he's not going to give me much time.

Eli jumps down onto the pavement, his cheeks still flushed from the heat of the stage. "Good," he says. "Because there is no 'us.' Never was."

I close my eyes so I can get through the next part. "I'm sorry. I never meant for you to find out that way. I was going to tell you, I swear. But I need to tell you that you might be in danger."

"Danger," he says incredulously. "Really."

"Yes. Someone has it in for me and Ava—"

The door to the club scrapes open, and Adam and Rebecca walk out in a wave of heat and noise. "I busted the last decent pair of sticks I had in my kit," Adam says, coming toward us. He stops when he sees who Eli's talking to. "Um . . . sorry."

Rebecca bumps me hard with her shoulder as she brushes by me to get to Eli. As soon as she reaches him, she wraps her arm possessively around his waist and gives him a deep kiss, one that he's quick to reciprocate.

I wait, standing awkwardly with Adam until they're through. "I . . . I still need to talk to you. In private."

"Anything you need to say to Eli you can say in front of

me," Rebecca says. "Bitch." She glares at me, and for a second I wonder what she's capable of.

I wait for Eli to say something to her, but he doesn't, just keeps his eyes steady on me. "I'm listening."

"How about after the show? Can you meet me by the bar, out in the open, for just two minutes?" Nobody says anything. "It's important."

"Fine." Eli gives a quick nod. "Two minutes."

"Eli, no!" Rebecca says, pounding one fist into the side of the van. "You don't have to listen to anything she has to say."

"Knock it off, Rebecca," he says, pushing her slightly away. "I don't need you involved in this."

"Thank you," I say before Rebecca can get another word in. It comes out stilted and formal. I walk back into the club feeling dazed and overwhelmed, my hands shaking and beads of sweat on my forehead.

"Lex!" Ava says, grabbing my arm through the crowd. She looks closely at my face in the dim light. "What's wrong? You look like shit."

"Nothing," I say quickly.

"Did you see him? What did he do?" Ava's eyes flash with anger. An anger I'm almost grateful for.

"We were talking out back in the alley . . . ," I begin, but I can't find the words to describe how I feel. I shake my head. "I'm fine, really. I'll be right back." I get that queasy excess-saliva feeling that happens right before you throw up, so I head for the bathroom. Screw Alicia's carefully applied makeup, I need to put some cold water on my face. Pushing past the line for the two tiny graffiti-covered stalls, I jam myself into the corner of the counter, run my hands under the faucet, and splash my face. It feels good. I grab a couple of squares of rough brown paper towel to wipe them off. I look in the mirror and am not sure who I see anymore—the girl staring back with the red cheeks and the smudged eyeliner could be either of us. Any of us.

Rebecca opens the door to the bathroom, walks straight toward me, and slams the back of my head into the wall before I can react. "Stay the fuck away from him," she hisses, her eyes narrowed.

I push her back until she bumps the sink. "Don't tell me what to do."

She takes another step forward. "I mean it, bitch. Stay away from Eli or you're going to regret it. I'll see to that."

The rest of the girls waiting for a stall have stopped talking to watch. I take one last look at Rebecca and push my way out of the bathroom. I can't afford to get into any more trouble at this point. My face feels hot and my hands are clenched into fists. There are a few guys milling around on the stage, but the band hasn't gone back on yet. I scan the crowd but don't see Ava anywhere.

Melissa walks up to me looking harried. "Have you seen Eli? Their second set is going to go over, and they're ballbusters about the noise curfew around here."

"He's out back with Adam," I say. I glance up to the stage and see Adam sitting behind the drum kit adjusting his bass drum. "Oh. I guess he's still looking for the guitar strap."

"Just what I need. Trying to get musicians to play on time is like herding cats," Melissa says, looking annoyed.

"I'll go get him," I offer. Maybe I can quickly say what I came to say and get the hell out of here. Sitting through their set is going to be torture now, and Rebecca's going to take every opportunity to make sure of that.

The alley is quiet when I open the door of the club. I don't see any movement near the van, and he doesn't answer me when I call. "Eli?" I say again, a little louder this time. There's no other sound out here except for the muffled music coming through the door that leads to the club. The side panel of the van is pushed open, and I'm sure he's inside it rummaging around, which is why he didn't hear me. When I'm almost to the van's back bumper, I see the bottoms of his Converse sprawled alongside the back tire, the toes pointing unnaturally into the asphalt. I run the last few steps, my chest tight with fear, until I can see him clearly—facedown in the street, his head turned to the side and his eyes open, a growing stain of dark red blood pooling on the back of his shirt from a wound on his neck.

It feels like a scream, but it comes out as a whisper.

"Eli!"

CHAPTER 21

Time seems to stop as I drop to the ground and put my hand on the back of his head, trying to stop the blood, but it seeps through my fingers. Panic fills my body, shooting sparks through my bloodstream. I'm desperate to find another explanation, another reality. This can't be happening! His beautiful blue eyes stare straight ahead, and there's no life or recognition in them. Eli's skin is warm to the touch, and I can still see traces of sweat around his hairline from being onstage, but his arms lie uselessly at his sides, and his body has a stillness to it that I've never seen before. Even before I put a hand up to feel for a pulse on his neck, I can feel the disbelief growing. I have to acknowledge what I don't want to admit. There's nothing I can do. Eli's already dead.

"Oh my God, I'm so sorry," I say, tears filling my eyes and spilling onto the front of his shirt as I hold him half on my lap and half on the ground. "I'm so, so sorry." I feel like curling up beside him, giving in to whatever's going on around me, because I couldn't protect him. I couldn't save him.

I don't know if I've been here for minutes or hours when I hear the door to the club scrape open and deep voices in conversation as someone walks into the alley. That tiny sound jerks me back to life. Eli's gone; there's nothing left of him in this body—no music, no understanding, no forgiveness. I look down the alley at two guys in sweat-soaked T-shirts as they lean against the building, their heads wreathed in smoke. My stomach lurches, and I know I can't let them find me here. With all the other evidence, there's no jury in the world that would believe I'm innocent. And if I go to jail for this, I'm sure Eli won't be the last victim.

Gravel grinds into my knees, and I brace myself on the van, my hand leaving a deep red smear on the white paint as I pull myself up. The metallic smell of the blood hits my nostrils, and I manage to step a few feet away before the hot vomit makes its way up my throat and splatters onto the asphalt. I stagger upright and wipe my mouth with my sleeve. I'm not thinking about the blood that covers my hands and stains the front of my shirt in big, wet blotches. I'm just relying on instinct and self-preservation as I walk quickly past the two guys by the door—the only way out of this alley.

"Hey!" one of them shouts as I walk by. I can hear the alarm in his voice, so I break into a run. "Hey! Stop her!"

The heels on Ava's shoes are too high, and I almost twist my ankle before I kick them off, gaining speed as my bare feet pound the pavement. The guys must give up the chase to see what I've left behind, because I'm alone as I turn the corner onto the main street. I can hear the faint bass rumblings from inside the club. The guys must be getting ready to go on for the second half of their set, not knowing that they've already played their last notes together. The world around me is a blur from the tears that stream down my face. Eli will never be onstage again. Never pick up his guitar. Never sing. And it's all my fault—I led Ava right to him.

I race down the sidewalk, the lights from oncoming cars flashing into my eyes. I run for blocks and blocks, trying to put as much distance as possible between me and the club. Finally my breath is so ragged, I can't run anymore, so I veer off into a side street lined with the loading docks of the stores that are in the front. I lean against a chain-link fence and try to force air into my lungs. I can't believe this is happening. I don't want to believe it, but it must have been Ava in the photo the night that Casey died, and she didn't just let Dylan off with a warning. She's been systematically killing all the guys that Alicia's gone out with. She's been lying to me. For how long?

My phone buzzes, and I pull it out of my pocket. Ava. I feel the vibrations and stare at her name on the screen until it just becomes a jumble of unfamiliar letters. After what she's done, I can't help her anymore. I hesitate, then press IGNORE, my chest heavy, the decision irreversible. I turn the phone off so that nobody can track my movements, and then look around, trying to get my bearings. I'm still downtown somewhere, but I don't come here enough to know the streets well. My hands are shaking, and for the first time I really see the blood that's dried, sticky and sheer, on my left palm, and the huge spots on my silver top. Eli's blood must be all over my pants too, but they're black, and in the dim orange light from the alley I can't see it. I pull the top over my head and immediately start to shiver, the black tank top underneath the only barrier between me and the cold misty air. There are several Dumpsters near the first loading dock, so I wad up the bloodstained shirt and smash it as deep into the rotten, sickly-sweet-smelling garbage as I can. The cops might find it if they look hard enough, but hopefully by then it won't matter. I need to stay one step ahead of them. And one step ahead of Ava.

It's the sirens in the distance, the high wailing that bounces off the buildings, that gets me moving again. I pass another club, dozens of people lined up under a red awning, and a few of them stare at me as I walk by with my head down, trying not to draw attention to myself, but it's hard to be inconspicuous with bare feet and bloodstained hands. I have to get somewhere safe to clean up and figure out my next move.

On the next corner there's a yellow neon sign advertising Topsy's Diner. Despite the fact that it's open twenty-four hours, I see only a couple of people on stools at the counter. There's a side door that leads to the parking lot. Most of the customers are in the front of the diner, so I slip in the side door and head straight for the bathroom. The tiles on the sink are cracked, but the water from the tap is warm the minute I turn it on.

I pull the last few drops of soap from the dispenser. The

suds are tinged with pink as they float down the drain, and nausea hits me again as I rinse off the last of Eli's blood. The face that stares back at me in the mirror is pale with a dark red blood smear on the cheek. I'm not sure I recognize myself anymore. The movements of my reflection follow me as I wet another paper towel and scrub my face; then I rinse my mouth to get rid of any traces of the night.

I'm alone in the bathroom, so I lean against the sink and pull out my phone. I have no idea who to call. Home is out, along with Maya, because she's the first person they'd expect me to ask for help. It's possible they've even put a trace on Dad's and Maya's phones already. Ava could be anywhere, and now that I know what she's done, I can't let her know where I am. We're both on our own. I don't owe her anything anymore. I turn my phone on to dial the only other possible number, quickly before I lose my nerve.

"Hello?" I can hear the caution in his voice.

"Zane?" My voice cracks with just that one word.

"Lexi? What's going on?"

Suddenly I'm not sure of anything. Not even Zane. He's been so helpful through all this—maybe a little too helpful. "Where are you?" I ask.

"I'm at home. Why?" His voice is wary.

"What's your home phone number?" That's the only way to be sure that he's not here somewhere, not involved.

"My what? Lex, this is crazy—you're already on the phone with me."

"I need to call you on your home number," I insist.

He sighs with frustration and gives me the number.

"I'll call you right back," I say, repeating the numbers under my breath as I hang up and dial again with shaking fingers.

I almost collapse with relief when Zane answers the phone on the first ring. "Now you have to tell me what's going on," he demands. "Where are you?"

"I'm at a diner called Topsy's downtown." I can feel the tears welling up in my throat as I think about what I have to say next. "Something bad happened. Really bad."

"I'll come get you," he says instantly.

"You don't understand." I feel the hot tears falling from my cheeks. "Eli's dead. I . . . I saw him. Ava did it. I'm sure of it now." My voice breaks, and it takes a second of deep breathing to get the rest out. "But they're going to think it was me."

"No, they're not," he says, his voice calmer than I can imagine. "You didn't do anything wrong."

"They will," I insist. "People saw me. . . . I had blood all over. . . . It's bad. . . ." I can feel the panic rising again as I picture Eli lying in the alley.

"Stay there!" he says. "I'm getting into the car."

Zane could get in so much trouble just being with me. I feel totally alone right now, but I don't want to drag anyone else down with me. "But what if they catch—"

"I'm leaving now," he says, his voice full of authority, and I lean on that for a moment. "Can you wait there for me? Are you safe?"

I look down at my dark clothes and bare feet. I look homeless but okay. "I think so. For a little while."

"Good. Sit down and get a cup of coffee and wait for me. I'll be there as soon as I can." He pauses. "And, Lex, take the battery out of your phone."

"I'll turn it off," I say.

"The cops can still trace it. You need to get something small—like a nail file or screwdriver—to take the screws off the back and pull the big square battery out. Can you do that?"

"I think so."

"Okay. I'll see you soon."

"Okay." I hear him hang up and silence take over. "Thanks," I say into the empty air, and hang up the phone.

I'm conscious of my bare feet as I slip into a booth near the side door, but there's nothing I can do about that right now, so I just tuck them under the table and hope that nobody will notice. There's a container full of toothpicks on the table, so I grab one and snap it in half. I take off the cover of the phone and see the screws just like Zane said. It takes a few tries with the toothpick, but eventually I get them off and pull out the big square battery.

"What can I get you, sugar?" a waitress says, slapping a laminated menu onto the table.

I jump back, startled, and lose one of the tiny screws under the table. "Um . . . coffee. Just coffee."

She looks me over. "Coffee and a piece of pie," she says, scribbling on her tiny notepad. "Coming right up."

"Just coffee," I say. My stomach is churning. I'm not going to touch it, but I need an excuse to take up this booth until Zane gets here.

"Look, honey," she says. I can see a piece of pink gum stuck to her back teeth when she talks. "The pie's on the house. You look like a girl who could use something on the house right about now."

I stare at my fingers on the table. There's a trace of dried blood on my cuticle. My eyes fill with tears. "Thanks . . ." I look at her name tag. "Rose."

She grins and taps the plastic tag with her pen. "Rose E. Rose. That's my full name, swear to God. My first name was Rose, and I married a man named Rose. Makes it easy to remember, don't it?"

I manage a tiny smile. "It does."

"Coffee and pie coming right up."

Without my phone, I have nothing to do but watch the other customers and stare out the window until Rose places a cup of coffee in a thick ceramic mug in front of me, along with a piece of apple pie almost obliterated by a scoop of vanilla ice cream. "You're such a bitty thing, I figured the ice cream can only help."

"Thanks," I say, trying to look normal by tearing packets of sugar and dumping them into the coffee. Rose walks up to the customers at the counter with a glass coffeepot, topping off each mug and leaning down to talk for just a second.

I poke at the pie with a fork. Lifting a bite to my mouth is impossible, but there's something in the smell that's comforting. Homey. Which is funny, because for all she cooks, Cecilia has never baked a pie in her life.

The ice cream has melted into a puddle and is dripping slowly off the plate by the time Zane slides into the booth across from me. Just the sight of him makes new tears threaten.

"Thanks . . . thanks for coming," I say, my voice barely above a whisper.

Zane gets up and moves to the seat next to me, surrounding me in a hug that I allow myself to melt into. I bury my face in his chest and inhale the scent of the sun and the sea, closing my eyes as if I can block everything out. "What happened?" he finally asks, his voice rumbling in my ear.

I pull away and grab a napkin to blot my eyes. "Ava killed Eli. In an alley in back of the club where he was playing."

His face is full of disbelief. "You saw her?"

"No. Not exactly. But I lost track of her when I was in the bathroom, and when I went outside to find him . . ." I trail off here, the grief threatening to overwhelm me. If only I could take that minute back. "When I got outside, she'd already gotten to him first." I lift my eyes to Zane's. "It had to be her. No one else knew we were going to see him, and she was so insistent about coming. It was one cut to the back of the neck, just like the others."

"And there's no way this was something else? An accident, or maybe he got mugged?"

I look straight at him.

"Okay, okay," he says, giving himself over to what I already know is true. "What did you do then?"

"I ran. Stopped once to get rid of my shirt and then found this place and called you."

"Your shirt?"

I nod. "It was covered in blood. I tried to help Eli before . . . before I knew he was dead. I stuffed it into a Dumpster in some alley."

Zane considers this. "You know the cops will find it."

"Doesn't matter. I left a nice big handprint in Eli's blood on the van when I pulled myself up off the ground. And a couple of guys saw me running away." I put my elbows on the table and my head in my hands. "I'm totally screwed."

"What about Ms. Alvarez?" Zane says, his voice full of renewed enthusiasm.

I lift my head. "Her job is to keep me out of jail, not necessarily to believe what I say. At best, she probably thinks Ava and I are in it together." I pause and take a deep breath. "It looks bad, Zane. Really bad. I just . . . I just can't believe this is happening." It feels surreal. It's one thing to see photos of dead guys after the fact but something else to feel the warm blood on your hands.

The bell at the front door jingles, and a cop walks in, one hand on the gun at his hip. I stiffen and glance out the side door, but the cop car is sitting there running, with his partner in the front seat.

"You stay here," I say, my mind in full panic mode. "I don't want to get you any more involved in this. I'm going to make a run for it."

I start to rise out of the booth, but Zane pulls me down. "Relax. He's just getting some coffee," he says, indicating the cop, who's now making jokes with Rose. "They have nothing to do with you."

The panic is rising in my chest until I feel like I can't breathe. I'm responsible for this mess. "I don't have time to just sit here—I have to get moving. I can't let anyone else get hurt."

"Where will you go?"

"I don't know," I say, my voice desperate. I feel trapped.

Rose walks up to our table, steam rising from the glass coffeepot in her hand. "A warm-up?" she asks.

"No, thanks, Rose." I pull a crumpled twenty out of my pocket and shove it toward her. "Keep the change."

She follows my eyes to the cop I'm trying desperately not to stare at. "You kids need a quiet way out of here?" she asks in a hushed tone.

Zane gives her a grateful smile. "Yes, ma'am."

She gives a barely perceptible nod backward. "Through the kitchen and out the back door by the walk-in freezer. Follow the alley down toward the streetlights. That'll put you on the corner of Lincoln and Cleveland."

"Perfect," Zane says. "I'm parked on Cleveland."

"Thanks," I say, following Zane out of the booth and into the unknown.

CHAPTER 22

"Here," Zane says, reaching behind his seat. He hands me a pair of black flip-flops.

I hold them up. "They're miles too big."

He glances down at my dirty bare feet. "Better than what you have right now."

"True," I say, slipping them on. "Thanks."

I watch the cars speed by in the other direction. I don't have a clue where we're going, but I want to put as much distance between me and the club as possible. I catch my reflection in the side mirror and marvel at how much has changed since I put the makeup and pendant on so many hours ago. If only I had it to do over—I never would have brought Ava to the club, never would have led her straight to him. And Eli might still be alive.

Reaching behind my head, I unclasp the diamond necklace, and then hold it in my palm. So many things have come from being Alicia, and not many of them good. Before I have time to think about it, I roll down my window and toss the pendant out, leaving it to be crushed by the cars behind us. It's way past time.

Zane glances over but doesn't say anything.

My mouth tastes sour, like a night that's gone on too long. "Do you have any gum?"

"In the glove compartment."

I flick it open and root around in the dim light among the parking tickets and expired insurance cards. I spot a bright green package in the corner, and when I lift it, I see something long and black underneath. It's heavier than I expect as I pull it out, and when I press a tiny silver button on the side, I'm so shocked to see a sharp blade pop out that I almost drop it, nicking my finger in the process. Zane has a knife—a very long, very sharp knife—hidden in his van.

"What the hell?" I demand, holding the blade out toward him.

"What?" Zane says, taking his eyes off the road to glance at me.

"I found a knife in the glove compartment!"

"So? When I surf, I change my clothes in the van, sometimes early in the morning, sometimes in sketchy neighborhoods. Everybody should have a switchblade on them. It's for protection."

I stare at the shiny metal blade, sharp on both sides and honed to a fine point. The perfect weapon to kill someone quickly. I feel panicked and sick. I knew Zane was being too nice to me, too helpful. Why after all this time would he want to help unless he's in on it somehow? It's not me he wants to help—it's Ava.

The yellow lines are whizzing by on the asphalt below our tires, but I reach for the door handle anyway. Anywhere is better than sitting here right now.

"Holy shit!" Zane says as the wind rushes in through the open door. He swerves across three lanes of traffic toward the side of the highway. "Shut the door!"

"No!" I say, waiting for him to slow down enough so that I can jump out. "I shouldn't have called you. You're in it with her!"

"Now you're just being crazy," Zane shouts, easing the van to a stop at the side of the freeway. The jerk as we stop is enough to slam the door shut. "You called my house! I wasn't anywhere near the club."

"You can get a house phone forwarded." If anyone can figure that out, Zane can. I should have known. I unbuckle my seatbelt and lunge for the door in one movement, but Zane grabs my arm and pulls me back into my seat. "Let me go!" I scream. I kick and claw at him, frantic movements that match my thoughts.

"Lexi!" Zane shouts. "Stop! This is crazy!" He grabs both my arms and holds them tight to my sides. We're both breathing heavily, and the sounds of the cars rushing by inches from the van fills the space around us. "I'm not in on anything! I keep the knife in my van for protection, that's it." His brown eyes are panicked as they search my face.

I stare at him, not knowing if I can believe anything he says. It feels like I can't trust anyone. Ever.

"I'd never hurt you. There's no way I would do anything to hurt you. All I want to do is help you." His voice is barely a whisper now as he slowly releases my arms. "You've got to believe that."

"You're in on it with Ava," I say, although my conviction is starting to waver. I want to believe him, but it seems like every little thing is stacked against me right now.

This seems to deflate him, and he reaches around me to open the door. "If that's what you think, then go ahead. Take off. Nothing I can say is going to convince you."

I look at the darkened ditch that stretches next to the freeway. If I get out here, where am I going to go? I glance up at Zane, but he's staring out the front window, his jaw sharp in the light of the oncoming cars. I have to trust him—at least for now. "I'm keeping the knife," I say, slamming the door shut.

"Fine," Zane says. He grins slightly. "How many serial killers would send their victim straight to the spot where they keep their weapon?"

"Only the stupid ones," I say, relaxing a little.

Zane glances up at the rearview mirror, the light reflected there illuminating the flecks of gold in his brown eyes. "Lex? I need you to duck down and slowly move toward the back of the van."

"Why?" I ask, turning to look.

"Don't turn around! There's a cop pulling up behind us. The van's windows are tinted in back, but they'll still see your shadow with the lights on us. Crawl into the back and get under the pile of old towels behind my board. Then don't move. I'll take care of everything."

Without thinking, I do as he says, and am getting to the back just as the van is flooded with bright white light. I pile the damp, musty-smelling towels on top of me, doing my best to make sure everything is covered. My chest is heaving and I concentrate on taking tiny, shallow breaths as I hear a voice outside the van.

"Yes, sir," Zane says, answering some question. "My phone rang, and I pulled over to answer it." His voice is amazingly steady. "I know it's illegal to talk and drive."

There's a pause and then more deep rumbling from outside. I realize that I'm still clutching the switchblade in my hand. I drop it, knowing that I'm not going to use it here. If we're caught, it's all over.

"Sure," Zane says. I hear the glove compartment open and him rustling around.

There's another pause that seems eternal. I'm getting so antsy, it feels like I'm going to jump out of my skin, but then I hear the voice again.

"Thanks," Zane says. Another pause. "Yes. Definitely, I will." I close my eyes and stop breathing entirely as he starts the van and pulls slowly into traffic. Neither of us says anything for what seems like hours.

"Stay down for a few more minutes," Zane calls toward the back. "I want to make sure they're not following."

I press my cheek into the floor of the van, bouncing along in the empty back until Zane calls that the coast is clear.

"What did they want?" I ask, climbing back into the passenger seat.

"Just to know why I was stopped on the side of the freeway," he says, his eyes on the road ahead.

"And you didn't give me up?"

"Jesus, Lex," Zane says, shaking his head sadly.

We stay quiet, each of us lost in our own thoughts, until I realize we're turning onto Zane's street. He and his dad moved here after the divorce, and I haven't been here for years. "No," I say firmly. "Not your house."

Zane slows and pulls into an open parking spot down the street from his building. "You have other plans?"

"I shouldn't have called you," I say, regretting letting him in this far. If he wasn't involved before, he is now. "If the police catch you helping me, you could go to jail too."

"I'd be pissed if I found out you were in this much trouble and *didn't* call me," he says, opening the car door. The street is empty this late. "Look, Dad's not going to be home until morning. He's been taking overnight shifts in the cab. It's after one—there's nothing else you can do tonight. At least come in and let's figure out what our next move should be." He tosses his keys into the storage space under the armrest and shuts the door.

"You're leaving your keys?" I ask as I get out and shut my door.

He pulls the surfboard out of the back. "Yeah. I lose the car keys all the time—this way I know where they are. Nobody's going to steal a fifteen-year-old van. And if they do, they'll be doing me a favor."

I follow him onto the sidewalk, feeling like eyes are watching from every curtained window. "What if you get caught? What if the cops find me here?"

Zane looks up at the building. Most of the windows are dark. "How are they going to find out? I'm not on your dad's radar anymore, and it'll be tomorrow before they can trace your phone calls." He heads for his apartment. "And besides, where else are you going to go?"

I hate to admit he's right, so I don't say anything, just follow him toward the apartment building. The metal gate to the courtyard clangs behind us and makes me jump, but there's no other movement as we walk up the concrete steps to the second floor.

"Come on in," Zane says, unlocking the door and holding it for me.

From the second I walk in, I can tell that only guys live here. Not that it's messy. It's just that it's full of necessities and nothing else—no pictures on the walls, unless you count surfing posters and a calendar from last year. The main decoration is a giant bookcase against one wall that holds years of gold surfing trophies of all sizes, behind a plaid couch that's probably older than I am. Zane looks around as if seeing the apartment for the first time. "It's not much," he admits.

"It's fine," I say, grateful to have four relatively safe walls around me for the moment. "Thanks for coming to get me."

Zane puts the surfboard against the wall and takes a few steps into the kitchen. "Are you hungry? Do you want something to drink?" He's suddenly strangely formal and uncomfortable.

"No." I look down at my pants. Even though I can't see it, I know that they're covered in dried blood. Eli's blood. I choke back emotion as I picture Eli on the ground—I have to keep it together. If I lose it, I can't help anyone, not even myself. "Can I . . . Do you mind if I take a shower?"

"Sure!" Zane rushes into the hallway and pulls a faded red towel out of a cupboard. "There's some shampoo and stuff in there already. Probably not what you're used to, but it should be okay."

"I just want to get out of these clothes," I say. "Do you have some sweats or something I could borrow?"

"Everything's going to be too big," Zane says, walking into his bedroom. It's surprisingly neat, and I'm a little shocked to find that his bed is actually made. He moves a heavy duffel bag from in front of the dresser and shoves it into the closet. "Here's a pair," he says, pulling some gray sweats out of a drawer. "You can roll these to make them shorter." He dives back into the drawer and comes up with a blue T-shirt from a Baja surf competition. "This was always too small."

"Thanks," I say, clutching the clothes and walking into the bathroom. After I shut the door, I realize that underneath the scent of laundry detergent, the shirt smells like Zane, and before I can stop myself, I bury my face in it and breathe deep. Like surfing and summer. And now safety.

I turn the water as hot as I can stand it, steaming up the small room within seconds. Long after my hair is washed and the dried blood is gone from my legs, I stand under the pounding spray, my normally whirling thoughts a total blank. After putting on Zane's sweats and shirt, I find a comb in the drawer and tease the knots out of my wet hair. I look like a wreck, but I feel a little better. Almost like I can handle whatever comes next. I pull my stray hairs out of his comb and am opening the drawer to put it back, when I notice a letter stuffed into the corner of the drawer. I pull it out and see the red-and-black logo of San Diego State.

I glance at the lock on the door. I really shouldn't be snooping in his stuff, not when he's been so great about everything. The envelope's already open, so it's not like I'm breaking and entering. This is just entering. Or removing. I pull the letter out and scan it quickly. *Dear Zane . . . pleased to offer you . . . congratulations.* I look at the letter in disbelief. He got in. And never even mentioned it.

When I walk into his room, Zane's lying on his bed watching the little TV that sits on the dresser. It's a queen-sized mattress, but he's so tall his feet still dangle off the end. When he sees me, he jumps up and clicks it off, but not before I see that he's watching the twenty-four-hour news channel.

"Is there anything about . . . ?" I ask, staring at the black screen.

"Doesn't matter," he says, shaking his head. He holds out a still-steaming mug. "I found some hot chocolate with the little marshmallows that you used to like."

"Don't lie to me," I say. "If I'm going to fix this, I need to know what they know. Was there anything on the news about Eli?"

I can see Zane's jaw tighten as he tries to decide what to tell me. I reach for the remote.

"Okay. Okay," he says. "I'll tell you, but you don't want to

turn that on." He sits back down on the bed. "They're looking for you," he confirms. "Had your picture up on the screen
and everything."

I sit down next to him. Collapse, is more like it. I knew
they were going to think it was me, but it's still hard to hear.
"What did they say?"

"They didn't show much—just a bunch of flashing lights.
But they interviewed one of the detectives. Lex." He turns to
me, his face serious. "They said that you should be considered armed and dangerous."

I bite the inside of my lip. "That means they're not even
looking for anyone else." I glance at the dark TV. "Did they
mention you?"

"No." He shakes his head. "Rose would never give us up."

"We can hope."

Zane hesitates. "They . . ." I can see that he doesn't want
to tell me.

"What? Zane, you have to be honest with me."

He swallows hard. "They showed video of Ava talking to
the police. She looked really upset and was gesturing to the
cops."

"Did they arrest her?"

"No," he says. "They interviewed her. On the news. It was
quick, but she was asking you to turn yourself in."

I get back up and start pacing the small room. "Liar! After
everything I did, she's still going to pin this on me! I can't . . .
I can't . . ." I'm so angry, I can't even form words, just point
to the darkened screen. "She's right there! Talking to report-
ers like she's totally innocent." I tried to protect her, and look

where it got me. I should have told the police what I thought before it was too late—they'll never believe me now. The reality of what she's done washes over me, and tears fill my eyes. I wonder if Eli saw her in the alley—if he thought for a split second that it was me who did that to him.

I sit down and put my head in my hands, not even trying to stop the tears that flow through my fingers. Eli's gone, and Ava's the reason why. It almost feels like she's dead too.

What if Ava figures out I called you?"

Zane smiles. "Honestly, we're not that close."

"Seriously! What if—"

"Stop," he interrrupts. "Let me worry about that. We'll be fine here until morning."

Zane doesn't say anything more, just moves closer and puts his arm around me. When the shaking stops and the sobs are coming more slowly, I wipe my eyes on the edge of the T-shirt I'm wearing. I lean into Zane, feeling his chest rise and fall with every breath.

"Eli seemed like a great guy," he says quietly.

"He is." I sit up and wipe the last of the tears off my face. "He was. Which is why I have to find Ava and make this stop. I know it sounds crazy. I know that nobody will believe me—"

"I believe you," Zane says simply.

I smile at him, his words dissolving the anger that was starting to rise again. He doesn't have to believe me. He didn't have to come get me. But he did, and I should be grateful. "Thanks. But now what do I do? The entire world thinks I'm a killer. Because the real killer looks just like me."

"Not *just* like you."

There's something in his voice that makes me hesitate. "You don't think Ava did this, do you?" I ask.

He looks up at me, his brown eyes intense. "I don't know," he admits. When he sees the look on my face, he continues quickly. "But I know you didn't—and that we need to find the person who did."

I want to agree with him. I want to nurture the tiny nugget of doubt that's sitting in my heart and find out that Ava isn't this person she's become in my head, this stranger who is capable of things I never even considered possible.

Zane sets his phone on the dresser. "It's too late tonight, but I'll text around first thing in the morning to see what people know. We'll come up with a plan, I promise."

I feel antsy, like I should be doing something instead of just sitting here, waiting to get caught. "What about school?" I say. "I mean for you. I don't want you to miss any on my account."

"I feel a sick day coming on," Zane says. "Maybe a couple of them."

I glance at the envelope that's still in my hand.

"Where did you get that?" Zane asks, unable to hide his irritation.

I gesture toward the door. "It was in the bathroom. I wasn't snooping." I hold it up. "Why didn't you tell me?"

Zane leans over and takes the envelope out of my hands. "Never came up."

"After all my talk about not getting into Stanford, it never came up?"

He shoves it into the bedside table drawer. "Doesn't matter, because I'm not going."

"Not going? How can you get in and not go?"

Zane turns on me. "I want to focus on surfing right now and see what happens with that. State will always be there."

I stare at him in disbelief. "But you got in! To college."

"So?" He squints up at me, and the expression on his face hardens. "You didn't think I was smart enough. You didn't think that some idiot surfer could actually get into a university."

"I . . ." I try to refute him but as I look at him, I know I can't. I know he's smart. I just never thought he'd go to college.

Zane slams the TV remote onto his bed. "You always have to put people into little labeled boxes." His eyes are flashing in anger. "The pretty one. The smart one. The surfer. The jock." He walks up to me so forcefully that I take a step backward. "The rock star. And your world is totally out of order if one of those people tries to step out of that box. Even you." He tosses one arm out to the side. "You're so busy being Stanford material that you can't see what's in front of your face. What's been in front of your face for years—ever since we were little."

I look up at him—he's easily a foot taller than I am. I'm not afraid, just a little confused. And ashamed—whether or not he goes to college is none of my business. "What are you talking about?"

Zane reaches down and strokes my cheek with the back of his hand. The air around us is thick and humming, and for a moment I imagine him bending down to kiss me. "You really don't have any idea what I'm talking about, do you?"

The tenderness in his voice makes my legs feel weak. Zane turns away, the tension between us broken, and I'm staring at the veins that run down his neck and into his collarbone. I want to reach out to him, to answer him, but suddenly I'm so tired, I can barely stand. "I'm sorry," I whisper. They're only two words, but they cover a multitude of sins right now.

Instead of answering me, Zane turns and pulls the covers off his bed. A sense of anticipation runs through me as I watch the muscles in his back bend and flex under his shirt. Zane spends so much time in surf trunks that when he's fully dressed, it looks a little staged, like he's wearing a costume.

"Get some sleep," he says quietly, all traces of anger gone.

I climb into the plaid flannel sheets, a mystifying sense of disappointment lurking inside.

He pulls the comforter up to my chin. "I'm going into the other room for a little while, but I'll be back soon."

"Okay," I answer, burying myself into sheets that carry his scent. I hear the door close and think that there's no way I'll be able to sleep, but I'm wrong. I must have dozed off, because the next thing I know, the room is dark and the mattress is shifting with Zane's weight as he settles in beside me. His motions are smooth and quiet, and I know he thinks I'm asleep as he slides one arm under his pillow just like he did when we had sleepovers at my house so many years ago. I can feel the cold few inches he's left between us like an icy river. The warmth from his body radiates across the space, and I'm suddenly so sad and lonely that I ache inside. Zane hesitates as I push my back up against his chest, fitting my body into the space made by his, the rhythm of his heart beating against my spine. Just for tonight, I want to feel his warmth and share his strength. He pauses, motionless for a few seconds, then gently puts one arm around me, and I feel him relax as he pulls me toward him, the two of us pressed up against each other in the middle of his big, wide bed.

CHAPTER 23

There's a phone ringing in the distance when I open my eyes the next morning. A feeling of dread has settled in my chest, and it takes a few seconds for what happened last night to tumble into reality—the club, the blood on my hands, Topsy's Diner. And Zane.

The light coming through the crack in the curtains is gray, and his room is still bathed in shadow as I sit up and try to get my bearings. His side of the bed is empty, and when I reach over, the tangle of sheets is cold to the touch. The phone is still ringing, and I can tell by the echo that I'm alone in the apartment. I creep out of bed and open the door a crack, just in time to hear the answering machine pick up.

"Zane! What the fuck? You're not picking up your phone— where the hell are you? Carlos called and said that you never showed up for the flight. They're halfway to Tahiti by now . . ."

without you. Don't blow this shit, dude. This is a big fucking deal! Call me. Now!"

Whoever's on the other end of the line slams the phone down, and I hear a loud dial tone until the machine clicks off. Tahiti. The tour! I try to remember when Zane said he was leaving, and then duck back into the bedroom and fling open the closet door. There on the floor is the duffel bag that he shoved in there last night. I pull it out and look inside. There are neatly stacked T-shirts and shorts, along with flip-flops and surf trunks. He was all packed to go. My heart races with panic. Where could he have gone so early in the morning? Did he change his mind and bail on me? What if he decides to turn me in?

I dash out to the living room, grab the phone, bring it back to Zane's room, and close the door. I stare at the receiver, knowing it can connect me to anyone in the world but that there's nobody left who can help me. A tear falls down my cheek as I think about everything I've lost. About what Dad must be going through right now. I can't help it, I have to talk to him.

I dial the number to the phone he keeps in his office. At least if he's not there, I can hear his voice on his message. I'm almost shocked when I hear his deep voice say, "Hello?"

"Daddy?" I whisper, as if anyone who's listening on the other end can't hear me if I'm quiet.

"Phil!" Dad says a little too loudly.

"It's Lexi. I . . . I need to talk to you."

"I know," he says. "Yes, we're all worried, but we have no

idea where she is." There must be someone else in the room with him. He pauses. "I know there are a lot of police cars on the street. I'll see what I can do to get some of them moved for you." I hear a noise as he cups his hand over the receiver, and muffled voices as he talks to someone. "Yes," he says, back on the line. "The detective who's here says that we can clear some of the cars away from the driveways. They're trying not to inconvenience the neighbors too much."

"I didn't do it," I say softly.

"I know, Phil," he says. "Definitely. There are definitely a lot of police in the house. We've got the house phone and the cell tapped so that if she does call, we'll be able to find her."

"Thanks, Dad. I'll be okay." My voice quavers as my eyes fill with tears again. I wish I were there, sitting on the couch watching some stupid movie with him. I miss home so much.

"You bet," he says, his voice cracking.

"I love you."

"You too, Phil," he says. "You too."

The phone goes dead, and I toss it onto the bed. I can't go anywhere near the house, he made that clear. I hear the front door open, and I freeze, wondering what time Zane's dad is supposed to get home. There's some rustling in the living room, and I'm about to duck into the closet when I hear Zane whisper my name as he opens the door. He's fully dressed and looks like he's been up for hours.

"You're awake!" he says brightly, then frowns at the duffel bag on the floor.

I feel stupid for thinking he'd turn me in. He's already

given up so much. "When were you supposed to leave?" I demand.

"For what?" He's stalling. I can tell I've caught him off guard.

"The tour."

He shakes his head but won't meet my eyes. "Not for a couple of days."

"You're lying," I say. "You were supposed to leave this morning."

"Doesn't matter," he says, closing the door behind him and putting a bag on the bed.

"It does matter! This is a very big fucking deal! The guy on the phone said so."

He winces. "Jorge called the house?"

"Yes. And he's pretty pissed." I zip up the duffel and shove it into his hands. "Go. Get the next flight. Don't screw up your future just for me."

He tosses the bag onto the floor and kicks it toward the closet. "I'm not going. I'm staying with you," he says calmly, folding his arms across his chest. "Maybe this is the future I'm not supposed to screw up. Yours."

My heart skips when he says that, and I feel instantly guilty. Part of me doesn't want him to go. Doesn't know what I will do if he picks up that duffel bag and walks out the door. "But won't you—"

"For once stop second-guessing everything," he says almost irritably. "Sometimes you have to trust your intuition. I'm here, and I'm helping until we fix this mess." Zane rummages in the plastic bag and pulls out some jeans and a pair of black flats. "I got you these—hope they fit. I figured . . . your other stuff . . ."

Is still covered in Eli's blood. I never want to see those clothes again. I take the shoes from him and check the size. "They're perfect. Where did you go?"

"The Target by the freeway opens early." He looks into the bag and tosses it to me. "There's a toothbrush in there, and a T-shirt. We should get moving. Dad's going to be home by nine, and we need to make it look like I'm gone."

I check the bag. He even bought deodorant.

"I just . . ." I'm so overwhelmed, I can't finish the sentence, so instead I just pull him toward me and give him a kiss on the cheek. If I can't go home, I want to be with Zane. "Thank you."

He hesitates a fraction of a second before he lets me go. "It was nothing. Now get your ass in gear before we get caught."

————

The crunching sound is so loud, it fills my head, and I look down to see yellow crumbs spilling all over the front of my shirt. Zane's shirt. He bought me a cute gray one this morning, but I put the surf shirt back on instead because it made me feel better.

He glances over at me from the driver's seat of his van. "How can you eat those?"

I pull another ring from the plastic bag and crunch down on it, sending a new shower of yellow dust down the front of me. "I always have sweet tea and Funyuns on a road trip."

"They stink," he says, peering out the windshield at the gas station parking lot. We couldn't think of anywhere else to go. I'm supposed to be on the run, and Zane's supposed to be on a plane. The more people who think that, the better.

"Breakfast of champions." I blow a hot mass of onion breath in his direction. "You're just jealous. Besides, someone whose fingers are red from Flaming Hot Cheetos shouldn't talk."

"Hmmm," he grunts, and takes a swig of his soda.

Zane's phone dings. "It's another email from Slater."

He's been emailing all morning, thinking that Zane's on a plane somewhere over the Pacific. "Anything new?"

"No. Ava still hasn't shown up for school. And there's going to be a press conference this afternoon." He looks up at me. "Sounds like everyone's really freaking out."

"Good," I say. "That means that they have no idea where I am. As far as anyone else is concerned, I vanished into the night somewhere downtown, and you're—" I still feel so guilty he missed the flight that I can't bring myself to say "on a plane," so I settle for, "Gone."

Zane types on his phone. "I'm telling him to keep the info coming." He pauses, and then continues typing. "And that they're serving the meal, so I have to go."

"A meal? Since when do they serve food on a plane?"

He grins. "They do in first class." He types a little more. "Also, apparently there is this seriously hot girl in the seat next to me that I'm going to spill some water on so that I'll have an excuse to talk to her. Probably a swimsuit model going to Tahiti for a photo shoot."

"Nice touch."

We spend several long minutes watching people pull up and pump their gas, as the silence in the van seems to get louder. Apparently we've run out of unimportant things to talk about. Something needs to happen soon, because I'm getting antsy.

"What do you think we should do?" I finally ask, more to hear myself talk than because I'm looking for an actual plan.

"I think we should find out who really killed Eli. Before . . ."

"Before the cops find me," I finish for him.

Zane turns his head away from me to watch a homeless guy walk into the bathroom on the side of the building. "We'll get this figured out."

"How? I already know who did it. I just can't prove it."

He turns back to me. "Why are you so sure it's Ava?"

I can almost feel him pulling away from me. He doesn't want to believe me. "The evidence. She was there last night because of me. She's been following me around taking pictures and making appointments as Alicia."

"But wasn't there a picture of her and that Dylan guy too? She couldn't take a picture of herself."

I've already thought about that. "She could have gotten someone else to do it. Makes her look even more innocent."

"You really think Ava is that much of an evil mastermind?"

I try not to let my emotions get away from me. "Why not? She's been putting incriminating Photoshopped pictures on Alicia's page. Who else would do all of this?" Never mind why.

"They're not Photoshopped," Zane says.

I stop, my mind rushing at full speed. "What aren't?"

"The pictures on Alicia's wall. That's what I was doing last night after you went to sleep. I analyzed some of the metadata on the photos, and they're real. Every photo you upload has a binary code attached to it, and some of them, like the selfie profile picture, were uploaded somewhere in Oceanside. Does Ava hang out in Oceanside?"

I feel a charge rush through me. "The address she gave at the salon was in Oceanside. And the DMV registration—that was in Oceanside too."

"Do you even know anyone there?"

"No." I pull my phone and the battery out of my pocket. Aside from the disposable phone, some crumpled bills, my license, and a useless ATM card, my phone is the only thing I own right now. "The address is in here."

We both look at the blank screen. "How fast can they track my phone, do you think?"

"Pretty fast," he says. "Especially if they've got a trace on it. The minute it's turned on, it'll ping the location and give a triangulation of the cell phone towers in the area."

"When did you get so technical?"

Zane shrugs. "I hear things."

"I'm not sure we have a choice. The only place for us to start is in Oceanside, and the only info is trapped in here."

Zane turns the key in the ignition. "Okay. Fire it up, but only for a few seconds. Long enough to get the info but not so long that they can figure out where we are. We'll be out of here before any cops can respond anyway."

I take a deep breath, push the battery into the back, and turn the phone over to watch the screen jump to life. Sixty-seven missed calls. I don't have time to process that, only look at the address in Oceanside and pop the battery out again as Zane makes a right turn out of the gas station.

"You get it?" he asks, pulling into traffic.

"Yep." I watch the side mirror, convinced that I'm going to see a black-and-white patrol car in the reflection any second now. "It's 12941 Sunderland in Oceanside."

"Put it in my phone for directions. Should take only about twenty minutes to get there."

And then what? Knock on the door and ask for Ava? I can't think that far ahead right now, but our movement makes me feel better, like we're actually accomplishing something. I stick my dead phone into the center compartment, slide down in the seat, and put on some oversized aviator sunglasses I find in there. Glancing out the side window, I expect every car we pass to honk when they recognize me, but everyone is just going on about their regular Wednesday, yelling at traffic and illegally texting on their phones. I wish we could stay on the freeway forever, speeding toward nothing, leaving all of the mess behind us.

Too soon, we pull off the freeway and follow the directions to the house on the map.

"It should be halfway down this street," Zane says, leaning forward to look out the window at the identical stucco houses that line both sides of the road. "12927 . . . 12935 . . . ," he says, reading the painted numbers on the curb.

"Why don't they just go in order?" I'm suddenly pissed. Pissed at the stupid house numbers. Pissed at what happened to Eli. At having to run from the cops and try to prove to everyone that I didn't do anything wrong. "It would be so much easier if each house on each street would just start at one, then two, then three. None of this skipping-around crap."

"Really?" he says, taking his eyes off the road to look at me. "The inconstancy of house numbers is what you want to talk about right now?"

I fold my arms across my chest. "Well, it's stupid."

"And 12941 is right there," he says, pointing to an off-white house with a red tiled roof.

"Holy shit!" I blurt out. "There's a blue Honda parked in the driveway. Keep going!" I smack his arm as he slows down. "We don't want to park right in front."

"Where do we want to park?"

"There." I point to the curb about four houses down. Close enough that we can see the front of the house and the driveway but far enough away that we won't be noticed.

"What's with the Honda?" he asks as he turns around and pulls over to the curb.

I stare at it, trying to make sure it's really there. "Whoever got the speeding ticket in Alicia's name was driving a Honda. And there was a blue Honda parked in the empty lot at WaterRidge that night. . . ." I trail off, trying not to think of that night with Eli, back when everything was still good.

"There are a lot of blue Hondas in the world."

"Don't even start," I say. "This particular blue Honda is

no coincidence. It has something to do with Ava, and I'm not leaving here until I find out what."

"So we wait?"

"I guess so." I can't think of a better idea at the moment.

Zane glances down the street. "Not a lot going on here in the middle of the day," he says, surveying the blank, staring windows and closed garage doors. Like a lot of neighborhoods here, the street has the feel of a ghost town, the sidewalks always empty in a place where nobody ever gets out of their cars.

I'm making deals with myself in my head. We'll wait here for five minutes . . . no, ten minutes, before I jump out and knock on the door, demanding answers. I have no idea what I'm really going to say, but the deadline makes me feel more productive. I'm watching the numbers tick by on the ancient clock on Zane's dashboard when I see her walking down the front steps toward the car. Ava's head is down as she searches for something in a white bag I don't recognize.

"There she is," I say, slumping down farther in the front seat.

"Jesus, you're right," Zane says, ducking down in his own seat.

I can't believe what I'm seeing. All the puzzle pieces fit together, but I never thought they'd actually form this picture.

"It doesn't mean anything," Zane says. "There could be a lot of explanations for why Ava's way out here."

"Right." We both know that the only explanation is that she's hiding something. Something big. I watch as Ava opens the door and slides into the front seat of the car in the

driveway like she's been doing it all her life. She's so preoc-
cupied that she doesn't even look around as she backs the car
into the street and takes off.

"Should I follow her?" Zane asks, turning the key in the
ignition.

"Yes! Go!" I look around for cops, but all I see is an old
man driving a white car past us.

Zane swings in behind him.

"This is perfect," I say. "She won't notice us now."

"She probably wouldn't remember my van anyway," he
says, careful not to take his eyes off the blue car. "We haven't
exactly been hanging out the past decade or so."

"We can't take that chance." My heart speeds up as Ava
heads for the freeway.

"Where do you think she's headed?"

"No clue. But we're going to follow her until we figure
it out."

We get on the freeway and lose the Honda in the
stream of cars. "I don't see her," I say, scanning the road
ahead of us.

"She's up there," Zane says, gunning the van so that I can
feel the engine straining to keep up. "I won't lose her."

After a few moves in and out of lanes, I see the back of
the Honda a few cars ahead. Zane slows down so that he can
keep up without getting any closer. I start to notice familiar
freeway exits up ahead. "What if she's going home?" I ask.
"There are probably cops all over the place. We can't follow
her there."

"If she's going that way, then we'll just pull over. We're not going to get caught, I promise."

The turn signal on her car lights up, and I check the green freeway signs overhead. "She's taking La Costa." Suddenly I know where she's going. But why? Does she have more information for them? "She's going to Ms. Alvarez's office."

Zane heads for the freeway exit. "She must have something that will clear your name. Otherwise she'd just talk to the cops."

His insistence on trying to pretend that Ava wants to help me is getting irritating. "Would you stop? If it was something that would help me, Dad would be with her. If he knew about it, he'd never let her go alone, not with all of this going on. For all we know, Ava's bringing Ms. Alvarez the bloody knife that she just happened to find in my room. With my DNA on it. That coincidentally matches her DNA."

Zane shakes his head but says nothing.

Ava turns into the parking lot. "Go past it and around the corner," I say. "There's another entrance on the other side, where she might not see us." It seems to take hours to go around the block. "There," I say, pointing to a clump of eucalyptus trees toward the back of the lot. "Pull in there." Ava's parked up at the front by the building. I see her head in the driver's seat, but she doesn't look like she's making a move to get out.

Zane quickly backs the van into a space at the edge of the lot near the exit. There aren't many cars in the lot, and I feel exposed. "What's she doing?" I finally ask.

"Texting, I think," Zane says. A few seconds later his phone chimes, and I jump.

"It can't be," I say, and pick it up to look at the screen. I exhale. "It's only Maya," I say, handing him the phone.

"Okay, this is weird," he says, reading the email. "Maya says that Ava is on her way to meet you, that you're going to turn yourself in."

I glance over at Ava, still in the blue car. "Do you think she knows we're here?"

He squints in that direction. "I don't think so. She hasn't looked up once."

Zane unclips his seat belt. "I'm going to go talk to her. You stay here, where it's safe."

"No way. I'm the one—" I begin.

"What's she going to do to me?"

"That's the point! I have no idea what Ava might do." I feel so unmoored. For seventeen years, I've known Ava as well as I've known myself—I could finish her sentences, anticipate her wants, and read her emotions, but none of that's true anymore. She's like a stranger to me.

"I'll be fine," Zane says. "But you need to stay out of sight. If somehow the cops follow her, take the van and get the hell out of here."

"She's moving," I say, my attention drawn back to the blue car. We watch as Ava gets out of the Honda and walks toward some trees at the other end of the lot. For the first time since the club, I'm able to see her clearly. She's got on jeans and low-heeled boots, but there's something about the way she moves that's off somehow. "Something's wrong," I say.

Zane glances at me. "What do you mean?"

"I don't know," I say, watching her lean against one of the trees. Over her shoulder she's got the white bag that I've never seen before, and she picked a spot where she can see the entire lot but is almost hidden from view. "I can't say exactly. She just . . . she just doesn't look normal."

"I'm going," he says, reaching for the door.

"No!" I say, suddenly afraid. "She's already killed three people."

"We don't know that," Zane says. "Besides, the only guys who are dead have been going out with one of you."

I can see how determined he is, and honestly I just want the not-knowing to be over. "Give me your phone, then," I say. I go to the home screen and press the video icon. "Put this in your pocket. We won't have any video evidence, but we might at least get some audio that could help."

"Street smarts too," Zane says, slipping the phone into his pocket.

"Be careful," I say.

"You be ready to tear out of here if you need to," he says. "Don't worry about me."

I slide into the driver's seat and watch Zane as he makes his way across the parking lot. He looks casual, as if he's heading for the office building. As soon as he's about to reach Ava, a guy dressed in a suit comes rushing down the steps and stops in front of him. I'm straining to see what they're doing. Is the guy a plainclothes cop? After a few seconds, Zane turns toward the main street and starts gesturing right and left. The guy must just be asking for directions. I can see Zane glancing worriedly at Ava, but even though she must see him, she hasn't moved an inch.

Once the guy's on his way, Zane heads straight for Ava. Before she can even say anything to him, my eyes are drawn to a familiar car that just entered the parking lot. The car parks next to the blue Honda, and the girl driving gets out, but I can't believe what I'm seeing. This is crazy.

I open the door to the van, jump out, and head for Zane as fast as I can. I hear Ava call my name, but I don't stop and don't even look toward her silver car. My eyes are glued to the girl talking to Zane—the girl who looks just like us but isn't Ava. In some part of my brain, all of the events of the past few weeks have started to make sense, but all I can do is stare in disbelief.

"What the hell?" Ava says as we reach them at the same time. Her voice has an angry edge to it that I feel but can't really express.

There's no mistaking it as we look at the girl standing next to Zane. She looks just like us. She has the same dark curly hair and green eyes that I've seen in my mirror for as long as I can remember. She's even wearing the diamond pendant that I threw out the window of Zane's van last night. It's impossible, but only one word escapes my lips in these first few seconds.

"Alicia?"

CHAPTER 24

"It's Rubi," the girl says calmly, as if she's been expecting this confrontation all along. I recognize the name from Cecilia's text. I knew that had nothing to do with Cecilia's sister's husband. This is who they were talking about. Worrying about. My stomach sinks—Cecilia has something to do with this. Out of all the ways I imagined this ending, no way I pictured what's standing right in front of me.

"What?" demands Ava. Her disbelief is almost palpable. We can't believe what we're seeing. Is it the makeup or the clothes that make her look so much like the two of us? I'm not sure, but whatever it is, she's doing a better job at being Alicia than I ever could.

"My name's Rubi, not Alicia." Even her voice sounds like Ava's. The girl's hand goes to the pendant around her neck. "I love that you think that."

By the tone of her voice, I can tell Ava's feeling threatened when she says, "You have two seconds to tell us what the hell is going on here before—"

"Before what?" Rubi says. A small smile crosses her lips. "Before you call the cops?" She glances at me. "We all know you're not going to do that. I'm guessing you were pretty careful to make sure that none of them followed you today."

Suddenly it all makes sense—the strange Alicia sightings in the surveillance photo, at the food trucks, and at the club, not to mention the angry guy at the party who we'd never seen before. She turns her head, and I see two faint parallel pink lines running down her neck and into her jacket. The exact marks fingernails would make if Casey grabbed her. It wasn't me or Ava behind all of this—it was this girl.

I notice her hand move toward the white bag. If she murdered Eli last night, she might still have the knife on her.

"There's something in her hand!" I grab her arm roughly, and her wallet falls to the ground.

"Take it easy," Rubi says, wrenching her arm away. "I'm not the killer, if that's what you're worried about. And neither is Ava." She bends down and gathers up the wallet and some papers that fell out of it.

Ava whirls on me. "You thought *I* killed Eli? What the hell? What about you? What am I supposed to think when one second you vanish into thin air, and the next the club is full of cops and Eli's dead?"

I'm suddenly not sure of anything anymore. "He was already dead when I found him," I explain quickly, trying to blink back from my mind the image of his lifeless body.

"Someone had gotten to him first. I saw you on the way to the bathroom, and then I couldn't find you, so I figured—"

"You figured I was the killer? I've spent the last twelve hours looking for *you*. Of all the ungrateful, insane ideas—"

Rubi holds out her hands to stop Ava just as she's ramping up. "Neither of you killed Eli. Or Dylan or Casey. It's all a mistake. There have been too many secrets for too long—I'm here to straighten stuff out." She opens the wallet and pulls out a driver's license. One with a picture that looks just like ours and with the name Alicia Rios on it.

"Where did you get that?" Ava asks.

Rubi turns it around so she can admire it. "Had it made. Took the test and everything."

Ava's cheeks are red, and I can see she's frustrated. "What the hell? I have Alicia's ID. And it's fake."

"Yeah, well . . . this one is more official." I picture the cops at our door, Alicia's license mysteriously on their computers.

"Which is why the police had a copy of it," I say. "Why would you do that?" Does she want so desperately to be like us?

Rubi shrugs. "I needed it in order to be Alicia, and a real one was a lot cheaper than a fake ID. And my parents said that if I got a speeding ticket they'd take my car away. It wasn't that hard."

"That's crazy." I study her face, and I can't deny that she looks the part—whoever did her makeup is amazing.

"This is bullshit," Ava says, echoing my thoughts. I can see from her face how much she doesn't like to be out of her element like this. "I don't care what the license says. Who the hell are *you*?"

Rubi straightens up, and I can't tell if she really is this calm or if it's all an act. "I thought you'd figured it out by now. I'm your sister."

Ava takes a step closer to me, solidarity apparently overcoming anger. "We don't have a sister. We're twins."

"Actually, *we* are triplets."

She says that like it won't change everything. Triplets. I feel like I can't breathe, like all of this must be some kind of sick joke. But I look at her and can't deny what I'm seeing.

Rubi looks from me to Ava. "I somehow thought you'd be happy when you guys finally found out the truth. I've been keeping the secret for months, and it's been killing me."

"Months?" Ava demands. "You've known about this for months?"

She shrugs, and it seems like Rubi is trying to look casual, like finding out you have another sister is something that happens every day. "I followed Cecilia to your house one day. They've always been so secretive about where she goes, and why I can never go along. You weren't home, but I saw your rooms and the pictures on the wall and started to put it all together. I promised them I wouldn't tell," she says. For the first time she looks a little bit guilty. "But it was harder than I thought it would be."

My heart drops. Cecilia knows about this girl. She's been lying to us our whole lives. "What does Cecilia have to do with all of this?"

Rubi raises her eyebrows at me. "Cecilia is our aunt. Our mother's sister."

Ava's face is bright red. "Dad would never lie to us like that!"

"He doesn't know there were three of us." Rubi shakes her head. "And he doesn't know that Cecilia had anything to do with it. As far as your dad knows, she's just an employee who volunteered to become his housekeeper when his wife up and bailed on him."

Ava steps toward her. "So your . . . mother . . . just got rid of two of us, like puppies in a litter that was too big? Dumped us on the restaurant steps like a bag of garbage?"

For a second I see the first cracks of doubt in Rubi's face. She doesn't like us talking bad about her mother. Our mother? It's so hard to believe, but the proof is standing here staring me in the face—telling me the story that I've always wanted to hear—at the totally wrong time and place.

Rubi's jaw clenches. "It wasn't like that. Mama was only eighteen and couldn't raise us all, so she did what she thought was best. You two were the chosen ones, with the big house and the new cars. How do you think I felt, seeing all the things you got growing up?"

"You got our mother." The words are out of my mouth before I can stop them. "Isn't that enough?"

Zane hasn't said a word this entire time, has just been looking from one of us to the next. He catches my glance. "What?" he says. "You have to admit this is pretty freaky."

I look around at the empty parking lot, suddenly feeling

very exposed. "We need to get out of here before someone recognizes me." I look at the two of them. "Us."

"That's why I'm here," Rubi says. "This has gone on too long. I need to turn in evidence that will help clear your name." She nods at me. "All of our names. Thanks to you, I can't show my face around town at the moment."

"What evidence?"

"I got a look at someone who pulled into the Cheesecake Factory parking lot that night. And part of a license plate. Find him and you'll find the guy who's behind the murders. I'm sure of it."

"What were you doing there in the first place?" I ask.

A look of guilt crosses her face. "I was being Alicia." She glances at me. "I'd gone out with Casey a couple of times. As Alicia. I didn't know what had happened with you the night before. I thought it would be fun to surprise Casey after he got off work." Rubi puts one hand up to her neck. "He thought it was a little less fun." She holds out a scrap of paper for us all to see. "When I took off, I saw another car pull into the lot. I should have turned this information in a long time ago."

I look at the paper. *7ETR*. "That's it? Four figures?"

"That's enough," Rubi says defensively. "It was a black pickup truck, and a guy in a dark hoodie was driving. It pulled up right beside Casey's car after I got out of there. I remembered the license plate when I found out what happened. I have kind of a photographic memory."

"Did you see him?" I ask. "Did you see this mysterious guy in a black truck kill Casey?"

"No. But who else would have pulled into an empty parking lot in the middle of the night?"

"All you have is a partial license plate and your word that this truck was in the parking lot that night," I say, anticipating Ms. Alvarez's reaction. "Unless you have a picture of him actually killing Casey, this isn't going to do us much good."

Rubi looks at the piece of paper again, the confident look slipping from her face.

"All we know is that the killer is someone who owns a hoodie and a black truck." I squeeze my eyes shut. "Not exactly narrowing the suspect pool."

"It's better than nothing," Zane says, taking another look at the paper. "I mean, at least we could get Ms. Alvarez to run the plate against black trucks in the area. It's a start."

"It's a shitty start," I say. "All it proves is that there was someone in the parking lot around the same time." I want what Rubi is saying to be true, but I just don't know how to prove it.

"Why should we believe anything you say?" Ava says to Rubi. "This is . . . this is insane!"

"Do you have any better suggestions?" Rubi asks. It's almost a taunt. She makes a sweeping motion with her arm. "Anything else that would explain what I'm doing here?"

I don't say a word. It feels like the world is closing in on me, fast.

"I'll go," Ava says, grabbing the paper from Rubi. "I'll take it to the lawyer."

I take a step toward her, already feeling guilty for suspecting her. "No, let me. This is my mess."

"You can't go in there," Ava says. "Every cop within fifty miles is looking for you. What if someone sees you? Or worse, what if Ms. Alvarez is under some kind of obligation to turn you in?"

"You look just like me," I remind her. "What's to stop them from arresting you instead?"

Ava waves her hands at me. "My fingerprints are different, and they fingerprinted me last night," she says. "If they do take me in, it won't take them long to figure out it's me and not you. But I don't think it'll get that far."

I'm starting to say something more, when I catch Zane's eye and the almost imperceptible shake of his head. I take a deep breath and let it go. "I'll wait out here, but the minute I see one flashing light on a cop car, I'm coming in to get you."

"I'm coming too," Rubi says, taking a few steps toward the building. "It's my evidence."

Ava whirls on her, more in command of the situation than I've ever seen her. "And she's *my* sister. You stay."

Zane puts a hand out to stop Rubi. "Let her go. No sense muddying up the water right now. Giving you up to the lawyer is only going to put a bigger target on everyone's head."

Rubi hesitates, and I can see her thinking about it.

"Zane's right. Instead of just being after me, they'll want all of us," I tell her.

"Okay," Rubi says. "But you've got to make her believe you. Tell her that they need to find this guy." She looks down at her hands. "I should have done this a long time ago. I just . . . I just didn't think this many people would get hurt."

"I got this," Ava says, straightening her back and walking toward the steps.

"I don't like being out here," I say, looking around at the open parking lot. "Can we wait for Ava in the van?"

"Let's go," Zane says, putting one hand protectively around my waist. Once we reach the van, he slides the door open, but I put a hand out to stop Rubi. "No way." I turn to Zane. "I don't want her in there."

Zane pauses. "Your suspect list gets longer by the minute. Why would she come here if she had something to do with the killings?"

Rubi smiles at Zane but says nothing.

I look away from her—there's something disturbing about seeing my face on someone who isn't Ava. "You've already admitted that you're a stalker. So now I'm supposed to invite you into a conveniently enclosed space?"

Rubi drops her bag to the ground and holds her arms out wide. "Frisk me," she says. "Go ahead, pat me down. Check my bag—whatever you want."

I know she's bluffing, so I call her on it and quickly run my hands over her pockets while Zane picks the white bag up off the ground.

"There's nothing in here," Zane says, handing it to me.

"Okay," I say, pointing to the open door. "But I'm watching you."

"If this is the way you treat family . . ." She peers into the van and then jumps back. "Holy shit! What is that?"

I look in and see Bettina in the corner. I'd forgotten

about her. "She's good at keeping secrets," I say. "And she doesn't track people like they're the wounded antelope on the Serengeti."

Rubi sighs and climbs in. "It wasn't like that," she says, settling against the back wall of the van.

"So what was it like, then?" I say, leaning against the back of the front seat. It's not that I don't want to sit near Rubi but that I want to get up the courage to look at her. I stare at her face and try to pick out the differences. They're there, just like there are differences between me and Ava, but it's almost impossible to put into words. We must have remembered Rubi deep down somewhere in our baby brains—even six-month-old babies must have some sense of the world—and made up Alicia not out of our imaginations but out of our half-formed memories.

Rubi shrugs. "I'd heard them talk about Raquel and Robin before, but I didn't know who they meant, and they always stopped talking when I came into the room."

"Raquel and Robin?" Zane asks from the driver's seat.

"Raquel and Robin. Alexa and Ava."

Robin. I roll the name around in my mind. I know without asking that my name was Robin.

"Mama's going to be pissed that the secret's out now. But I think she knew you'd find out someday."

"So, what—they just told you all about us?"

"No," Rubi says. "Like I said, I followed Cecilia to work one day. You weren't home, but there were pictures on the walls and stuff. They had to tell me then."

"Did you get that from my room?" I ask, pointing to the diamond *A* pendant around her neck. The same one I thought I'd lost and Dad replaced.

She lifts it up as if seeing it for the first time. "Yeah. I told myself I was just borrowing it. I was going to put it back, I swear. I just wondered what it would feel like to be one of the chosen twins."

Dad always said that we were chosen just for him, but until now I never really thought about it much. I can't imagine growing up alone and then finding out I had two sisters somewhere else. I almost feel sorry for her.

Rubi reaches behind her neck. "You can have it back."

"I don't want it," I say quickly, remembering the feeling that I got dropping mine out Zane's car window. "Alicia's gone."

Rubi nods knowingly. "I knew she would be sometime. She was fun, though."

"So you really pretended to be Alicia?" Zane asks.

Rubi hesitates. "A few times. Some guy at a party thought I was Alicia, and I figured it might be fun to play along, so I did." She looks down at her fingernails. "Made me feel like I was one of you. At least for a little while."

"So you just *became* Alicia? Told people that was your name?" I look at her hard. "Made appointments as her?"

Rubi looks surprised I figured that out. "Not all the time. But it was nice when people would call me Alicia. Made it feel more real."

"How long have you been following them around?" Zane

asks. I've been so involved in the conversation, I almost forgot he was there.

"I don't know. A while, I guess. To get it right I watched how Alicia acted and dressed—"

"The sunflower seeds!" I say suddenly. "That's why the DNA on them came back as mine. Ours. You were sitting outside Ava's room watching us, weren't you?"

Rubi bites the inside of her cheek, something I've seen Ava do a million times. "Look, I know it sounds creepy, but . . . I just really wanted to be part of it, you know?"

I'm relieved and sad at the same time. "I thought some guy was stalking us. You scared the crap out of me."

"Good," she says, suddenly serious. "Because someone is stalking you. Whoever's in that black truck killed Casey, Dylan, and Eli, I'm sure of it."

I look out the window at the office door, but there's no movement. Each second that ticks by makes my nerves feel tighter. "But why? I mean, Casey was an ass and Dylan cheated on Ava, but Eli didn't do anything." If anything, I lied to him—it should have been me who ended up dead.

"I don't know," she says. "All I know is that anyone either of you goes out with ends up dead."

Zane's phone suddenly buzzes, breaking the tension that's settled over us. "It's Ava," he says, flipping it to speaker. "Hello?"

"Get out of here," she says, her voice panicked and her breathing heavy. "Get in the van and get out of the parking lot as fast as you can. There's a warrant out for me now too, and I'm pretty sure the cops are on the way."

"Ms. Alvarez would never turn you in!" I say. "She's my lawyer."

"She didn't," Ava says. I can hear a door shut behind her. "But she got a call while I was in the office. Lexi—they found traces of Dylan's blood on your backpack. There isn't anything she can do."

As she speaks, I can hear the shrill wail of a siren in the distance. I look out the window and see her on the steps of the building. There's no time even to process this information. "Get in your car!" I tell her. "You have time."

"They'll follow me."

"Wait there," Zane says, revving the engine. She's only thirty feet away, but she's not moving fast enough. He swings the van out of the parking space and barely slows enough for her to jump in the open side door.

"Get down on the floor, all of you," he says.

"Once I shut the door, Zane slows down to the speed limit as he pulls onto the street. Ava curls into a ball, and I wrap my arm around her, feeling the pounding of her heart against my body, while Rubi sits on the other side of the van, watching us intently.

We're already camouflaged in traffic and waiting in a long line of cars at the stoplight by the time the parade of police cars pass us, lights and sirens wailing.

CHAPTER 25

"I didn't mean for you to find out this way," Elena says. She glances worriedly at her sister across the table. Cecilia has had tears in her eyes since we showed up at the door in Oceanside. It doesn't feel like the right time for this, but we had nowhere else safe to go. "Please don't be mad at Cecilia. She was my connection in the first place. She worshipped your dad and knew he'd make a great father for you girls once I decided I had to give you up. After his wife left, she got the job with your dad even though I didn't want her to. Part of me wanted a clean break, but over the years, it's been nice to have someone there behind the scenes, making sure you were okay, letting me know what's going on with the two of you."

I've thought about this moment my entire life, but looking at Elena just makes me feel numb—all this information is bouncing off me like hail on a sidewalk. I don't feel like this woman is my mother; there's no instant moment of recognition like I always imagined would happen. I figured our birth mother would pass me on the street one day or get in line behind me at the grocery store and I'd know in a second, from somewhere deep down and long-buried, that it was her. Elena's just a stranger dressed in a pink sweatshirt sitting in a kitchen in Oceanside.

Ava, however, is openly hostile. "I'm not okay with this. Any of this!" She's standing against the wall with her arms crossed over her chest. Her fierce loyalty to Dad doesn't surprise me.

I give her a look, because I don't want Elena to stop talking. I figured I'd find my birth parents someday. I just didn't think it would be today, and it feels like a million questions are floating through the air waiting to be plucked. I focus on the wedding ring on Elena's finger, how the diamond sparkles in the light from the kitchen windows. "You're married, right? Is he . . . is he our birth father?"

"No." She shakes her head. "I was very young when I had you—I didn't marry the boy. He doesn't even know. Leo came along a few years later, and he's been a good father to all the girls." She glances at Ava, whose expression hasn't changed.

All the girls except us. I know I'm staring at Elena, but I can't help it. As hard as I try, I can't see much of a resemblance. She has dark hair and green eyes like we do, but that's about it. I imagined our birth mother would look exactly like us. Older, but otherwise the same.

"We should call your dad," Cecilia says suddenly. "He's been sick with worry about you."

"We can't," I say quickly, turning to look at Zane. He's on

the couch in the living room, giving us as much distance as he can. "I tried. The phones are tapped. . . . He basically told me to stay away."

"But we have to let him know that you're okay."

"No!" I say. "If I get arrested, then I won't have the chance to fix this. If it weren't for Alicia, three boys would be alive right now."

"But they'll know you didn't do these things," Elena says. "They can't put you in jail if you're innocent."

"Doubtful," I say, thinking about everything that's stacked against me. "And in the time it takes to clear my name, more people might die."

"What can you possibly do?" Cecilia asks. "If there is a madman out there, how can you stop him?"

"And how are you going to find him alone?" Elena asks. She's got a worried look on her face that belongs on a mother.

As she speaks, an idea starts to form in my mind. It's a small chance, but it's better than none. "If what Rubi says is true, then maybe we won't have to find him." I glance at Zane, who's listening carefully. "We can let him find us."

———

"What if it doesn't work?" I ask Zane. "There are so many things that can go wrong. What if he doesn't show up? Or the cops find us? What if you get hurt?"

Zane puts his hands on the top of the old wooden swing set in Rubi's backyard and stretches his shoulders. "And what if it does work? We catch him red-handed. It's a great plan, Lex," he says. "And right now it's the only plan."

I'm sitting on the platform by the slide, the wood warm against my legs. I glance at the sliding door, but I don't see anyone inside. Zane walks over to where I'm sitting, and at this height, I can see the gold flecks in his brown eyes. "Don't worry about me," he says. "The biggest advantage this guy had is the element of surprise, and we're taking that away. If we can catch him with the weapon, the detectives will be able to link him to all of the crimes. Case closed."

"I know, but—"

"Stop with the 'buts.' We can do this." He playfully punches me in the arm. "You can do this. The biggest question is where."

I try to stop dwelling on the negatives and pretend that I feel a tenth as confident as he does. "We know that he follows the guys, learns their routines, figures out a time when they'll be alone."

"For all we know, he's already following us," Zane says. "He could have been watching the whole time from the minute you left Eli in the alley."

I don't want to admit he might be right. "How about the beach?" I say. "We've both been there a lot, and after five, Eighteenth Street really clears out."

Zane nods, considering it, the sun shining through the ends of his curls. "It might not clear out enough, though. Cardiff could work—secluded enough that there won't be too many people around but close enough . . ."

I know what he's thinking. Close enough to people for them to hear someone screaming.

"Close enough that it's safe," he finally says. "But when?"

"Tonight," I suggest, mostly because if I have too long to think about it, I'm sure I'll lose my nerve.

"Okay." Zane smiles, his support unwavering. "I'll post on my page that I'm going there, in case he's checking."

"Doesn't everyone think you're gone?" I get a pang of guilt whenever I think of the trip to Tahiti. He should be on an island in the Pacific Ocean right now, getting ready for the surf competition, not plotting to catch a killer with me.

"Not that many people know about it." He smiles at me. "It'll be fine." Zane tilts his head like he's thinking about something. "There's one more thing. We have to make it believable."

"Believable how?"

"That we're together. In order to get this guy to strike, he has to think we're going out. I think we should . . . practice." I must have a weird look on my face, because he quickly adds, "Just so it looks right. Believable. We can call it a rehearsal."

"Okay." I study the wooden surface of the swing set, unable to look at him. I always say I don't think about Zane this way, that we're just old friends, but I realize now that's not true. I'm very much thinking about him this way. I feel so guilty. Twelve hours ago I was holding Eli's lifeless body in my lap, and now I'm having thoughts about Zane. I shake my head. I'm not betraying Eli—I'm trying to find him justice. This is all just a rehearsal.

Zane puts one hand on either side of where I'm sitting. His face is dangerously close to mine, and I realize this is what I've wanted since we were in bed together last night. Since before last night. I'm a terrible person.

"So what should we do?" I whisper.

He seems to consider that question for a second. "I think you should kiss me. On the lips, just once, to see if it looks authentic."

Zane's smile is wide as he bends toward me, and despite how casual I'm trying to make this moment, I inhale sharply when his lips touch mine. There's an electricity between us in even the smallest contact, and it feels like my insides are spinning. He pulls away from me, and it's like a light has gone out, but I do my best to cover my reaction. After all, this is just pretend.

I cough a little to clear my throat. "Like that?" I'm sure he can hear my heart beating, the pounding is so loud in my ears.

In response, Zane leans in again, until there is no space between our bodies. He pulls me toward him as he brushes his lips against my neck and traces my jaw before finding my mouth again, the desire in his kiss echoing through my body. We stay like that for several long moments, my hand raking through his hair as his holds the back of my neck. When he finally pulls away, I feel like I've come home.

"I'm thinking more like that," he says with a broad grin.

I burst into tears.

"Oh, shit!" he says, first putting one arm around me and

then awkwardly dropping it to step back and look into my eyes. "I'm so sorry! Lexi . . . talk to me. I'm so sorry. I didn't mean anything, I swear. . . ."

I take a couple of deep breaths and try to regain control. This is all just pretend. We're just putting on a show—no different from when I kissed Steve Miller in *Guys and Dolls* in eighth grade. I wipe my face with both palms. "I'm sorry," I say finally. "It's just . . . it's just been a hard couple of days."

Zane walks a few steps away from me and laces his fingers behind his head. "I should have known not to mess around like that." His face is a mask of worry. "With everything that went on last night—"

I wave one hand at him. "It's okay." I sniff and sit up straight. "I think that will do fine."

CHAPTER 26

"No way," Cecilia says the minute we tell them the plan. "It's too dangerous."

"She's right," Ava says, and I'm surprised she's agreeing with anything Cecilia says at this point. "It's crazy."

"Any of you have a better idea?" I ask. The living room is silent for several seconds.

"Then I think we have to try," Zane says, rubbing at the beads of moisture on the outside of the glass of water he's nursing. He's been shooting me anxious looks since we came inside, which only make me feel worse.

"I don't like it either, but we can't just hide out here waiting for the cops to find us. The only suspects they're looking for are sitting right here in this room," I say. "It's up to us to find the real killer."

Ava slaps her hands on the arm of the sofa. "How can we find the real killer when we don't have a clue who that is?"

"It's someone who hates you enough to want you both in jail," Zane says.

"And smart enough to plant evidence," I say. "Did Ms. Alvarez say anything else about Dylan's DNA on my backpack? What it was? Where it was?"

"No. She barely had time to get that out before I bailed," Ava says.

Zane turns to me. "You're sure there's no way Dylan had your backpack? Maybe there's a logical explanation for how it got there."

"No! I always keep it on the island in the kitchen. The only time I met Dylan was in our hallway one night. That's it." I glance at Ava, but she looks down at the coffee table. "There's no way that his DNA could have gotten on my backpack accidentally. Someone had to have put it there. On purpose."

"So who could hate us that much?" Ava asks.

Everyone hesitates, and it's a little disturbing to think about who might have it in for us. Some crazy person we pissed off without even knowing it.

"How about that guy from the party? The one with the tarantula tattoo?" Zane says, glancing at Cecilia.

I shrug a tiny bit. It's too late to keep secrets from her now. "I've thought about him."

"I have no idea who that guy even was," Ava says. "But he was pretty pissed off."

We all look at Rubi. She glances at the ceiling and then down at her hands. "That would be Brian." She catches my eye. "Okay, okay. He was my one and only solo experiment as Alicia. He's kind of a jerk, but I don't think he's a killer."

Zane rubs his cheek where Brian hit him that night. "I'm not so sure about that."

"What happened with this tattooed Brian person?" Cecilia asks.

Rubi shrugs. "We went out a couple of times, but he was kind of a thug." She breaks into a little smile. "Which was fun at first. But then, not so much. I basically just avoided him after that, didn't return his calls, you know?"

"And when he saw me at the party that night, he wanted Alicia to know how he felt," I say.

"But Casey had already been killed by then," Zane says. "When did you go out with him?"

"Before Casey," Rubi says. "Just after Valentine's Day."

"Which would put him in the right time frame," Ava says. "He would have been the last guy Alicia dated before Casey."

I feel closed in, the clues overlapping on themselves until they're just a confusing jumble. "I'm going to get some water," I say, standing up and pushing my way past Ava and Rubi.

I don't notice that Zane is following me until I get to the kitchen and he reaches out to touch my arm. "Listen, Lex. About what happened—"

"It's fine," I interrupt. I can't look at him, so I stare out the window. "I don't want to talk about it."

"Maybe I do," he says quietly.

"I totally overreacted," I say. "You were right—we needed

to practice to make sure it looks right. It's not like either of us meant anything by it."

"Right," he says quickly. "I just wanted to make sure we were both clear on that."

"Well, we are. Don't worry about it."

"I thought you were pissed at me." Zane's face is as serious as I've ever seen it. "I'd never do anything to hurt you. You know that, right?"

I nod. Standing next to me is the Zane from years ago— the one who'd let me run his train set too fast until the engine flew off the rails, and who pushed Gordon Faulkner into a puddle because he tried to look at my underwear on the swings. I didn't realize until recently how much I missed that Zane.

I fill my glass with water from the faucet and turn to him. The awkwardness in the room is almost palpable. "We should get back."

"Right," he agrees.

In the living room, Zane slides into the chair farthest from my spot on the couch and focuses on Rubi.

"I still don't think Brian would do this. I'm not sure he's smart enough to plant evidence and all that," she's saying.

I shake my head. "So far, this Brian guy is the only one with any motive that I can see. And motive is what we've been missing. He was sure mad enough that night at the party."

"And he already thinks I'm going out with Alicia," Zane says.

Cecilia raises her eyebrows but doesn't say anything.

Zane leans forward. "Look, we're all sitting here thinking that whoever did it was trying to frame you." He looks around the room. "But what if we've got it wrong? What if the killer was actually out to protect you?"

"What in the hell are you talking about?" Ava snaps.

"No—listen. Casey is killed right after he hurts you. Or whoever he thinks is Alicia. And Dylan is killed right after he humiliates Alicia by cheating on her."

"That's crazy," I say. "What did Eli do?"

He shrugs. "I'm not sure. Maybe whoever did this thinks Eli hurt you too. Or was going to."

"Nobody is going to go around killing people just because they hurt Alicia," Ava says.

"What about the photos online? In every one of them, the guys are angry. What if those aren't to show the motive, but to show that the guys had it coming in some weird way?"

"I put the photos on Alicia's page," Rubi says.

We all turn to look at her.

"It was just for fun. Some selfies, the photos from shows I went to, stuff like that," she says.

"What about the pictures of us with the guys?" Ava asks. "Were you following us around and taking photos of us too?"

Rubi looks confused. "I didn't take pictures of you with any guys. I haven't actually been on Alicia's page in weeks."

Zane pulls up the page and hands the phone to her.

"I didn't do these," she says, shaking her head. "I didn't take any of these last ones. Someone else put those there. Wow. Whoever it is really wants you to go down for this."

Leave it to Zane to make the killer out to be someone trying to help. "She's right. This is somebody who wants to set Alicia up as a cold-blooded killer."

"Fine," Zane says, looking at his phone again. "It was just a theory."

"What about Rebecca?" Rubi says, turning toward me.

I stare at her. "How do you know about Rebecca?"

She narrows her eyes at me. "I know things."

"Rebecca's crazy, I'll give you that," I say. "But why would she kill Eli? And I didn't even know her when Casey was killed."

"I did," Ava says. "She tried to start something at a club in the North Bay about a month before Casey was killed. Got pissed that Eli was hanging out with me."

"She did try to start a fight in the bathroom last night," I say. "After she saw me and Eli talking . . ."

"Maybe she thought he was getting back together with you?" Rubi offers.

I remember their kiss in the alley. "I doubt it. She looked pretty sure of her position."

"Putting you in jail would be a good way to keep you away from her boyfriend."

"But why would she kill him?"

"Suspicions aren't going to do us any good," Ava says. "We need evidence, not theories."

"I agree," Rubi says. "We'll put the bait out there and see who it attracts." She looks at Zane. "No offense."

He grins. "No worries. I'll be the bait all day long."

Thank God he doesn't look at me when he says that.

"We're coming with you. And Leo too when he gets home," Elena says. "We should at least call the police, let them help."

"We will," Ava says, though I'm not sure she means it. "As soon as we know who we have, we'll call them."

Cecilia stands up. "Well, we can't do this on empty stomachs. How about I go and get some food?"

Trust Cecilia to think about food at a time like this. But as soon as she says that, I realize how hungry I am. I haven't eaten anything except Funyuns all day.

Nobody objects, so Cecilia grabs her keys off the counter. "I'll go to Los Pericos and pick some up." She gestures to Zane. "Why don't you come with me, help me carry the bags?"

Zane glances at me. "I'd rather stay here, if that's okay."

I smile at him, thankful that I have him on my side. Even if some of it is just pretend.

"You should come." She gives Zane a not-so-subtle wink. "Leave them to catch up a little bit."

Zane gives in. "Okay. I'll go." He walks over to me, picks up a pen from the table next to the sofa, and writes some numbers on my hand. "That's my cell. Call me if you need anything, okay?"

"Okay." I don't want him to leave, but I don't say anything else as I watch him close the front door behind them. Now Ava's the only one left who's familiar.

Rubi sits back on the sofa and looks at her mother. "I didn't really tell them about how it all happened. You know . . . about dropping them off."

Elena turns in her chair. "You didn't? Why not?"

"Because I thought you should."

Elena pulls out her phone and turns it toward us. On it is a picture of Rubi and two younger girls on merry-go-round horses.

"Those are your half sisters," Elena says, her face beaming with pride. "Lara and Jasmine. They're at school, but they'll be home after three."

I wonder what it would have been like to grow up in a house full of girls. I have to ask the question I've wondered my whole life: "Why did you give us up?"

"I grew up in a small town in Colorado. We had a little rancho—a couple of horses, some cows, things like that. It was nice. That's where you were born." Elena's voice is quick but steady, like she's reciting a script she wrote a long time ago. "I was so young, and then when you came, you were so small and needed so much help in the beginning." She glances toward Ava. "Raquel was really sick with the tubes and the doctors. . . . After you came, I knew I didn't want to give any of you up. I thought I could do it, that I could raise all of you together." She hesitates. "I tried. But it was just too hard."

"They think you dumped them, like puppies," Rubi says.

"It wasn't like that," Elena says, turning back to me, tears in her eyes. "I wanted what was best for you. Rubi was the oldest. It just seemed right this way."

"Rubi's the oldest?" I ask. I've always felt like the oldest.

Elena nods. "Rubi was born first. Then you and then Raquel." She glances at Rubi, and then back to me. "But it wasn't just that, just because of the order you were born in.

You and Raquel were so close, always sleeping with your arms around each other. . . . I couldn't bear to separate you." She looks at Ava. "I prayed and prayed until I realized that I would rather lose you to another family than have God take Raquel too early. So I left for California to make a new life, and then Cecilia suggested your dad and the restaurant. It was all safe. . . . I knew you'd be taken care of."

I know Dad's going to be upset when he hears about Rubi, hears that he unknowingly separated triplets. Despite everything that's happened, he wants what's best for us. He always has. "We were," I finally say. "Even though I'm on the run from the cops at the moment, Dad did a good job."

Elena nods gratefully, holding on to the small amount of forgiveness I can give her right now. "Thank you," she whispers.

CHAPTER 27

"No heels," I say to Ava as she looks at herself in Rubi's mirror. "We all have to look the same. And be able to run if we need to. Those things are a liability."

"But they're so cute," she says, spinning around in Rubi's strappy red sandals. Finally, she's found a sister who shares her taste in shoes.

"Try these," Rubi says from inside the closet, tossing out a pair of black flats remarkably similar to the ones I'm wearing. She emerges with another pair that are the same except for tiny bows on the front. "I'll cut these off, and then all three of us will look the same." Ava slips the flats on reluctantly and stands in front of the mirrored closet door with us.

I have to admit, the effect is a little creepy. By digging into Rubi's clothes, we've managed to find jeans for the two of them to match the ones I'm wearing, and three long gray T-shirts that match closely enough. With the same high ponytails and the same red lipstick, nobody will be able to tell us apart. "Freaky," Ava says under her breath.

"Yep," Rubi agrees.

"I just wish we had something to bling it up," Ava says, picking at the hem of her shirt. "This stuff is all so boring."

"Would you get serious!" I say. "We're not going to a party, for God's sake. We're trying to catch a killer. We don't need to be flashy, we just need to be identical."

"It's working," Elena says from the doorway.

All three of us turn in unison. "Can you tell us apart?" Rubi asks.

Elena points to Rubi. "Rubi." Then to me and Ava. "Ava and Lexi."

I laugh. "Close, but no."

She looks astonished. "I got Rubi right, though."

Rubi walks over and stands in front of her. "Maybe. Maybe not."

Elena steps back, confusion written all over her face. "Okay. Now, that's not funny." She looks panicked.

"You got Rubi right." I laugh. "That's Ava," I say, pointing to my sister.

She shakes her head. "I'm going to have to mark you guys somehow."

"When we were little, Dad pierced our ears and put purple stones in mine and pink stones in Ava's. That way our teachers could tell us apart." I see Rubi's posture slump as the words escape my lips, and I can tell I've hurt her feelings a little.

"Mine were red," she says. "But only because my name is

Rubi." We all mentally finish that for her—there was nobody else who looked like her.

"Zane and Cecilia should be back soon," Elena says. "Let's go clear off the table."

"Can I use your bathroom?" I ask as we all file out of Rubi's room.

"Sure," she says. "Down at the end of the hallway."

I use the bathroom and am about to walk out when I hear something buzzing on a shelf above the sink. It's a new phone—the kind Ava wants to get as soon as Dad will let her. The screen lights up as a text comes through.

"Someone left their phone in the bathroom," I say, holding it up as I walk back into the kitchen.

Rubi glances over. "That's Aunt Cecilia's. She's always leaving her stuff around."

I look at the shiny new touch screen. "This isn't hers. She has an old one with the keyboard that Dad gave her years ago."

Elena looks at the phone in my hand and shakes her head. "No, that's the phone Cecilia just got a few months ago. She's always wasting her money on every new gadget that comes out. I tell her all the time that an old phone makes calls just as well as a new one, but she never listens." She points down the hall. "Why don't you go and put it in her room so she won't lose it. Last doorway on the right."

I don't know what to say. I've never seen Cecilia with anything but Dad's castoffs. And I can't imagine her wanting every new gadget that comes out. She can barely even change the channel with the remote. "Okay," I say, turning and walking down the short hallway.

The door is closed, but as soon as I open it, I smell Cecilia's world—a familiar combination of roses and spice—and know I'm in the right place. I recognize the white iron bed as one that used to be in our rooms before Dad redecorated a couple of years ago, but as I look around, I get uneasy. There's a new laptop sitting on the dresser and a tablet next to the bed. I've never in my life seen Cecilia willingly interact with a computer. I'm running my fingers over the brushed aluminum of the laptop's lid, when I hear someone pounding on the front door, followed by some startled cries. The bedroom door is still open, so I rush to it, but pause as I hear orders being barked by a deep voice, and the crackle of police radios. Shit! They found us!

Without thinking, I jump into the closet, slide the door closed, and huddle in the corner, covering myself with some long coats and dresses that have been pushed to the back. The action sends up clouds of Cecilia's perfume. My heart is pounding, but I force myself to take short, shallow breaths, because every time I move, the plastic hangers click together. I can hear something going on in the living room. How did they find us? We did everything right—we left Ava's car in the parking lot and I took the battery out of my phone. A sinking realization washes over me. We took the battery out of my phone, but in the craziness of getting out of Ms. Alvarez's parking lot, we left it in Ava's. She still has her phone on her, and it's working. And easy to track.

I stay as still as possible as heavy footsteps clomp down the hall toward my hiding place. I can hear the squawk of the radio as one of the cops gets closer, and then a bang as the door to Cecilia's room opens. I squeeze my eyes shut, waiting to be discovered, as a hand ruffles the hangers above my head. I can hear the cop's heavy breathing as he searches the closet, and I know that any second a gloved hand is going to reach out and pull me up and into the daylight. It's over. A rushing sound fills my ears, and I bite my bottom lip in order not to cry out. It seems to go on forever, but in a few moments, I hear the boots shuffling on the bedroom carpet and the cop shouts, "Back bedrooms are clear!"

I sink farther onto the floor as I wait for him to come back, but all the noise is coming from the front of the house. I want to stay hidden, want to crouch in this closet forever in the ultimate game of hide-and-seek, but even more, I want to know what's going on, so I silently push the dresses aside and creep toward the half-open bedroom door. I can't see anything, but I can hear the cops' voices a lot better, along with the unmistakable metallic click of handcuffs and a girl's calm, soothing voice repeating that it's going to be okay. Another radio crackles, and a voice at the front of the house says, "We got them both. Two in custody. We're bringing them outside now." I lean against the wall for support as I realize what's happening: they think Rubi is me—and Rubi is letting them. She's going to go to jail in my place. Like Ava said, they'll figure it out soon enough, but Rubi has bought me half a day at least.

My brain spins as I try to think of my next move. What

if they take Elena too? I have to tell Zane and Cecilia not to come back. I have to at least try to get out.

The window above Cecilia's bed leads out to the backyard. I quietly stand on the bed so that I can peer outside. From what I can see, there are no cops back there—which makes sense if they think they've already got me in custody. The window clicks as I lift the latch, and I freeze, but nobody else in the house hears it. Inch by inch I slide the window open, and then pop the screen out as quietly as I can. I fully expect to be surrounded by cops as soon as I stick my head out, but there's nothing back here but a patchy lawn and the old wooden swing set. I hook one leg over the ledge and then the other, and let out a slight yelp as I drop the five feet to the ground.

I'm sure the front is swarming with police cars, so I turn toward the wooden fence that lines the side of the narrow yard. The whole thing is only a little higher than my head, so I put one foot on the cross brace and pull myself up to the top. The neighbor's yard is a similar size, but paved and completely empty. After I slide down the fence to the other side, it takes only a dozen steps to make it to the far side of the yard, where I repeat the process and sink into a lawn on the other side. This yard is empty too, but a small white dog starts barking and scratching at the glass patio door, so I race across the grass as fast as I can. This fence is taller than the others, and as I put my foot on the wooden slat, I know I'm not going to make it over. I drop back down and look around, and spot a large ceramic pot next to a lawn chair. I barely notice its weight as I move it next to the fence, and then I wobble on the top as I use it as a stool to give myself the height I need to get my leg over the top. I'm four houses away from Elena's now, and I land on the deck of a covered hot tub. Instead of crossing this yard, I run along the side of the house to the gate that leads to the front. Quickly I lift the latch and duck down past the living room windows in case anyone is inside.

There's a bush at the corner of the house, and it makes a good cover as I look down the street at all the activity. There are four cop cars and a big black SUV parked at various angles in front of Elena's house. I don't see Rubi and Ava anywhere. They must already be gone, which means that the minutes until the cops find out Rubi's true identity are ticking by. One cop is leaning into the open window of a car, talking to another cop, who is obviously typing something on a computer. The mood seems less urgent and more casual now that they've gotten what they came for. I look the other way at Zane's van, parked behind a silver SUV one more house down from where I'm standing. Thank God there wasn't room to park in front of Elena's house when we got here today.

Nobody seems to look my way as I walk down the front yard next to the shrubs, then quickly along the sidewalk to Zane's van. I say a silent prayer and find the door unlocked. I slip into the driver's seat, duck down, and find the keys in the armrest right where he usually keeps them. I peek over the dashboard at the cop still standing at the open car window. He tilts his head back and laughs at something the other cop says—just another day, as far as he's concerned.

"Go inside already," I say under my breath as the minutes crawl by. Finally he bangs twice on the door of the squad car and waves as it begins to reverse. Then it pulls forward, and I press my face against the passenger seat while the car speeds off, inches from the van I'm hiding in. I glance back up in time to see the other cop take a quick look down the street, say something into the radio that's attached to his shoulder, and turn toward Elena's front door.

As soon as he's out of sight, I slip the key into the ignition, and the van's engine roars to life. I don't even glance at Elena's house as I turn in the middle of the street and head toward town. I can't see out the back in the rearview mirror, so I sit up and tilt the mirror toward me until I see the end of Elena's driveway receding into the distance. I hold my breath until I'm around the corner. Nobody on the street is paying any attention to the beat-up white van as it rolls away. After a few minutes of driving, I pull off the main road and into the parking lot of a strip mall. Surrounded by other cars, I feel a lot less conspicuous. I reach into my pocket, pull out Cecilia's phone, and stare at the screen as it waits for me to enter the passcode. In the background there's a photo from a couple of years ago of Rubi sticking her tongue out at the camera. Why would Cecilia pretend that she hates new phones? And laptops and tablets? I stare at the four empty boxes on the screen and on a hunch type in the four numbers of our birthday—at least, the date that Dad decided was our birthday—but the phone won't let me in. What else would she use? I type in her birthday, but that's not right either. The address at Elena's house is too long. I've got to call Zane! I try to calm down enough to think straight. I type in our birthday again, but only the month and day, 0620, and let out a whoop when the screen clears and her icons pop up.

I punch in the numbers Zane wrote on my hand and hear it ringing on the other end. I'm impatient for him to answer. Just as I think it's going to voice mail, I hear him pick up, but there's only a rustling on the other end.

"Zane?"

There's no answer, and I wonder if they've already gotten back to the house.

"Zane?" I ask again.

I can hear muffled voices. He must not realize he picked up. I hang up and put my head on the steering wheel, then bang on it, tears in my eyes. Pick up the phone! Come on, Zane! Pick it up. Looking out the windshield at the liquor store, dry cleaner, and Baskin-Robbins, I wonder what I'm going to do if I can't find him. I can't go back to Elena's. I can't go back to my house. Or Zane's. For someone who hates technology, Cecilia has pages and pages of icons for things I've never even heard of. I go back to the home screen, and my finger hovers over the photo icon. She obviously has photos of Rubi. Does she have photos of us growing up too? Was she taking them all along and we never noticed? I click on it, and it takes a few seconds for the image that appears to make sense in my brain. It's me and Zane in the backyard of Elena's house. I'm on the platform of the swing set, my hands covering my tears as Zane leans away from me. That's creepy— why was she spying on us? I flip to the next photo and drop the phone when it comes up. Fumbling on the floorboard of the van, I find it, but I don't want to look again. I take a couple of deep breaths and look, but it's still there—a picture of me and Eli in the alley of the club last night, his face twisted into a mask of hatred and betrayal as I try to convince him he's in danger. Cecilia was there. Right there, just before he was killed.

Flicking through some more photos, I can't believe what I'm seeing, but it's all right in front of me. The photo of Eli and me at the party, the one of Ava and Dylan at the beach, along with the picture of Casey standing outside my car that night in the parking lot. Cecilia took them all and then posted them to Alicia's page. She's not afraid of technology. That was a lie.

I flick back to the first picture and study it, a feeling of dread seeping into my limbs. My hand shakes as I toss Cecilia's phone onto the passenger seat and turn the key in the ignition. Zane guessed right—she was trying to protect us in some twisted way. And now he's the only one left alive. I have to find them before she can finish the job.

CHAPTER 28

I'm driving just to be moving, when I realize I don't know where I'm going. Where did she say she was getting the food? Los something? Shit. I pull over again and grab her phone. It sounded like someplace they go all the time. I scroll through her address book and see it—Los Pericos. I quickly push the CALL button and wait until a guy with a heavy accent answers the phone.

"Hi," I manage, trying to sound calm. "What's your address?"

"Two seventy-eight East Fourteenth Street," he says, the background noise almost deafening. They must be busy.

"Where is that?" I say, looking at the green street signs hanging on the traffic lights above my head. "Exactly?"

"In the Pelton Center. Next to the Bank of America," he says abruptly, and hangs up.

I'm already on East Fourteenth Street. I see a neon sign

a few blocks ahead that starts with a *P*, and I pull into traffic. I slow down as I realize that they might not have even gone there. What if making Zane go with her was just an excuse to get him alone? I remember how he didn't want to go, how she basically guilted him into it. I feel time slipping away—it must have been close to an hour ago now.

The parking lot of the Pelton Center is pretty big, but I spot Cecilia's gold Lexus right away, parked directly in front of the restaurant. It has the dent above the back left tire that Ava put there when she was learning to drive, back when it was Dad's car. The restaurant is packed, and I can't see inside very well, but I keep my eyes trained on the front door. It feels like hours, but the clock says I've been here only a few minutes when the glass door swings open and Cecilia walks through, followed by Zane carrying several plastic bags full of food. They're talking and relaxed, and I can barely believe the relief that floods through me. Zane's fine, at least for now.

Before I can decide what to do, the back lights of the Lexus come on and Cecilia pulls out of the parking space. I try to pull out behind her, but my aisle is blocked by an old man in a giant Cadillac with his turn signal on, waiting for a car to pull out from in front of the bank.

"Come on!" I shout, honking my horn, but he just waves into the rearview mirror and keeps waiting. I can't sit here. I have to get to Cecilia and Zane before anything happens. Reaching over, I pick up Cecilia's phone to call Zane again, but it goes straight to voice mail.

I finally back all the way down the aisle, which is harder than I thought it would be in Zane's giant van full of blind spots, and turn toward the exit, but I don't see the gold Lexus anywhere. I crane my neck to see down the busy street and spot them at a light about a block away. I hit the gas, pull in front of a bus, and manage to make it to the light four cars behind them. The light changes and they cross the intersection, but instead of turning right like she should to get back to the house, Cecilia keeps going. I only sort of know where we are, so she's probably using a shortcut. I swing around two of the cars in front of me so that there's only a VW and a small red car between me and the Lexus. I'm trying to figure a way around the cars, when Cecilia takes a quick right, and I'm too slow to react. I watch the Lexus disappear down an alley between two strip malls.

Damn it. I can't turn around in the middle of the busy street, so I turn right at the next light and then right again at the end of the next block. If I'm lucky, the alley will come out directly in front of me. I see an alley, but I don't see the Lexus, so I turn into the narrow space between the buildings, and the gold Lexus screeches to a stop about ten feet in front of me.

Thank God I found them! I'm reaching for the door handle when I sense that something's wrong. Cecilia's eyes go wide as she sees me in the van, and it's not just surprise. There's guilt there too. I know without a doubt that she's behind everything that has happened. She didn't cut herself making dinner the other day—that was all for show. She cut herself struggling with Dylan that morning. Right before she put a blade into the back of his neck.

I need to get Zane away from her. I'm up much higher

than they are, and I don't think she can see my hand as I reach for Cecilia's phone, barely glancing down as I dial 911 and hit SPEAKER. Cecilia's staring at me through the windshield of her car, so I turn to the side and rub my nose to cover my actions as I give the dispatcher our location.

"Do you need police or fire department?" the dispatcher asks.

"Police," I say. "Hurry!" Zane's already at my window.

"Lexi! What's going on?"

I'd better be right, because there's no turning back now. I leave the phone on the seat and climb out of the van. I have to play this right—not let on that I know anything and stall until the police get here. "Oh my God, you guys! You'll never believe what happened at the house!" Even to me, my words sound false and hollow.

Cecilia plasters on a fake smile as she slides out of the driver's seat. "Lexi!" she says with surprise. "Is everything okay?" Her left hand is empty, but her right hand is in her coat pocket as she steps out of the car. I'll bet everything that she has a knife in there. This was no innocent shortcut. She was planning on killing Zane right here, next to the filthy green Dumpster.

"What happened?" Zane's eyes are full of concern as he stands next to me.

I have to keep going like I don't know what Cecilia is doing. Who she has become. "The cops came. To the house." I'm standing awkwardly by the hood of the van, but I can't think of what else to do without giving anything away. It's taking everything I have to stay in this one spot. I have to keep her here and keep her talking. "They took Ava. And Rubi, because they thought she was me. I hid in the closet until I could get out through a window."

Cecilia looks shocked. "So they think they have you already?"

"Yeah. But it won't take very long for them to figure it out." I let the built-up frustration come to the surface, and my voice breaks. "And I don't know what to do now."

Usually Cecilia would be the one to put her arm around me, to tell me that it's going to be okay, but this time it's Zane. I can feel his heart pounding as I press into his chest. I pull him down toward me even more. "The cops are coming," I whisper into his ear.

He leans away from me, looking confused. He doesn't understand.

But Cecilia does. "You need to get away from her," she says, a menacing tone in her voice that is totally out of character for the person I know so well.

"Why?" He grabs my hand and steps slightly in front of me.

"Because Cecilia is the one we've been looking for," I say, my eyes steady on her.

A strange sort of calm seems to come over her as she gestures toward the Lexus. "Look, why don't we all get back into the car and get out of here? We can talk about this rationally somewhere else."

My heart's pounding. What's taking the cops so long? "I know what you did," I say, stepping out from behind Zane.

"I found your phone. The one you didn't want us to know about. And I saw the photos."

Cecilia's face pales as she absorbs the information. She stands up straighter, and I can see her resolve strengthening. "I did it for you. For both of you. To protect you, because that's been my job since the day you were born."

"To protect us? Are you serious?" It feels like I've been punched in the stomach. I knew that Cecilia did this, but to have her actually admit it almost knocks me off my feet. Cecilia's been my mom, my nurse, and my shoulder to cry on. And now she's my enemy.

"Those boys were bad. All of them. They hurt you, and I knew that if I didn't do something, it was going to get worse."

"So you killed them? You really killed them?" I know in my head that it's true, but it's so hard to picture Cecilia plunging a knife into Dylan's neck and then coming home to pack my lunch for school. It's crazy.

Cecilia shrugs like it's no big deal. "It wasn't even that hard—I just pithed them like we used to do to suckling pigs when I was a kid." She makes a twisting motion with her right hand, like she's putting a key in a lock. "You should have seen the look on Casey's face, so surprised and bug-eyed." She smiles a little wistfully, her eyes flat and emotionless. "He deserved it the most."

There's stunned silence. I look at Cecilia, really look at her: at the wiry strands of gray that are starting to pepper her dark hair, the hands that changed our diapers when we were small, now with nails bitten down to the skin. These are the hands that ended Eli's life. And Dylan's. And Casey's. It's like the Cecilia I've seen almost every day of my entire life doesn't really exist. It doesn't seem possible.

I shake my head, trying to make sense of her reasoning. "But why? Why would you do something like that and make them think it was us?"

"That was an accident. I never meant for the cops to suspect you. I put the photos up on Alicia's page to help you—to show that you were the victims here." She takes a step toward us, her eyes glassy as she seems to stare past me. "None of those guys was good enough for you. They all hurt you."

"But you don't just *kill* people," I say, my voice rising in anger even though I try to stop it. Zane and I both take a step back.

She looks confused, even hurt. "I only did what I had to do to keep you safe. That's my job, to keep you and Ava safe."

Zane's left arm is twitching against mine, and I put a hand out to keep him calm. It's not time yet. "Get into the van," I say to him, tired of all this talking. Cecilia is still at least five feet away from us.

"I wouldn't do that," she says.

"Why not?" I glance at her, but she hasn't moved. "You have a knife. What are you going to do to the two of us from over there?"

Cecilia pulls a small black gun out of her pocket with her right hand.

I take another step backward.

"Now just leave Lexi alone and get back into the car with me," Cecilia says, flicking the gun in Zane's direction.

"Zane hasn't done anything," I protest. "He's been help-ing me."

Cecilia looks at me, the gun still level in her hand. "But don't you see, baby girl? He's only going to hurt you in the end. They all are. This is all for your own good. Besides, Zane knows too much—he practically said it back at the house. He'd go running to the cops in a second."

Zane squeezes my hand one last time and then lets it drop as he starts toward Cecilia.

"No!" I can't believe he's just going to give up.

She keeps the gun trained on him as he walks toward her.

Just as he reaches the Lexus, he lunges for Cecilia, and the gun goes off into the air as he forces her hand upward. I run to them, and she starts to fight him off, kicking and jerking as he forces her up against the alley wall. The gun clatters to the ground and is kicked to the side. She's no match for his strength. I should have known he wasn't going to give up so easily.

"Check her pocket for the knife," Zane says, his breath ragged as he presses Cecilia's hands against the wall. With one last effort, Cecilia twists away from him, shoving him with both hands so that he loses his balance. In a flash, Zane goes after her, and they struggle on the ground before he hauls her back to her feet and pushes her back up against the bricks. The fight seems to have gone out of her, and she sags under Zane's grip, her eyes fixed on the ground.

"Okay," I say, patting her jacket pocket. We need the knife—it's the only thing linking Cecilia to all the murders. It's Ava's and my key to freedom and she's got to have it on her. As I search, something wet drops to the dusty asphalt, and I follow the dark rivulets of blood up Zane's arm to his shoulder. "Don't move," I say, my voice as steady as I can make it. "I found the knife."

"Damn," Zane says as he sees what I see: the handle of the knife sticking out just below his collarbone.

"No, don't!" I shout, grabbing his free hand as he reaches for it. "You have to leave it. If you pull it out, you could bleed to death."

"I'm okay," he insists. I look at the beads of sweat on his upper lip and the waxiness of his skin and know that he's not.

"You're losing a lot of blood," I tell him. "Try not to move. Can you hold her?"

Zane presses her against the wall with his good hand. "Yeah." He nods quickly.

I yank the door of the van open and find a beach towel wadded into the corner. I grab it and race back to the two of them. Cecilia hasn't moved, but Zane's eyes are mirroring the panic he must be feeling.

"Here," I say. "I'm going to wrap the knife in the towel so it won't move. And hopefully we can stop the bleeding. Okay?"

"Okay." He nods just the smallest bit.

My hands are shaking as I press the towel up to the wound. His shirt is already soaked red with blood. Zane winces as my wrist bumps the handle of the knife.

"I'm sorry," I whisper.

"It's okay," he says, managing a half smile.

Cecilia says nothing as I finish wrapping the wound. She's

defeated, all the fight gone out of her. I look and see blood already welling up under the towel—all of us frozen in our positions. My heart sinks, and I realize the cops had better hurry. "Does it hurt?"

"Not really," he says, looking down curiously. His words are thick in his mouth. "I'm getting kind of dizzy, though."

"I'm going to call for help again," I say, looking down the empty alley. What's taking the cops so long?

I'm halfway to the van when I hear the screech of tires and the sirens wail as both exits to the alley are suddenly filled with cop cars, their flashing blue and red lights flickering over the high walls of the alley.

"They're here," I say, rushing back to Zane. I've never been happier to see cops, and they swarm the alley and start barking orders over the car's loudspeaker.

"Everyone! Hands where we can see them!" a rough voice booms over our heads.

I put my hands up, and Zane follows as much as he can as Cecilia slips down onto the asphalt. "Zane's hurt!" I shout. "We need an ambulance!"

Two cops approach cautiously, guns drawn.

"It's Cecilia," I say, nodding to her on the ground. "She had a gun. It's over by the car." The tall officer spins me around and slaps handcuffs hard around my wrists, while another cop yanks Cecilia roughly to her feet and cuffs her hands behind her back.

"Zane's been stabbed," I say as calmly as I can. "The knife is still in him. He needs help!"

The cop hesitates, but he radios the information to the

arriving cars. He shines a flashlight in Zane's face. "Can you walk?"

Zane doesn't say anything, just gives a short nod. His tan has disappeared and his skin is pale and mottled. "Wait!" His voice is strained. "Lexi . . ."

"I'm fine," I say. "Just go with him. Don't worry about me."

As soon as they start to move, Zane leans on the cop, taking tiny steps toward the cars until more cops come and half support, half carry him to the ambulance that has just pulled up at the entrance to the alley. People are swarming the street now, drawn to the show by the lights and sirens.

The cops set Zane down on the bumper of the ambulance, and he's swallowed up by people in uniform barking orders at each other. The first cop pulls me aside and shines a flashlight into my face. "What's your name?"

"Alexa Rios," I answer, still trying to see past the commotion at the ambulance door. Zane has to be okay. He has to be.

Cecilia is led to the open door of a cop car. I can see the top of her head as she slides into the backseat.

"You too," the cop near me says. "Let's go!" He grabs me by one arm and starts to lead me away.

"What the hell is going on here?" Dad's voice booms over the chaos.

I spin around and see Dad and Ms. Alvarez flanked by Detective Naito. "Lexi?" he asks in disbelief as both he and Ms. Alvarez ignore the cops and rush toward me. "They told me you were already in custody."

"That's not me," I say, not having a clue how to explain the past twenty-four hours.

"What happened?" Dad asks, his face red with emotion. He turns me toward the sunlight coming in from the end of the alley. "Jesus, are you okay? Look at you!"

I look down and notice the bloodstains that are all over my shirt and hands. "No, I'm fine." I take a deep breath and nod toward the ambulance. "Zane got cut. It's pretty bad. It . . . it was Cecilia the whole time," I say, looking toward the cop car where Cecilia is sitting in the back, staring straight ahead.

"Cecilia?" Dad asks, sounding lost and uncertain. He turns back to me.

"She did it all," I say, my eyes filling with tears. I don't even recognize her anymore—the Cecilia I knew died with Casey. "She thought she was protecting us. . . ."

"And you took it upon yourself to find her?" Ms. Alvarez says, sounding more concerned than angry.

"You realize how dangerous this was?" Dad asks. "You could have been killed. You should have called the cops the minute you knew."

"I know. But this was the only way I could get anyone to believe me."

"It's over now," Dad says with a finality that I wish I felt. It feels like it's all just beginning. He gestures to my shirt. "Can we . . . do something about this mess?"

"Not here," the detective answers. "It's evidence now. We'll have to go down to the station."

"I'm not going anywhere until I find out how Zane's doing," I insist.

"We'll call his parents as soon as we can," Ms. Alvarez says, her voice surprisingly kind. "And we'll make sure he gets the best care available."

One of the cops leans over and whispers something into Detective Naito's ear. His eyes get wide and he holds out three fingers. "Three? Really?" He turns to look at me.

I glance at Dad to see if he's following the conversation, but he's absorbed in watching some of the other cops surround the scene in bright yellow crime-scene tape. Explaining Rubi is going to be one of the hardest parts of this day.

"Care to explain?" the detective asks me.

"It's kind of a long story," I say. I hear a door to the ambulance slam, and I turn in that direction, only to be stopped by one of the cops. "I have to see Zane!" I say, trying to get around him, struggling against the cuffs on my wrists.

"I'll take her. She'll cooperate," Detective Naito says, nodding in that direction. As we approach the ambulance, he reaches back and uncuffs my wrists. "We're all going to have a long night down at the station. Don't make a liar out of me."

I smile gratefully—he believes me. "I won't."

One of the back doors of the ambulance is still open, and I see Zane lying on the gurney, one arm wrapped in bandages held tightly to his chest and the other connected to tubes dripping fluid from plastic bags held up high by one of the paramedics. His eyes are closed and he still looks pale. "Is he okay?" I ask.

"Lost a lot of blood," the paramedic says, squeezing one of the little bags.

"Hey, Lex," Zane says, his eyes fluttering open.

I step into the ambulance and crouch down beside him, stroking his hand while avoiding the tubes. "We got her. It's going to be okay."

He breaks into a weak smile. "And you saved my ass in the process."

"Not true," I say. "You had it under control."

"I thought it was a shortcut," he says. "I had no idea she had a gun. Or a knife."

I look at the bandages and realize how close we really came. How close I came to losing Zane again—this time forever.

"We need to get going," the paramedic says, opening the back door wider.

"Okay." I turn back to Zane and run my hand along his cheek, memorizing the spark in his brown eyes. I lean over, careful not to jostle his arm, and give him a long, hard kiss on the mouth, one that I hope holds a combination of apology and promise.

"I'm not pretending anymore," I whisper into his ear.

Zane reaches up with his good hand, causing all the tubes to sway, and pulls me to him, his lips soft but insistent on mine.

"Damn, Lex," he says, his voice faint in my ear. "I never was."

CHAPTER 29

There's a squeal and then a splash as someone else is pushed into the pool down below. I turn back to Dad and the remainder of his friends sitting around the patio table and realize it's that time of the night when the adults are going to head indoors and turn the party over to the rest of us. Paper streamers flutter from the pergola above our heads, and cheesy paper signs reading CONGRATS, GRAD! sway from the awning. I look around at the table full of gifts and the other table still groaning with food, despite the fact that we've been out here for hours. The past few months have felt so empty without Cecilia here, I never thought I'd be so happy for a simple graduation party in our own backyard. Nothing is ever going to be the same. I know she thought she was doing the right thing down deep in her illness, but that doesn't change the fact that three boys are dead because of us and Cecilia is going to spend the rest of her life in jail. Because of what she wanted to do for us.

I pick up a small exquisitely wrapped box and look at the card, surprised to see that it's from Ms. Alvarez. She's been really helpful these past two months, even though, thankfully, we didn't need a defense lawyer anymore. Dad tried to hire her for Cecilia and her insanity defense, but Ms. Alvarez didn't take the case because of a conflict of interest.

"Quite the haul," Dad says, nodding to the gifts. There are two identical-looking piles, one for me and one for Ava.

"It is," I answer, wondering if there's anything in there I actually need.

"I brought you something," he says, handing me an Andy Bar.

"Ha, ha," I say, taking it from him.

He looks down at the Cal Dad T-shirt he's wearing. "And thanks again for my gift."

I give him a hug, knowing how painful it is for him to be wearing Cal blue and gold instead of Stanford Cardinal red. "It's the least I can do. You're paying for it."

"Just keep that in mind," he says with a grin. "Eyes on the prize."

He's also wearing the Long Beach State hat Ava got him after accepting their offer. We'll still be hours away from each other, but I'm not so worried about that anymore—being apart might do us both some good. As long as it's not that far apart.

"Did you see this?" Dad asks, holding out a big square envelope.

"I did," I say. I look at him sideways. "It's from Elena." She's had a constant pinched, worried look ever since Cecilia was arrested. As much wrong as Cecilia did, she is still Elena's sister, and Elena owed her a lot. Dad still hasn't come to terms with Elena and her choices. I've been to see her in Oceanside a few times, but I try not to mention her in front of Dad because he doesn't like it. Ava still refuses to go over there at all.

"Did you see what it is?" Dad asks.

"Yeah," I say cautiously. "I opened it earlier." I should have put them away. They're only going to get him annoyed again, just when we were having such a good day.

"Can I look?" he asks.

"Sure," I say as nonchalantly as I can. "Ava got the same thing."

Dad slides the photos out of the envelope and spreads them on the table without a word. They're a document of our first six months—pictures of the three of us in matching tiny, frilly dresses, lined up in a row on couch cushions and propped up on our stomachs with little bows attached to our heads with stretchy bands. My favorite is a picture of all three of us in one crib, so tangled together that it's hard to tell where one baby ends and the other begins. I want to frame that one for my dorm, but I don't want to get Dad upset.

To my surprise, that's the one he picks up first, stroking the paper as if the image were real. "You were such beautiful babies," he says softly. Then he looks up at me. I know he's noticed the fact that I'm making more of an effort with how I look. Nothing approaching Alicia-style, just some mascara and lip gloss, but it's a start. "Still are."

I put my arm around his neck. "Thanks, Dad."

At the sound of the word "Dad," tears fill his eyes, but he wipes them away angrily. Ms. Alvarez—excuse me, Elisa—comes over and puts one arm around his waist.

"I think we're going to head inside," she says, looking up at him with adoration. I always thought it would be weird seeing him with a woman, but so far it's not bad. "It's getting a little chilly out here." Which it isn't—it's still almost eighty degrees, despite the fact that the sun set an hour ago.

Dad smiles at her and then looks down at all of our friends out by the pool. "You should see if anyone needs anything."

I know this is his way of giving me permission to go and have fun. "You sure you're okay?" I ask.

He gives me a weak smile. "I'm perfect. Now go."

I walk down the stone steps away from the patio and watch everyone splashing in the pool as the DJ that Dad hired switches songs on the PA. As the first guitar notes come through the speakers, the song reminds me of one Eli used to play, and I'm hit with a wave of regret. It's like that part of my life was severed the night Eli died. I saw Linzey and Melissa at Cecilia's hearing a few weeks ago. Linzey gave me a sad smile, but we didn't speak to each other. I can't blame them. If it wasn't for Alicia, Eli would still be alive right now. Everyone tells me that I'm not responsible, that the way Cecilia's mind twisted logic isn't our fault, but in quiet moments I still see Eli lying beside the van, and I can't help but feel responsible.

"Hey!" Rubi says, tugging on my arm. "Tell your boyfriend to give up his half of the court—some of the rest of us want to play."

I grin at her and pull myself out of the dark place my mind likes to wander to. "You know I can't make Zane do anything."

"Well, come make out with him or something," she says, dragging me in the direction of the tennis court. "Slater challenged me to a match, and we need a diversionary tactic."

I watch through the fence as Zane swings a racket with one hand and sloshes the liquid out of a red plastic cup with the other. Slater's on the other side playing just about as well, his flip-flops hindering any chance at returning the ball.

Zane breaks into a smile when he sees me, and waves the racket, just as a line drive of Slater's hits him squarely in the head. "Hey!" he yells over the net.

"Match point!" Rubi screams, and jumps over the net to take the racket.

"That was a setup," Zane says with a smile as he walks over to the sidelines. He leans down and kisses me firmly on the mouth. "I got distracted."

From this angle, I can see the pink scar that runs along his collarbone—the only physical evidence left of that horrible day in the alley. I wrap my arms around his neck and pull him toward me. "You don't know anything about distracted," I say, kissing him back, grateful that I still have the opportunity.

"God, get a room," Maya says, coming up behind us.

"I wish," Zane says, nuzzling my neck so that I involuntarily yelp.

"Speaking of," Maya says. "When do you guys leave?"

"Next week," I say. I can hardly believe I get to spend a week alone with him in Brazil. After missing the event in Tahiti, he wasn't sure that the ASP was going to give him another chance.

"The competition's not until that Saturday," Zane says. "So we have a few days to look around first."

"I can't believe your dad's letting you go," Maya says. "Pretty nice graduation present, if you ask me."

I glance up to where the adults are still sitting around the patio table. In the wake of everything that's happened in the past two months, it didn't even take that much convincing. I'm actually excited about the trip and about going to Cal in the fall. Maybe I'll go for a business degree, maybe I won't, but at least it's up to me to decide. "It is," I agree.

"And all I got was a new car," she says, shaking her head sadly.

I put my hand on the new pendant hanging around my neck. It's a Scrabble tile with the letter *L* on it. "This is still my favorite gift," I say, nudging Zane. "Better than diamonds and gold any day."

"Diamonds and gold aren't until our fiftieth anniversary," Zane says. I laugh, but his face is dead serious.

"What are we talking about?" Rubi asks, draping one arm around my neck, her face flushed from the exercise.

"Old people," Maya says, making a face.

"Good Lord, why?"

Slater comes over with his racket. "Anyone want a game? Just don't play Rubi," he says, nodding to her. "She cheats."

"I do not!" she says, bumping him with her hip.

Zane and I exchange glances. Looks like more than friendly competition to me.

"There you are," Ava says, walking up to us in mock frustration. She's wearing a skirt and a bikini top both so small that there's not much left to the imagination.

She reaches over and loops her arm through Rubi's. "I need you for a second. Joel Macy bet me twenty bucks that we weren't really triplets. It's time to collect." She looks back at me as they walk toward the pool house. "You too."

"Go ahead," Zane says, giving a squeeze before he drops my hand. "I'll be here when you get back."

I give him one last look, amazed at how much can change in such a short time.

"Wait up!" I call to Ava and Rubi as I catch up to them in the doorway.

Chatter stops and people stare as they always do when we walk into the room—the three of us together—exactly alike but so different at the same time.

"You guys know Lexi," Ava says, nodding to me.

"And this is Rubi," I say, grinning at the identical face next to mine.

Ava smiles, the pride in her eyes unmistakable. "Our sister."

ACKNOWLEDGMENTS

This is always the hardest page in the book for me to write because I'm afraid I'm going to leave out one of the many people who made my book possible.

First, there's my agent, Sarah Davies, whose guidance took a confused jumble of words and made them into a sellable novel. Thanks to my editor, Wendy Loggia, for her unwavering enthusiasm from the very first chapter, and to the entire team at Delacorte Press and Random House Children's Books for their support. Thanks to my writer friends: Heidi Kling, for figuring out the third twin; Robin Mellom and Eve Porinchak, for running away with me; Heather Mackey, for tacos and advice; Malinda Lo, for always thinking that I have good ideas; Daisy Whitney, for always answering frantic texts; and Cheryl Herbsman, for listening to me moan. Thank you to all the gals (and the guy) in the desert who gave me brilliant insights while we were floating in the middle of the pool. A special shout-out goes to Erin Murphy, who suggested I turn a comedy into a thriller.

Finally, thanks to my friends and family, who don't understand the special brand of crazy that writers share but put up with it anyway. Thank you to Commander Rocky Medeiros for advice on all things police related; any legal errors are mine alone. I'm glad he wasn't on this case, or there would have been nothing for Lexi to do. Thank you to my good friends Karen Ryan, Barbara Stewart, Jessica Romero, and Jill Raimondi for always looking interested when I talk, and to Hayley Proctor for college advice. Thanks to my family—the Jaynes, the Robisons, and the Dorans—whose lore is always great fodder for the stories I write. Finally, thanks to Bayo, Jaron, and Taemon for their unwavering support and understanding when I talk to myself in the car. They're the reason I can write realistic boys. And the reason I write anything at all.